Chicks with Sticks
(It's a purl thing)

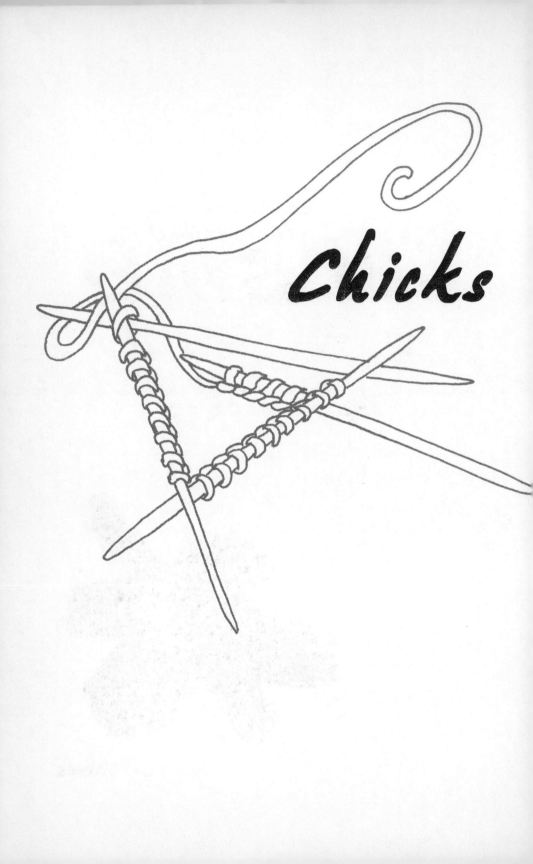

Chicks

with Sticks

(It's a purl thing)

ELIZABETH
LENHARD

DUTTON BOOKS

DUTTON CHILDREN'S BOOKS A division of Penguin Young Readers Group. Published by
the Penguin Group · Penguin Group (USA) Inc., 375 Hudson Street, New York, New York 10014, U.S.A.
· Penguin Group (Canada), 90 Eglinton Avenue East, Suite 700, Toronto, Ontario, Canada M4P 2Y3
(a division of Pearson Penguin Canada Inc.) · Penguin Books Ltd, 80 Strand, London WC2R 0RL,
England · Penguin Ireland, 25 St Stephen's Green, Dublin 2, Ireland (a division of Penguin Books Ltd) ·
Penguin Group (Australia), 250 Camberwell Road, Camberwell, Victoria 3124, Australia (a division of
Pearson Australia Group Pty Ltd) · Penguin Books India Pvt Ltd, 11 Community Centre, Panchsheel
Park, New Delhi - 110 017, India · Penguin Group (NZ), Cnr Airborne and Rosedale Roads, Albany,
Auckland 1310, New Zealand (a division of Pearson New Zealand Ltd) · Penguin Books (South Africa)
(Pty) Ltd, 24 Sturdee Avenue, Rosebank, Johannesburg 2196, South Africa · Penguin Books Ltd,
Registered Offices: 80 Strand, London WC2R 0RL, England

CIP Data is available.

Published in the United States by Dutton Children's Books,
a division of Penguin Young Readers Group
345 Hudson Street, New York, New York 10014
www.penguin.com/youngreaders

Designed by Irene Vandervoort   Printed in USA   First Edition
ISBN 0-525-47622-9
5 7 9 10 8 6 4

For my parents

Acknowledgments

Tremendous thanks to . . .

Jodi Reamer, for making it all happen and cheering me on the whole way.

Julie Strauss-Gabel, for her always calming, wise, and witty presence.

The many editors who came before her and put me on this path. Julie Komorn falls into this category as well.

Jen Bonnell, for her font of knit-knowledge and pattern expertise, and Mia Sorcinelli, for her funky mitten pattern.

Patti Ghezzi, my knitting guru, friend, and all-around yenta.

The bloggers, both knitty and writerly, who helped jump-start each writing day, including Bonne Marie Burns, "Wendy Knits," Meg Cabot, Sarah Dessen, Jennifer Weiner, and Laurie Halse Anderson. I also got tremendous help from knitting books, chiefly *Stitch 'n Bitch: The Knitter's Handbook,* by Debbie Stoller; *Teen Knitting Club: Chill Out and Knit Some Cool Stuff,* by Jennifer Wenger, Carol Abrams, and Maureen Lasher; and *Knitting Without Tears,* by Elizabeth Zimmermann.

The very inspiring "BC" of Chicago: Reva Nelson, Rachel Plotinsky, Jen Clark, Allison Cowett, and Cathy Kaneti.

The many other friends who helped me breathe during deadline panic, among them Alissa Citron, Kristen Rosich, Beth Berkelhamer, Ellyn Davidson, Wendy Lenhard, Amy Donsky, Dorit Naftalin, Mia Barricini, Sara Berliner, Elory Rozner, Julie K., Diane Dragan, Eileen Drennen, and Amy Greene.

My parents, Bunny and Bob Lenhard, whose faith in me has been exceeded only by their enthusiasm.

My super-supportive extended family of Lenhards, Donskys, Davidsons, Craines, Berkowitzes, and Lucille Miller.

Most of all, Paul, who is officially my family now; who never laughed at my starter scarves (and even promised to wear them); who cooked and cleaned so that I might write. A more nurturing, joyful partner there never was.

Chicks with Sticks
(It's a purl thing)

1 *(Cast On)

Screeeeee!

Scottie's body jumped awake first. It took a few seconds for her mind to catch up. As she lurched into hazy half consciousness, an image from her dream evaporated before she could even begin to wrap her brain around it.

She flopped her arms over her head and groaned in disappointment. But when her elbow sank into a tearstained spot on the pillow, it occurred to her that this was probably one of those dreams you'd rather not remember.

Screeeeee-CLUNK.

She groaned again. She'd forgotten it was Monday, which, like every Wednesday, Friday, and Sunday, was freight-train-chugging-through-Chicago-at-4:00 A.M. night.

Scottie lived in an old bread factory right on the railroad tracks on the north side of the city. The bread was long gone, of course. What was left were giant lofts with oversize ovens converted into kitchens, exposed air ducts, chinked brick walls—your basic urban hipster's heaven.

Scottie's parents were the urban hipsters, not her.

She was the one who dreamed about walls. Not the floating partitions that boxed off her bedroom—and stopped about four feet short of the ceiling—but actual walls. Complete, *private* walls. Scottie yearned for them the way other girls craved kisses. (Kisses, she wasn't really up to, yet.)

She was also getting *really* tired of having a train for a next-door neighbor.

When she was little, she'd loved it. The last commuter train, the 10:04, had been her sandman. She *couldn't* fall sleep before it arrived. While she waited, she'd turn restlessly in her bed—right side to stomach to left side to back. She'd stare up at the ceiling rafters, which were so far away, they made her feel as tiny as Tinker Bell. She'd suck on the ends of her fine, light brown hair—something she couldn't do in front of her parents, who thought it was gross.

Finally, the 10:04 would *whoosh* by her window and toot its whistle— a quick hello and good-bye. It was as effective as *Goodnight Moon*. By the time it cleared the building, Scottie would be out cold, like a good Pavlovian puppy. After that, she could sleep through anything: the cars hissing through puddles on Ravenswood Street; the chatter from her parents' art parties, ebbing and flowing out of their loft's gallery space; the clunk of the 4:00 A.M. trains.

Now that she was fifteen, her head wasn't nearly as obedient. Her insomnia couldn't get enough of those trains, kicking Scottie awake every time they *chugga'd* by.

"I hate you, train," she moaned now, propping herself on her elbows to glare at the trundling boxcars. They looked cloudy and wavy through her window's small, square panes of glass. They were gone within five minutes, but the damage was done.

Oh, Scottie went through the motions of trying to fall back asleep. She turned her back to the windows and smashed her cheek into the dry end of her pillow. She squeezed her eyes shut and made herself take deep, even breaths.

She put in a good thirty seconds of effort before she gave up and let her eyes snap open. Why bother? She knew the drill by now. If she kept the light off, she'd only toss and turn until about six, finally drifting off . . . right before her alarm rang.

Scottie rolled to the edge of her bed and turned on her reading lamp. The tall stack of books on her nightstand was immediately unappealing, but Scottie sifted through them anyway. On the top was *Hamlet*, the bane of every sophomore at the Olivia Stark School—because their Shakespeare-mad English teacher made everyone dress up and read the play aloud.

Scottie actually considered it, if only for its anesthetic value, but then she remembered *Hamlet* wasn't just a bad fashion statement. It was also filled with death.

No way, she thought, dropping the book to the floor and moving on.

The Iranian graphic novel had too many pictures. The book she'd checked out from the library didn't have enough. *Twist* magazine? Just . . . no.

As Scottie dropped the last of her stash down to the shag rug, something else fell with it—a folded piece of pink paper.

One of the guidance counselors at school had pressed it into Scottie's hand a couple of weeks ago.

"Come by and have a chat if you need to," she'd urged. Scottie should have seen it coming. The Stark School was Progressive with a capital P, and the counselors *loved* it when they had traumatized students to talk off the school's turn-of-the-century granite ledges.

To put it mildly, Scottie was *not* in the mood to open up her heart to some earnest adult who barely knew her. She'd put the thera-chat on the bottom of her to-do list. In fact, she hadn't even looked at the pink pamphlet. One glance at the title had been more than enough. She'd wedged it into the stack of books in her backpack and forgotten all about it.

Now? Well, a pamphlet was a lot shorter than Shakespeare.

Scottie swiped the flyer off the floor.

For a Grieving Teen, she read, adding in her mind, *A very special episode . . .*

Sighing, Scottie spread the pamphlet out on her pillow and read on.

Grief is much like a bad case of the flu, it said in a plump, teen-friendly font. *Like any sickness, it has side effects including depression, loss of appetite, insomnia. . . .*

But grief resembles illness in other ways, too. The pain eases over time, even if it feels like it never will. Talking about it helps. . . .

Okay, duh, Scottie thought, tossing the pamphlet back to the floor.

Good thing I made an A in algebra or I might not have been able to put it all together. She rolled her eyes. *Let's see, favorite aunt dies; a month later, favorite niece still can't sleep.*

Scottie closed her eyes. She could see the glow of the reading light through her lids. She opened her eyes.

Well, she thought irritably, *looks like* For a Grieving Teen *was about as helpful as a can of Red Bull.*

She couldn't completely blame her grief, though. The truth was, this wasn't a new phenomenon, cursing at trains at 4:00 A.M. Scottie had been losing sleep long before her Aunt Roz had died four weeks earlier.

The pink pamphlet only told her why it had gotten worse.

A second train screeched in the distance.

"GOD!" Scottie sputtered, burying her face in her pillow in frustration.

Enough already! she railed silently. *I'm sick of this. I want my life back!*

She wished her REM state would get over itself and go back to business. Or she wished there was somebody she could call—movie characters always had some die-hard friend who didn't mind when you woke her up in the middle of the night for a little split-screen handwringing. She wished . . .

I wish . . .

The voice in her head was whiny and pathetic. And suddenly Scottie's covers felt so hot and sticky, it wasn't enough for her to throw them off. She had to kick them to the floor, too.

I wish I wasn't always wishing! she screamed inside her head.

She bolted upright and grabbed her MP3 player off her nightstand.

Scrolling down to an old Ani DiFranco album, she shoved the little ear-buds into her ears. She needed something thrashy to drown out her thoughts.

Scottie listened for five minutes before she determined that Ani *so* wasn't working for her. She couldn't focus enough to get through one surly stanza, much less an entire album. Apparently, her thoughts were louder even than Ani's rage.

Sighing, Scottie plucked out the earphones and considered TV. But she'd tried that last night, and all the commercials aimed at geriatric insomniacs had depressed her. Besides, her parents might hear it over their wall partition. Too many noisy nights and they were definitely going to start whispering to each other about Prozac vs. Zoloft for morose teenagers.

Scottie got out of bed and began to pace, avoiding her fluffy white area rug and sticking to the cement floor. She wanted that cool-smooth feeling to travel from the soles of her feet all the way up to her burning head. Unfortunately, it seemed to stop somewhere around her knees.

Meanwhile, the fretting in her mind traveled downward and settled in her stomach.

In defeat, Scottie sat on her rug, shoving aside a pile of clothes to make room.

She got the entire mound—which had basically been serving as her closet for quite a while now—out of her way except the dregs at the very bottom. Her pink velour sweats with the hole in the hip were as flat as a pressed flower. And *there* was the striped sock she'd been looking for forever. Underneath that was a chunky high-heeled Mary Jane and a shiny black purse.

Her funeral gear. Scottie hadn't seen them since she kicked them off at the end of that awful day. Now all she wanted to do was bury them again.

She used her toes to shove the shoes back under the clothes pile, but when she tried to scooch the purse, too, she only managed to knock it over. Random stuff spilled onto the rug—a ChapStick and a tin of curiously strong mints, a few wadded-up tissues, and . . . a tangle of yarn.

Scottie stared. She'd completely forgotten about that fuzzy blue wool. She hadn't seen it since the funeral.

Actually, it had been after the funeral, when everybody was sitting shivah at Aunt Roz's house in Evanston.

For Scottie, sitting shivah was almost worse than the service. At least at the synagogue, you had to stay with it enough to stand up, sit down, and read prayers.

At a shivah, there was nothing to do but watch everyone mill around looking stricken and sad, yet somehow manage to devour a ton of cold cuts while they were at it. Scottie had curled up on the living-room window seat, gazing at the mourners in their crepey suits. She felt like she was viewing them from far away—the back row of a dark movie theater. Men shook their heads sorrowfully, then exchanged business cards. Women scurried about, slipping coasters under sweaty glasses and refilling the bread basket with dense little squares of rye. The little kids crawled around on the floor, scuffing up their patent-leather shoes, and the old people honked into handkerchiefs.

Was it any wonder that Scottie's eyes had glazed over? But she'd probably checked out for only a few minutes when she was jolted back awake. The space she was staring into had suddenly gone blue. A really beautiful indigo—deep and rich and much more interesting than the blue in a pair of jeans. It was so vivid, it shook her out of her stupor.

When Scottie had returned to a somewhat interactive state, she realized that the blue was a ball of yarn in the lap of the only other stationary person in the room—her great-aunt Lucille, who was tucked into a corner of Aunt Roz's favorite smushy green couch, knitting.

She spotted Scottie and patted the seat next to her.

Scottie had groaned quietly.

She *really* didn't want to make polite conversation with her Aunt

• • Chicks with Sticks

Lucille. Of course she didn't want to have to live with that wormy I-dissed-my-lonely-old-aunt feeling either.

She went over, sat down, and braced herself, but Aunt Lucille ended up surprising her. She didn't go through the usual, shaky-voiced litany about Aunt Roz, the "how tragic/too young/such a horrible car accident" speech. She actually didn't say anything at all. She just sat there and knitted.

Scottie found herself zoning into the rhythm of it. She'd never actually seen someone knit up close. She'd always pictured the needles poking up like old TV antennae, but Aunt Lucille had them cupped beneath her palms. The little knobs at the end of the needles brushed against her tweedy skirt every once in a while as she whisked through the stitches.

It felt like a lot of time went by in that little bubble of quiet. Scottie didn't know her Aunt Lucille very well, yet she had felt utterly comfortable cuddled into the couch next to her. The little clicks of the wooden knitting needles seemed to be conversation enough.

Or so Scottie had thought.

After a few minutes, Aunt Lucille had turned to her and said, "You seem intrigued, honey. Why don't I show you how?"

Scottie had tried to squirm her way out of it. Of course. Because . . . please, *knitting?* Wasn't that pretty much for, you know, people who are old enough to use handkerchiefs? Or weird girls who wore rainbow hair ribbons and striped leggings to school?

Turned out, Scottie didn't really have a choice. Without listening to her feeble protests, Aunt Lucille had shoved her yarn and needles into Scottie's hands and arranged her fingers around the whole business. Scottie might as well have been a marionette as Aunt Lucille talked her through the motions of knitting.

It was pretty simple, actually, once Scottie had wrapped her brain around the sequence. Spear a circle of yarn with one of the needle tips, loop the tail around, drag the second loop through the first one, then scoot everything onto the second needle.

Scottie had messed up a few times before she'd gotten it, but finally, she'd spike-loop-swished her way through an entire stitch. The success had made her feel strangely buoyant. She'd smiled creakily—for the first time in days—as she'd finished it. She'd even done a second stitch, just to prove that it hadn't been a fluke.

"You're doing it!" Aunt Lucille had cried.

"Yup," Scottie had said. She did two more stitches, maybe because she liked the feeling of the soft wool shifting in her hands.

Then she'd done yet another one for no reason in particular, other than to listen to that *click-swish* sound of the needles. Finally she did three more to get to the end of the row. She was surprised to feel a little hum of satisfaction as the final stitch fell off the left needle, leaving it light and unencumbered in her hand.

"Ah, I see it already," Aunt Lucille had said. "You *love* knitting."

Again, it wasn't a question.

Okay, Scottie thought, *I've knitted for a total of one minute and a total of seven stitches, and Aunt Lucille thinks she's got me hooked? Gee, it must be nice to think people are that simple.*

"It's instant, isn't it?" the old woman went on, oblivious to Scottie's incredulous stare. "That's how I felt the first time I learned to knit. I was eight, and my mother's knitting looked like magic to me. I begged her to teach me, and finally she did."

Okay, I don't recall even asking *to learn how to knit, much less begging.*

Out loud, though, Scottie did the polite thing. She thanked her aunt as she handed the knitting over.

Aunt Lucille, though, pushed it back at Scottie.

"You keep it, dear," she said. "It was going to be a belled sweater sleeve, but it's just narrow enough to be a scarf, which is much easier."

Scottie had sighed.

"Listen, Aunt Lucille, that's very nice of you, but knitting isn't really my thing."

"It *wasn't* your thing. Perhaps it is now," Aunt Lucille had replied.

She patted the puff of blue yarn absently. "Knitting has gotten me through a lot of hard times."

"I'm . . . I'm not going through such a hard time," Scottie had said, even as she felt her eyes go wavery with tears. "I mean, of course I miss Aunt Roz. I miss her . . . really bad, but . . ."

"Take the knitting dear," Aunt Lucille had pressed. "If it turns into a dust mouse under your bed, so be it. But if you need it, it'll be there for you."

Scottie didn't know what about Aunt Lucille's offer had gotten to her—the sweetness or the smugness. But suddenly she'd felt a flash of irritation.

All right already, I'll take the knitting, she'd thought, shoving the snarl into her funeral purse and squeezing out another thank-you. *Why is it that every time an adult gives you a gift, it's more for* them *than for you?*

As she'd hurried to the upstairs bathroom, hoping it wouldn't be mobbed with more crepey suits, she'd had to bite the inside of her cheek to keep from bawling loud and angry tears right there.

And now, here Scottie was at four in the morning, about to lose it again.

And *again*, there was that blue—a four-inch swatch of fuzzy fabric hanging off a long, wooden needle and a scraggly ball of yarn stuck through with the second needle. Scottie glared at the whole mess.

What *a coincidence,* she thought. *I wonder if Aunt Lucille hid in the closet to plant that little "sign."*

She pulled the free knitting needle out of the ball and began tapping it on the cement floor, giving her agitation a rapid drumbeat. With her other hand, she dug her fingers into the soft yarn. Aunt Lucille's nice, neat ball had become so undone, it was just a free-form blob now. Scottie stopped drumming and unraveled the yarn. Then she wound it back up until it had become a nice, spongy grapefruit attached by a foot-long tail to the knitted swatch.

Scottie glanced at the clock and cringed: 4:20.

She grabbed the free needle again—and jabbed it through the top-most loop in the swatch. She didn't know why she was even trying. She was sure she couldn't remember the stitch Aunt Lucille had shown her.

Except, a few fumbling twists and turns later, she did remember it! At least her fingers did. Her index finger caught up a loop of yarn, then wove it around, through, and across the needles. It was as if Scottie's hands had been itching to knit and her mind hadn't had a clue.

Ohhhh-kay, this is weird.

Scottie glanced furtively at her closed bedroom door before clicking her way through another stitch. It worked again, swishing from stick to stick with a satisfying little *sizzzzz.*

Clearing her throat quietly, she did it again.

And again.

By the time she reached the end of the row, she almost had a rhythm going. It wasn't anything you could dance to, but . . .

Almost without thinking, she started another row. She propped the four inches of blue onto her bare knees, enjoying the fuzzy feel of it as it shifted back and forth to the loops, tugs, and scrapy-clicky shifts of her needles.

The long string of yarn was flowing through her cupped right fingers now, whispering against her palm. Scottie thought of the way cats nudged their heads under your hand, petting you as much as you did them.

The softness. The zinging. The way the swatch began to grow, row by halting row, inching over Scottie's knees— all of it began to replace the agitated buzz in her head.

She sighed with relief.

But she also worried that her black-sky, middle-of-the-night empti-ness would come back if she laid the needles down. So she kept on knitting.

She was on her twenty-eighth row when the alarm went off two hours later.

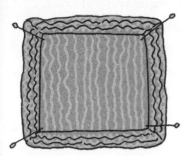

2 ✦ (Check Tension)

Post-alarm, Scottie's morning routine—shower, cereal, blow-dry hair while simultaneously glancing at *Hamlet,* then dash out the loft door—made her feel almost normal. But every time she rubbed her burning eyes or stumbled into another piece of furniture, she was reminded of her surreal, middle-of-the-night knitting.

It was like I was another person, she thought as she began her walk to the "L." *But who? Martha Stewart? Granny Weatherall?*

The whole crafty thing was *very* not Scottie. Every time she thought of doing something artistic, all she had to do to talk herself out of it was think of her mother, otherwise known (to Scottie, anyway) as the Creator.

Scottie's mother was a painter. A real painter, who splashed giant canvases with wild swirls of color that Scottie didn't really get. Plenty of other people did, though, or at least pretended to. After several art critics had written reviews (which Scottie also didn't really get), collectors started showing up at their loft. They arrived, almost always, in the Art Collector's Uniform: black-on-black outfits, chunky, plastic-rimmed glasses, and spiky, cropped haircuts.

They had matching taste in art, too. Enough of them had bought up the "utterly original Carrie Shearers" that several years ago Scottie's dad had quit his job on Michigan Avenue. Scottie didn't really get what *he'd* done at his office, either. He'd simply called himself a "corporate drone." Once he got out, though, he'd put singular glee into knocking out a wall between the family's loft and the one next door and setting up "Shearer Space: An Art Gallery."

The gallery became her dad's life. Scottie barely recognized him now if he wasn't chattering into his hands-free phone, buttering up potential buyers, booking caterers for art openings, or consulting with experts about humidity and lighting.

Despite all Dad's labor, everyone in the family knew that Scottie's mom was the only Shearer at Shearer Space who truly mattered.

There was a lot of reverent tiptoeing around the Creator, especially when she was in the middle of a piece. Her painting came in frenetic bursts that would stop for nothing—not Scottie, not her dad, not dinner. Her bright red hair—usually gelled into perfectly arranged spikes—went all askew. She wore the same clothes for days. She went on autopilot, looking past Scottie—looking *through* her—as she was asking about her day at school or performing some other mandatory momism. When she was painting, she wasn't really there. She was inside her art, consumed with its colors and shapes.

How self-absorbed can you get? Scottie thought as she shuffled toward her stop on the Brown Line.

She regretted, now, shoving her yarn and needles into her backpack right before she'd left home. She'd done it on impulse as she'd been hunting and gathering her gear for the day—trig notebook, clear lip gloss, train-fare card. Tossing in the knitting, too, had seemed to make sense. If she took the yarn with her, there was no way her parents—or God forbid some art buyers helping themselves to a tour of the loft—could stumble upon it.

Plus, it's not like a little bundle of yarn is a big deal to lug around, right? Scottie had told herself.

Now, though, as she heard the distant rumble of her train clatter-

• • Chicks with Sticks

ing toward the station, she wondered if she should have reconsidered. Her backpack felt like dead weight dragging her down as she began to run.

The rattle got louder as she darted into the station, shoved her card into the entry slot, and hurried through the turnstile. The train was just hitting the station now. If she skipped every other step, she'd make it. She raced up the stairs, dodging around passengers coming down.

But she didn't make it. She hit the platform just as the train doors were rattling closed, shutting her out. As the elevated train clattered its way down the track, Scottie threw her pack onto the tar-spattered platform and completely stunned herself by bursting into tears.

Things pretty much went downhill from there.

The first person Scottie saw when she got to her locker at school was Amanda Scott.

This, of course, was not a surprise. Scottie and Amanda had signed up for side-by-side lockers in the sixth grade, the first year all Stark kids started switching classes. Together, the girls had plastered the inside of their lockers with matching contact paper and little bulletin boards, where they left themselves notes like, "I ♥ Rodney" and "19th century poetry SUCKS!"

After school, Scottie and Amanda had been side by side, too. Scottie's extracurriculars were ballet and Amanda. Amanda's were tutoring and Scottie. They thought they were fated to be BFFs. Come on—Amanda *Scott* and *Scottie* Shearer? That was a sure sign.

But that was then. Now—Scottie and Amanda's sophomore year—it seemed like their names were the only things they had in common. Scottie found that, lately, she couldn't think of a single thing to say to her best friend.

So now . . . she didn't. Say anything. Taking advantage of the fact that Amanda was engrossed in reglossing her lips, lotioning up her hands, and adjusting the elastics on her perfectly tousled pigtails,

Scottie silently whizzed through her locker combo and started unloading her backpack.

She was almost done when Amanda slammed her locker shut. As the latch caught, Scottie heard a faint crackle that made her pause. It was the Scotch tape.

Every year, when she and Scottie got their new locker assignments, Amanda wadded tape into the latch in the door, jamming her locker into a state of permanent unlockedness.

Most people didn't know this, of course. Amanda was great at faking the precise twirl of her lock before she hitched her locker open. It was possible, in fact, that Scottie was the *only* one at Stark who knew about Amanda's totally fake lock twist.

The daily performance was just one of many Amanda used to hide her big secret. Numbers freaked her out. So did words, at least written ones. The reason? She had a learning disability. She read super-slow (when she chose to read at all), and math tied her up in knots.

Amanda had sworn Scottie to secrecy when she'd first been "diagnosed" in second grade. The LD had made them quiet and careful around each other for a good week—before they'd fallen back into their groove of playing with each other's hair, crank-calling each other nightly, and begging their parents to let them have a sleepover virtually every weekend.

Now, of course, Scottie knew what Amanda's learning disability was really all about. Amanda had described it to her once last year, when she and Scottie had just left Barnes & Noble. One of Scottie's favorite writers had given a reading there, and Scottie had begged Amanda to go. Amanda hadn't wanted to, but Scottie had used her best guilt-rending tactics *and* bribed Amanda with frozen yogurt.

It had been at Windy's, their favorite fro-yo stand, that Amanda had started talking about what reading and writing felt like to *her*.

"It's like my brain is an electrical wire that's all frayed and rusted at the ends," she'd said, staring into her cup of peanut butter yogurt to avoid meeting Scottie's eyes. "Reading and stuff makes that wire start sparking and spewing smoke. My tutor keeps saying that if I just wade through the smoke, the fire will die down. But sometimes it's so thick, I feel like I can't get through it. I choke, and the only way I can breathe is to run away."

"You mean, from the book?" Scottie had squeaked.

"Or the math problem or the locker combination," Amanda said. "Whatever. My tutor says I could do a lot better if I just got over myself."

"She said that?!" Scottie had been aghast. Amanda had suddenly seemed so . . . fragile.

"Well, she wasn't *that* harsh," Amanda'd said. "My parents are practically paying her entire grad school tuition, so she has to be nice to me. But in so many words, yeah, that's what she said. Maybe she's right, but I don't know. She has no idea what it feels like to be in my head. Nobody does."

"Except me," Scottie had said, slipping her arm through Amanda's. In the process, she'd jostled Amanda's yogurt cup, spilling the now-melted stuff down Amanda's arm.

Amanda had laughed, finally looking up at Scottie as she'd licked the drips off her wrist.

"Except you," she'd agreed.

How did we get each other so easily back then? Scottie wondered. She was beginning to think all that bonding had just been a figment of her imagination.

As Amanda turned away from her locker, and almost plowed into Scottie, her theory gathered even more evidence.

"Oh, I didn't see you there," Amanda said accusingly. "Don't even say hi, why don't you?"

"Sorry," Scottie mumbled, sort of meaning it.

Amanda shrugged and glanced around, scanning the hall for distraction.

Sorry, girlfriend, Scottie said silently. *Looks like you're stuck with me.*

"So . . . how was your weekend?" Scottie finally said lamely.

Amanda propped her chem book on her hip—just visible over the low-rise waistband of her little pleated skirt—and grinned.

"You're gonna regret blowing us off for our movie night!" she taunted.

"I didn't . . . blow you off," Scottie said. "I was just . . . I had a lot going on."

Which you might know about, if you had any interest in my life anymore.

"Okay, whatever," Amanda said, sighing ever so slightly. "I'm just saying that it couldn't have been as good as this."

"An Ashton Kutcher film festival?" Scottie said, arching her eyebrow.

"Okay, okay, you'll be happy to know I've finally come over to your dark side . . ." Amanda said.

Thanks and pass the Prozac, please, Scottie thought.

". . . and I agree that Ashton really *should* stick to TV."

"Really?"

"Yeah." Amanda replied. "In movies? He sorta sucks! But that's not the point. So Maryn and Tiff *did* come to movie night, right?"

Scottie couldn't help but flinch. Maryn and Tiff had been at Stark for as long as Amanda and Scottie had—since first grade. But Amanda had only become tight with them recently.

It had been bound to happen. Amanda, Maryn, and Tiff shared the same vital stats: they all lived in a manicured neighborhood called the Gold Coast, where no building was without a doorman and no condo without a maid's quarters. They all had trust funds, which bought them amazing clothes and lots of makeup. And they all had been recently anointed by the bod gods with brand-new curves.

The curves had quickly led to tiny tube tops, high-heeled shoes, and invites to virtually every happening on the near north side.

They had become official party girls.

Because Scottie preferred her red suede Pumas to Stuart Weitzmans she couldn't possibly afford, because she couldn't hold up a tube top without double-sided tape, and because she was too self-conscious to dance on coffee tables, she had been dubbed the anti–party girl. She was broody girl. A buzzkill. An ex-BFF.

"So, we started with Ashton's attempt at a serious movie," Amanda was saying. "That thing about the butterfly?"

"Uh-huh."

"Well, it creeped us out so much, we decided we just *had* to get out of the apartment and be among people. So we went to the Eight Bar and they actually let us in! No carding or anything!"

Scottie blinked. After her crying jag, her eyes felt swollen and heavy and her reactions were seriously delayed, but this was huge enough to give her a jolt.

"You went drinking at the Eight Bar?" she asked. "The Eight Bar which is next door to your building? The building where your parents live?"

"First of all, my parents were out at some benefit thing," Amanda said, rolling her eyes. "And second, I didn't say we went drinking. It was just about . . . going there. We danced a little, and this old guy started flirting with Maryn. Oh my God, it was disgusting. He was thirty-five, at least."

"Sounds like loads of fun," Scottie said sarcastically.

"It was!" Amanda retorted. "You had to be there. Which you weren't. What *were* you up to this weekend, anyway?"

"I . . . I . . ." Scottie looked down suddenly. Her eyes felt worse, and she wondered if they were super-red. Would Amanda notice?

"Hey, Pigtails."

Scottie looked up as Amanda froze and her eyes glazed over.

Okay, so she won't *notice. Not when Matt Altman is strolling up behind her, smirking at the back of her head.*

Slowly, Amanda flipped one of her carefully shagged ponytails over her shoulder and turned around.

Needless to say, she forgot Scottie was even standing there. Now it was she who was staring at the back of Amanda's head.

"Hey, Matt," Amanda said. She glanced down at his baggy cargo pants. "Aren't *you* the skater punk today."

"Oh yeah," Matt replied. "Come by the skate pool after school, I'll show you my ollies."

"Oh, don't you wish," Amanda said.

"More than you know," Matt quipped.

Oh, aren't they clever! Scottie thought. She slammed her locker door shut. Amanda didn't even flinch.

As Scottie stalked away, she berated herself.

Will Amanda notice my red eyes? Please. She won't even notice that I've left.

Scottie slouched through the entirety of her history class, then struggled to stay awake through English. (It helped that nobody died that day in *Hamlet*.) She practically wept with relief when, in Spanish, Señora Kent turned off the lights to show a video about *churros y chocolate*. As the cool darkness settled over the room like an afghan, Scottie quickly propped her head on her fist and dozed off, wondering before she conked if the Spanish were *really* as obsessed with fried dough and hot chocolate as Señora Kent made them out to be.

Finally, it was lunchtime. Scottie stumbled to her locker. In a way, she realized as she grabbed her math book, she was glad for the fatigue. It had taken over her brain, filling it with fuzz that canceled out thoughts she didn't want to think. It had also killed her appetite, but she headed to the cafeteria anyway. If nothing else, she needed some more caffeine. She had a trig quiz at the end of the day that she couldn't afford to sleep through, even if she hadn't really studied for it.

As she waited in the lunch line, her eyes wandered to the dead bunny painted on the wall right next to the dessert station.

Lovely.

The Stark School was all about kids following their creative impulses. The language arts teachers encouraged students to stage guerrilla Brecht in the courtyard. In poli sci, people were always proposing schoolwide boycotts and writing letters to their congressmen. Scottie's own older sister, Jordan, had created an underground film festival at Stark; now she was making movies at NYU.

The mural on the cafeteria wall, though, wasn't the sort of creativity that made it into the shiny pamphlets that they handed out at Stark fund-raisers. It had been painted by a bunch of seniors when Scottie was in the lower school. She remembered signing a petition about it, which the seniors had then presented to the principal. It had said something about kids being allowed to take ownership of their lunch hour. Art, they insisted, would make the cafeteria "a haven from the rigors and pressures of the prep school pressure cooker."

The touchy-feely psychobabble got the Stark administrators right where they lived. They'd even provided a huge array of paints and brushes.

It wasn't until the tail end of the painting process that the student artists had added the subversive elements: the two kids French kissing in a sea of smiling, multiracial faces; the teacher sleeping in front of a class of attentive students; and the gory dead bunny painted to protest the serving of meat in the cafeteria.

Scottie usually averted her eyes from the bloody animal so she could eat her spaghetti and meatballs in peace, but today, she couldn't seem to stop staring at it as she inched down the line.

Needless to say, she *didn't* go for the sloppy joes but, instead, grabbed a grilled cheese and an apple before heading to the soda machine. Just as she fed a dollar into the slot, Amanda appeared. She leaned into the Coke machine like it was a tall, supportive boyfriend and gazed at Scottie sideways, as if she was too tired to hold her head upright.

"Oh . . . hi," Scottie said.

"Don't sound *too* glad to see me," Amanda said. Her curvy hip was blocking the Diet Coke button.

Guess she hasn't quite gotten the hang of those things yet, Scottie observed.

Of all the changes Amanda had gone through in the past year, this was the one that fascinated Scottie most. She often had to stop herself from staring at Amanda's new body. Not in the same way *Matt* was always staring at it, of course. Scottie felt more like a kid with a science project—a cocoon that had hung around on its little branch for so long, she'd thought it would stay that way forever. Then one night, out of the blue, the cocoon had erupted and out had walked this beautiful monarch butterfly, poised to fly away.

That's pretty much what had happened to Amanda. She'd gone to Europe over the summer with her parents and little brother and come home a changed woman. She suddenly had hips to fill out her hip-huggers and a new drawerful of underwire bras. More than a month into the school year, she still seemed thrilled with the development.

"So, are you eating with us?" Amanda asked Scottie, cocking her hip out even farther. Scottie glanced at their usual table. Tiff was already there, flipping the top slice of bread off her veggie sandwich.

"I thought I might sit by myself and study trig," Scottie said. "I've got an evil quiz in sixth."

Amanda shifted her weight in the other direction, finally allowing Scottie a window. She jabbed the Diet Coke button. As she bent over to fish the can out of the opening, Amanda said, "You ran off this morning before I could finish my story. C'mon. Why don't you sit with us?"

Scottie glanced up.

I guess that was, maybe, an apology?

If it was, it was a lame one. On the other hand, Scottie was too tired to generate any drama. What's more, she was too tired to study trig, so she nodded and followed Amanda to the table.

Luckily, the moment they arrived, Maryn burst through a crowd of kids and practically fell into her usual seat.

"Oh my God," she screamed. "Guess what?!"

"Hello to you, too," Scottie said with false chirpiness. She felt

Amanda shoot her a look. Scottie, in turn, began tearing her sandwich into bite-size pieces.

"I just stopped in the computer lab," Maryn shrieked, "and you'll never guess who e'd."

"Steve?" Amanda proposed.

"Roddie?" Tiff said.

"Keller?" Scottie offered.

"No!" Maryn said as the girls rattled off the names of her top three crushes (not to be confused with the seven other guys on her love list). "Ted!"

"Ted," Scottie said. She looked at Amanda and Tiff, but they were as blank as she was.

"TED!" Maryn shouted. "From the Eight Bar?"

"The old guy?" Tiff said. She was squealing now, too. "*Quelle* disgusting!"

"What a loser," Amanda said, fishing a grape tomato out of her salad.

"But how did he get your e-mail?" Scottie asked Maryn. She was totally confused.

"Oh . . ." Maryn said, waving her pearly pink nails through the air dismissively.

"No, seriously, Maryn," Scottie said, dropping her bit of greasy sandwich. "I mean, what if this guy's a creepy stalker? Did he see your learner's permit or something? Did you tell him your last name? I bet he Googled you and found your e-mail address."

"No, I don't think so," Maryn said. She was suddenly really interested in her red Jell-O. Obviously, she hadn't spent any quality time with the dead bunny today.

She was also clearly hiding something.

Amanda and Tiff began whispering to each other and snorting behind cupped hands.

"Guys," Scottie demanded. "What's the deal?"

(It's a purl thing)   23

"She gave it to him!" Tiff suddenly screamed. "I saw it. While Amanda and I were dancing, Maryn wrote her e-mail address on the guy's business card!"

"Mare," Amanda said, shaking her head. "You're such a tease."

"Takes one to know one," Maryn said, glancing back at the food line. Scottie looked, too. Matt was at the cashier, paying for a double serving of sloppy joes and shooting Amanda a cocky grin, which she returned with a sassy waggle of her fingers. Scottie tamped down her annoyance and turned back to Maryn.

"Hello?" she said. "Am I the only one who thinks it's really screwed up to flirt with a guy who could practically be your father?"

"Where's your sense of humor?" Maryn said dismissively. She pushed away her Jell-O and pulled a lip gloss out of her purse. As she swabbed the sticky stuff on, Scottie wondered how many of those lippies Maryn went through in a month. Maryn declared to her friends (often) that she *hated* having naked lips. Whenever she ate, she reglossed between almost every bite, especially when she was IVOB. In the Vicinity of Boys.

"Hey, new color?" Tiff said suddenly, grabbing the spongy lip gloss wand out of Maryn's hand.

"Bobbi Brown," Maryn said. "Very fall."

"Love it," Tiff burbled.

Amanda grabbed a napkin and tossed it onto the table in front of Tiff, who scribbled on it with the lip gloss.

"Nice," Amanda said, examining the pinky brown smear closely.

Scottie coughed, but nobody at the table looked at her.

Okay, not only can they not stick to a subject for longer than, like, two minutes, they can't even speak in complete sentences.

Scottie propped her chin on her fist and picked at her sandwich. It had quickly gone from lukewarm to stone cold. And her apple had a big, ugly bruise on it.

You know, gum is starting to sound like a very tasty lunch, Scottie told herself. She reached into her backpack to grab some Dentyne. To get to it, she had to shove aside a wad of yarn. Finally, she found the gum, popped a piece into her mouth, and stared at the ceiling as she chewed. Maybe she'd been wrong. Trig *was* more appealing than lunch with Amanda, Tiff, and Maryn.

She tried to pop her gum by stretching it between her top and bottom molars. It didn't work. All she could muster were some pretty gross, wet grinding noises.

"Um, *what* are you doing?"

Scottie stopped chewing and came back to earth, smiling sheepishly at Amanda, Tiff, and Maryn.

"I'm gum-impaired," she explained.

That's when she realized that nobody was concerned with the offensive wad in her mouth. They were staring at Scottie's lap.

Scottie looked down and was surprised to see that her hand was inside her bag and her fingertips were skimming back and forth, back and forth, over her bumpy-soft swatch of knitting.

"What have you got in there?" Tiff said, a giggle lurking in her voice like a soap bubble on the verge of popping. "A puppy?"

Amanda just looked embarrassed, like Scottie had been caught scratching her crotch in public.

"Oh, please," Scottie said. She pulled the knitting out of her purse and waggled it at the girls. "Happy?"

"What is that?" Tiff screamed. "Did a sweater explode in there?"

"It's knitting," Scottie muttered.

"What?" Maryn said, grabbing the swatch out of Scottie's hands. Scottie felt a quick pang in her stomach as she watched Maryn's long nails pull at the stitches she'd worked on that morning. "Knitting? *Tell* me you didn't do this."

"Whatever!" Scottie said, snatching her beginning-of-a-scarf out of Maryn's hands. She stuffed it back into her backpack and zipped it up. But as she locked the soft fabric out of her sight, she felt the pang again.

In fact, she felt dangerously close to bursting into tears. She could sense her cheeks going pink. She knew her nose would be next, followed by a ring around her mouth. Soon her entire face would be red and squashy. Then the tears would break through, right there in front of the dead bunny and everyone.

Scottie swallowed hard and stared down at her pack, fiddling with the zipper and trying to swallow back her emotions.

"Scottie?"

Amanda sounded half-concerned, half-irritated. Scottie ignored her.

Slowly she opened her backpack again. The yarn burst out of it, almost as if it had felt cramped and resentful when she'd locked it away.

Wait a minute, Scottie suddenly said to herself. *Cramped? Resentful? We're talking about* yarn *here. Keep a grip on reality!*

Scottie looked up at Amanda, Maryn, and Tiff. Their faces were blushed and glossed and hardened. It struck her that her friends weren't exactly poster girls for reality themselves.

The tears were really threatening now, swelling up in Scottie's chest and making the back of her throat prickle.

What do I do? she thought in a panic. She heard a plaintive edge in her silent question, but at this point she didn't have the energy to berate herself for it. All she wanted was a solution.

She completely unzipped her pack and pulled out the blue wool. She inhaled as she wrapped her yarn tail around her finger and speared her first loop. As she completed the stitch, she exhaled loudly. She felt as if she'd just emerged from a long, underwater lap. She felt relief.

Another three stitches and the lump in her throat began to dissolve. Her breathing evened out, falling in line with the rhythm of her knitting's clicks and swishes.

She was halfway through the row before she remembered Amanda, Maryn, and Tiff. When she looked up, they looked even more aghast than before.

"Oh my God," Tiff said. "You're really knitting."

· · Chicks with Sticks

Amanda's top lip curled just slightly. "Well, *that's* new. Or I should say, old. As in, as old as my grandmother."

"I learned how a few weeks ago," Scottie said curtly. Needing to avoid Amanda's beautiful, bewildered face, she ducked her head and speared another loop of yarn with her right needle. But as she whisked her way through the next stitch, she realized she didn't really feel embarrassed. In fact, she was a little proud of the even, little wavelets of yarn building beneath her fingers.

She didn't expect Amanda to understand. Scottie barely understood it herself.

Breathe. Spike. Click. Breathe. Loop and swish. Breathe. Spike. Click . . .

"Ohhhhkay."

That was Maryn, using her best "Am I the only one who thinks Scottie's a freak?" tone.

Go back to your lip gloss, Maryn, Scottie scoffed inside her head.

But the thought immediately conjured an image in Scottie's mind. She pictured herself, last year, just before Amanda's Paris trip. Scottie remembered showing Amanda her new mascara before launching into a long discussion about lash lengthening vs. thickening.

Scottie had been these girls once. And now, somehow, she wasn't. Now she was knitting, of all things.

Can the real Scottie Shearer please step forward?

Watching her hands weave the yarn, looking as if they had minds and motors of their own, Scottie realized, *No, actually. I don't think she can. I'm not sure exactly who she is.*

Scottie had once read in a teen magazine that you should take a brisk walk whenever you felt the urge to take a nap. The exercise, the article promised, would be much more invigorating than sleeping through the afternoon.

Brisk walks were also the miracle antidote for vegging in front of the TV or devouring an entire bag of Oreos.

Normally, Scottie had about as much respect for chirpy teen-mag advice as she did for Chinese-cookie fortunes, but this afternoon she was desperate. She was so exhausted as she emerged from trig, and her possibly failed quiz, she was willing to try anything. She trotted up the stairs to Stark's third floor, then pumped her arms as she motored to her locker.

It worked about as well as a tranquilizer dart. As she pulled her homework out of her locker, she could only think about her bed . . . her pillow . . . the couch and its chenille afghan . . . herself cuddled beneath the afghan, snoozing away. . . .

Scottie tapped her locker shut and headed for the exit, only to be intercepted by Amanda, who was doing the brisk walk thing, too. Hers looked anything but weary, though. Amanda stomped to her locker and threw it open, not even trying to pretend she'd spun in the combination. Sensing Scottie looking at her, she glared over her shoulder.

"What?" she spat.

"I didn't say anything!" Scottie shot back irritably. "Jeez, what's wrong with you?"

Amanda opened her mouth but couldn't seem to find any words. She was clutching the handle of her pistachio-green purse so hard, her knuckles were white. Scottie also noticed that her nails were a mess—her always-perfect polish was chipped to shreds, though it had been perfect at lunch.

Except for her purse, Amanda's hands were also empty. She wasn't holding any books.

And suddenly Scottie just knew: something had happened in Amanda's last class. Maybe a teacher had made everyone read aloud or had people do equations on the board. Maybe Amanda had had to follow a chemistry recipe in front of a lab partner.

Whatever it was, she'd let the smoking fuses in her brain get the better of her. She'd freaked.

Scottie was surprised to realize that she wanted to hear all about it.

Yes, Amanda had become a flippy party girl. And, yeah, she'd made Scottie feel like the biggest of dorks at lunch. But the truth was, Scottie still cared about Amanda. She missed her. And she was hurting for her. At that moment, actually, it almost felt like a relief, hurting for Amanda instead of hurting for herself.

As far as this yucky turn in their friendship? Well, somebody was going to have to budge first, and suddenly Scottie wanted to be the one to do it. She wanted to kick all their new baggage to the curb and just be friends again. She wanted to start over from this moment.

What happened, Amanda?

All Scottie needed was for Amanda to answer her unspoken question—to spill out her trauma the way she used to.

Too bad Amanda couldn't read Scottie's mind like she used to. And clearly Scottie's expression wasn't sending out "talk to me" vibes either. Because Amanda just rolled her eyes, snapped her mouth shut, and turned back to her locker.

"Nothing's wrong with me," she said, banging a few books around. "Forget it. Go knit or something."

Sudden heat prickled around Scottie's hairline.

"What's that supposed to mean?" she demanded.

"Nothing. Whatever," Amanda sputtered, her back still to Scottie. "Forget I said it."

"Fine!" Scottie said. She started to stalk away, but somehow she couldn't get beyond their bank of lockers. Almost against her will, she turned back. A moment later, she found herself clutching Amanda's locker door, leaning into her sullen face.

"Knitting may be an incredibly dorky way to deal with my problems," Scottie whispered, the teary throat lump from lunch resurfacing, "but at least I'm *dealing* with my problems, which is more than *you* can say."

Amanda flinched and met Scottie's eyes. They both knew exactly what Scottie meant, but the queen of denial wasn't going to admit it out loud.

(It's a purl thing)

"Problems?" Amanda said to Scottie. "What problems could you possibly have? I've never met anyone more normal than you."

Now it was Scottie's turn to flinch.

Amanda was saying *normal* but she meant *boring*.

Scottie imagined what she must have looked like last night, sprawled on the terribly stylish white shag rug that her mother had chosen for her room, her knobby knees hunched up, her feet planted and pigeon-toed, her skinny fingers doing the same loopy stitch over and over and over.

The sobs were coming now, and they weren't going to stop.

"What do you know, Amanda?" she said, before her voice choked up. "Nothing! You don't know anything!"

Scottie whirled around and dashed away, making the door to the stairs just before her tears arrived.

The magazines hadn't mentioned another handy reason for that brisk walk—it was the perfect way to make an escape.

3 ✦ (Pick up and Knit)

All day long, Scottie had thought about nothing but sleep. Now she could barely blink, much less contemplate a nap. As she raced down the stairs, she couldn't tell if she was angry or exhilarated or just halfway down the pike to a nervous breakdown.

Only when she hit the sidewalk did she pause.

If she didn't want to take to her bed, where *did* she want to go? Drowning her sorrows at Joe was out of the question. Amanda always hung out there with Maryn and Tiff, trying to seem sophisticated by ordering espresso.

Never mind that she looks like she's sucking on spinach every time she forces the stuff down, Scottie thought.

Great—now she felt a fresh round of tears starting. She stared down at the sidewalk, where a cigarette butt was smoldering on the cement, and fought them off.

No more thoughts about Amanda allowed, she ordered herself.

She stomped on the cigarette and started walking. Because she still didn't know where she wanted to go, she let her legs lead the way.

They took the route they knew best—down the block back to the Brown Line. As she walked, Scottie distracted herself with the bustle on the street. She breathed in the cloud of beefy grease outside the hot dog stand, and then the sickly-sweet smoke wafting from the corner where a cheery Rasta guy always sold incense from a tiny card table. She peered carefully at the row of newspaper boxes blaring their "buy me, buy me" headlines.

But she still had more exorcising to do when she chunked through the "L" turnstile. So, instead of taking her usual route home—north to Ravenswood—she headed up the southbound stairs.

A few minutes later, she was sitting in a forward-facing seat, directly behind a seat that pointed at the center of the train. Scottie loved to prop her shoes on this sideways seat, tuck her knees under her chin, and sink into her fiberglass throne. From there, you could just veg and watch the skyline sparkle as you headed straight for its belly.

The train rounded a curve, jostling its riders violently. A couple of tourists gripping poles near the doors lurched backward and almost fell. Their countless shopping bags went flying.

Scottie knew it was mean, but she loved the "L" for this. *She'd* been riding this rickety train ever since she was fetal (according to her parents), and she knew exactly how to brace herself against its particular bumps and grinds. Visitors *didn't* know when to shift their weight, when to lean backward, and when it was safe to let go of the handrails. This was one place, at least, where Scottie had the inside scoop.

Maybe that's not so impressive to some, Scottie acknowledged, hiding a smile behind her hand, *but when your house is an avant-garde art gallery and your school is the sort of place that has dead bunnies painted on the walls, you take what you can get.*

Scottie kept smiling as she gazed out at the back porches of the flats that lined the train tracks. She knew their quirks so well—the lime-green flower boxes on the back of the graystone with the gargoyles; the hand-scrawled I ❤ OBAMA sign; a dog pacing on a rooftop deck, barking its head off as the train passed.

Soon the train careened into the downtown loop and immediately slowed down to a chug. It skirted the mammoth buildings so closely, you could have touched them if not for the Plexiglas windows. The

• • Chicks with Sticks

stone was carved with cornices and elaborate vines and mysterious-looking Grecian women, who'd been thrusting their chests out at "L" riders for decades.

Bye, boys, Scottie always imagined those granite women saying. They'd been sculpted to greet commuters of a hundred years ago, the mustachioed, big-shouldered types every Chicago kid learns about on field trips to the historical society. Now they were gazing imperiously at Scottie. She stuck her tongue out at one of them.

As the train completed the loop and headed back north, Scottie's eyes drifted away from the window. With her rage dulled and the train rocking her back and forth like an urban cradle, Scottie was pricked by a sudden urge, one that felt familiar and foreign at the same time.

This time, though, Scottie didn't hesitate. She reached into her bag and pulled out her blue scarf.

Hell, she thought as she dug eagerly into her first stitch, *if other people on the train can break into song or make out, complete with visible tongues, then I can play with my yarn and sticks.*

The swatch felt right in her hands, warm and fluid. She spiked her second stitch and almost hummed as she swished it from needle one to needle two. She began to knit to the rhythm of the train's jerky turns and grinding stops.

It was feeling less and less weird, this Aunt Lucille thing. Scottie even found herself gazing back out the window as she knitted, confident enough to simply feel her way through the stitches. She propped her hands on her knees and watched the sun begin to set. For a moment, a shaft of light cascaded through the window, bathing Scottie and her growing swatch in warmth.

The thing was, for the first time this whole wretched day, she didn't need it. Warming up, that was. Her blue scarf, long enough now to tumble over her knees and cover a good few inches of shin, was doing an excellent job of that all on its own.

❧ ❧ ❧

(It's a purl thing)

By the time the train let her off at her stop, Scottie was in total Zen mode.

And it lasted just until she made it to her building. She sighed as she walked down the long, echoey hallway to her loft. Before she unlocked the door, she was careful to tuck any errant bits of yarn into her backpack and zip it up completely. Even so, she actually found herself tiptoeing inside to avoid a Mom-interface.

Not that she needed to. Turned out her mom was at work and wanted to be sure everyone knew it. Music was blaring out of her studio. Angry, thumpy, anthemic, movie-sound-track type of music. Scottie had to cock her head and listen for a moment before she wrapped her brain around the voice—the completely familiar, teenage voice.

It was an old Avril Lavigne CD.

Way to act your age, Mom, Scottie thought. *And, oh yeah, feel free to borrow my music. No problem.*

Glancing through the glass doors that separated the loft's living space from the gallery, she spotted her dad, pacing and gesticulating as he talked into his hands-free phone. Scottie could have tapped the glass and waved hello, but instead, she went straight to the kitchen and tossed her bag onto the island, which was made, of course, of stainless steel. When your kitchen was basically a giant oven, it didn't really lend itself to cute little spice racks and wallpaper.

Scottie heaved open the fridge door. The fridge, too, was less than cozy since her parents had gotten an oversize Sub-Zero to handle all the hors d'oeuvres they served at the gallery's openings.

You could fit a body in here, Scottie noted as she peered inside. *Too bad there's no actual food.*

As usual when her parents were between parties, the shelves held little beyond jars of aioli and capers and forgotten takeout boxes. Her stomach was growling after her aborted lunch, so she grabbed a couple of the boxes. One held a slice of pizza that was looking a little gray. In another was mu shu that was way too khaki.

"There's gotta be *something* color-appropriate," Scottie muttered as she dug deeper into the fridge. She emerged with a white, Styrofoam box and took a peek.

No way.

Inside the box was a big pile of rolled-up deli meat, each coil shot through with an AstroTurf-green toothpick. Scottie's stomach lurched, and not just because the turkey and salami rolls were—pungently—many weeks old.

It was their source that repulsed her.

My parents brought home leftovers from Aunt Roz's shivah.

Scottie gripped the edge of the island so hard, her fingers tingled.

Am I the only one who thinks of Aunt Roz dying as a tragedy instead of an opportunity for a little takeout! she screamed inside.

And just like that, Scottie *really* felt the pain of losing her aunt. She felt as awful as she had on the day of the car accident. Worse, actually. Because it was really sinking in now—Scottie was never again going to make a date with Aunt Roz for a chick-flick double feature. They were never again going out for dim sum on a Sunday morning. No more sleepovers at the little house in Evanston. No more of the orange-glazed sweet potatoes Aunt Roz brought to every Thanksgiving.

Scottie tossed the deli back into the fridge, slammed the door, and snatched her backpack off the island. Emerging from the kitchen, she gave the tall canvas curtains that cordoned off her mother's workspace a long glare and headed for her room. She slammed the door, locked it, and flopped onto her bed. After staring at the distant ceiling rafters for a moment, she slid to the floor. She snatched a rubber band off her nightstand, pulled her hair back into a haphazard bun, and yanked her knitting out of her backpack.

Spike. Loop. Swish.

Avril sang along to her stitches.

'Cause you weren't there, when I was scared,
I was so alone. . . .

Scottie bobbed her head to the song and shot through a row. Sure enough, she felt her ragged breathing even out. The sweat prickling the back of her neck began to cool. Two rows later, Scottie was singing along to Avril under her breath. She kicked off her shoes and dug her toes into her shaggy white rug.

As she flipped her needle over and started another row, she started singing louder. It wasn't like anyone could hear her over Mom's top-volume Creating.

The Avril song ended with a breathy, angry shriek, and Scottie let loose and just shrieked along. Even as her voice reverberated around the ceiling rafters, she slapped a hand over her mouth.

Okay, what *was that?*

More important, was her mom wondering the same thing? Scottie cocked her head, listening for the *slap, slap, slap* of her mother's bare feet on the cement floor.

After a few moments of excruciating silence, another burst of music filled the loft—this time it was Liz Phair, the later, poppier version.

Scottie's mom didn't even know she was home, much less have an interest in her little moment of drama.

So why did Scottie feel more empty than relieved?

Maybe, she realized, it was because her grapefruit-size ball of wool had dwindled down to a small, blue plum. A few more rows of knitting and she was going to be yarnless. She'd have the whole night ahead of her with nothing to knit.

Scottie glanced at her watch. It was 4:30. Her parents preferred that she get home before dark, and with the October days shortening quickly, she knew she'd never make it if she left now.

But if I don't find myself some yarn, I might not make it, either.

Scottie told herself to just go and ask her dad for permission and tell him where she was going. He'd be cool about it, or maybe even give her a ride.

But that would mean telling her father about her knitting. For some reason, this felt about as revealing as asking him to buy her tampons.

Scottie shook her head and jumped to her feet. She walked around the bed and plopped herself down at her desk. As she did a quick Web search on her computer, she shimmied in her chair to her mom's music.

I couldn't fight it, I couldn't wait to get awaaaay, Liz sang.

Scottie sang along. She was riding a sudden burst of energy and didn't want to give it the opportunity to fizzle out by being careful.

Besides, she wasn't going to get caught. Her mother was obsessed with her painting, her dad was deep into his cold calls, and Scottie, for the first time in a long time, knew exactly where she wanted to be.

Well, sort of.

The moment she'd gotten into a cab, she realized she'd left home without the address she'd scribbled down. All she remembered was the block.

I'm sure it'll be easy to find, she thought as the car dropped her off and zoomed away, leaving her in the middle of the 1600 block of Foster Avenue in Andersonville. *A store full of yarn can't be too easy to miss, right?*

Scottie hooked her purse over her shoulder and began to walk up the block, scanning the storefronts. She passed a seedy currency exchange and one of those Middle Eastern bakeries whose front window was crammed with copper teapots and giant bags of rice. A shoe store, a hot dog joint, of course, and a used-record store. But no yarn.

Scottie swallowed hard. It was easy to feel confident walking around Chicago as long as she knew where she was. But she hated being lost, *hated* having to ask for directions.

Especially to a place called KnitWit, she thought as she trudged along. *How can that not sound like an insult?*

Scottie walked up and down the block but saw no sign of yarn or needles or anything knitty at all, in *any* of the windows. She was trying to decide between using the five-dollar 411 on her cell and giving up completely, when something caught her eye.

It was a little shingle swinging over a window on the second floor of a building on the south side of the street.

On that sign were two letters: KW.

Next to the initials was a little ball of blue yarn—blue!—and a criss-crossed pair of needles.

Scottie dashed across the street, her heart thumping away again. So KnitWit wasn't a storefront but an old, second-floor apartment, the kind of place where you usually found tarot-card readers or some ancient tailor who'd been making men's suits since the Depression. Scottie always imagined these shops as dusty and underlit, smelling of cabbage soup or too many cats.

Sighing, she found a narrow glass door tucked between a minimart and a travel agency. She could now see the word *KnitWit* decaled onto the glass. The loopy letters looked like they'd been arranged out of bits of yarn.

Scottie climbed the steep, narrow stairs until they dead-ended at a landing with two rickety doors. One of them—the one with the purple glass knob—was hung with a big blackboard. A cup of colored chalk was nailed to the spot where a doorbell might have been. On the chalk-board, *KnitWit* was drawn in the same bubbly pink and green letters that middle-schoolers use to decorate their notebooks. Flitting around the name were scrawled messages.

Alice, I'm holding your honey milk hostage at the coffeehouse. Meet me there with the Debbie Bliss—3 p.m.

Alice, I finally finished the sleeve! Call me. ☺ B.

Hey, Purlicue, I need more lilac cashmerino. Can you save me????? Tiny

Scottie's stomach swooped. All the chummy chalk scrawls made her feel like she was walking into a clubhouse without the password. Should she knock? Or should she just give up and dart back down the stairs?

While she was still frozen on the landing in wimp mode, the door swung open. A wind chime, which must have been hanging on the other side of the door, jingled loudly as a young woman with pale green hair and an armful of yarn skeins plowed right into Scottie.

"Whoops!" the woman cried, stepping back into the shop's foyer. Compared to the murky stairwell, the little room was like a sunburst, painted orangey pink and bathed in yellow-gold light. It smelled faintly, and pleasantly, of toast and warm candle wax.

"See, that's why you never leave KnitWit needle-first." Greenie chortled. She waved Scottie inside.

Scottie laughed weakly as she walked in.

"Are you closing up?" she asked. "I didn't know the hours. . . ."

"Oh, this isn't my place. I *wish!*" Greenie said, taking another step backward so Scottie could come all the way in. She looked around the little foyer. It was plastered with flyers from floor to ceiling. On quite a few of them, Scottie noticed woebegone kittens looking for a home.

Guess, they've got the knitting type pegged, she thought.

She glanced again at the girl with the green hair, fishnets, and hot-pink fingerless gloves. *Then again, maybe not.*

Greenie was sizing her up, too.

"You've never been to KnitWit before?" she said. "Hard to find, huh? But now that you have, you're gonna get addicted, I assure you. Don't even try and fight it. You'll get the shakes."

"Great," Scottie muttered. "Sounds fun."

The woman grabbed her elbow and pulled her deeper into the shop.

Scottie found herself in a room dominated by a giant, round table laden with yarn. Skeins and hanks and balls of the stuff spilled out of bowls and buckets and boxes. There was yarn that looked like cobwebs. Like eyelashes. Like paper. Fuzzy balls of undyed wool squished together like a family of sleeping hamsters. Yarn as deeply red as cherry juice. Yarn as translucently blue as watercolor painted on a pure-white page. Yarn that Scottie wanted to touch and hold and string around her needles.

(It's a purl thing)

As all those yearnings came to a quick boil within her, Scottie literally gasped.

Whoa! I am addicted.

She also had a burning curiosity about the other stuff piled on the table. She spotted a basket of short needles connected by curvy stretches of wire and a box of metal cards with holes in them. A cracked ceramic bowl held cute little rings dangling with charms, and another had rubber pencil cappers (or something) in the shape of socks and sweaters.

Scottie couldn't believe how excited she was about all this stuff, but she also felt too shy to paw through it the way she wanted. She didn't even know what to look for.

"Alice!" Greenie called through a door with a mint-green frame. "I've got a newbie for you!"

"You make me sound so predatory," said a voice. Scottie held her breath until Alice herself appeared in the doorway. She waved Greenie out of the store with a laugh, then gave Scottie her full attention.

Purlicue. Now Scottie got it. Alice had black ringlets sproinging off her head in every direction. A few of the curls were clipped back with some glittery pins, but the 'do was relentlessly wild nonetheless. The same went for the collar of frizzled yarn capping her long, fuchsia cardigan. For good measure, the sweater was clipped around her voluptuous torso with a scattering of tiny, rhinestone pins. On her feet, Alice wore turquoise socks and flat-footed, suede clogs, the kind that made you walk in a leisurely lope, whether you wanted to or not. But clearly, Alice wanted to. As she floated around the table, she smiled easily. Her smile made Scottie think of . . .

. . . *of fullness,* she realized. Like she just finished a big cup of full-fat hot chocolate.

Alice looked at Scottie as she walked toward her. Then she nodded quickly and turned to pluck a skein of coppery brown yarn out of a crockery bowl on the table. She slapped the skein onto Scottie's shoulder and laid a hank of her pale hair over it.

• • Chicks with Sticks

"Just as I thought," Alice said, showing the yarn to Scottie. "This color really brings out the red highlights in your hair. . . ."

"Scottie," Scottie filled in. "And, I don't have red highlights in my hair!" She glanced down and saw the same thing she always did—the stick-straight ends of her long, dishwater-brown hair.

"You'll see the red when you're wearing a sweater made out of this," Alice said. She held the coppery yarn up to Scottie's hair again, and suddenly Scottie *did* see it—a glint of light that she'd never seen in her hair before.

"What is that, magic yarn?" she asked with a nervous laugh.

"Just some good old Lion Brand Wool-Ease," Alice said, giving the skein an affectionate stroke. "I'll show you what *is* magic, though. A friend of mine—a spinner—just gave this to me."

Alice pulled a twist of wheat-colored yarn out of another bowl on the table. She thrust it beneath Scottie's nose.

"Smell."

Scottie took a tentative whiff. The yarn smelled sort of warm and sort of grassy and sort of waxy. Scottie thought she detected just a trace of barnyard, too, but not in a bad way.

"It's Wensleydale wool. Really rare stuff. Can you smell how sheepy it is?" Alice purred. She buried her own nose in the yarn and took a deep sniff. "*Mmmm,* I love it."

Scottie didn't quite know what to say. All she knew was all this yarn was intoxicating! When Alice handed her the Wool-Ease, she cradled it in the crook of her arm.

"Maybe I could make a scarf from it," she said, gazing down at the twists of copper. "Instead of a sweater, I mean. Scarves are all I really know how to make."

Scottie reached into her bag to pull out her blue swatch, but when she glanced again at Alice's finely woven sweater, she hesitated. Her own scarf, with the occasional holes formed by dropped stitches, the gathers in spots where she'd pulled the yarn too tight, and the pockets where she hadn't pulled tight enough—it seemed so childish in comparison.

So, what are you going to do? she asked herself. *Just run away?*

Scottie felt like she'd been doing that a little too often today. And besides, something told her that Alice would say the right thing when she pulled out her little beginner's swatch. So she did.

And Alice did.

"Oh, merino," she said, her voice deepening to a purr as she examined the scarf. "Oh my God, this blue. It's perfect. So you want to finish it, huh? I have just the thing. . . ."

Alice handed Scottie's scarf back to her and gave the dining-room table another once-over. She shook her head this time and headed into the next room. Scottie followed her.

This room was bigger than the dining room. It must have been the living room back when KnitWit was a flat—a railroad-car apartment whose rooms were lined up one after another, with the bedrooms jutting off the sides.

Now the room looked like a classroom, of sorts. All the furniture— a few broken-down recliners, some straight-backed, cane-seated chairs, one antique love seat upholstered in a shiny peach fabric, and a couple beanbag chairs—were arranged in a circle. As Alice began to poke around, Scottie noticed there were baskets and big bowls and old, wood-slat soda crates all over the place—stashed in corners, tucked between chair legs, tossed into a tall bookshelf against the wall. Inside each of these random containers was, of course, more yarn.

After a bit more digging, Alice whirled around with a triumphant smile. In each hand, she held a skein of blue yarn. One was fuzzier than Scottie's wool and two shades lighter. The other was a couple of shades darker. It looked as if it had been dipped in navy ink, yet it still had a shimmer to it that Scottie instantly loved.

"I could put the light blue on one end of the scarf and the dark on

•• *Chicks with Sticks*

the other," Scottie said, reaching out for the skeins. She couldn't wait to dig her fingers into the spongy coils. She could already picture herself unraveling the yarn and knitting, knitting, knitting.

"That's exactly what I was thinking," Alice said. "The part you've already knitted goes in between."

Alice gave Scottie a searching look.

"I think you're a fringe girl," she said with a decisive nod. "Do you know how to do fringe?"

"I barely know how to knit!" Scottie blurted.

"We both know that's not true," Alice said, looking Scottie directly in the eyes.

This solid, wild-haired woman felt strangely familiar, even though Scottie already knew she'd never met anyone like her. Scottie held Alice's gaze for a moment, noticing that her eyes were the same coppery color as that first skein of yarn. Then she felt herself flush, and she looked down at her blue scarf—which was really still just a swatch. She picked at it nervously, running her fingers over its flaws.

"You've clearly got the knit stitch mastered," Alice said. "What about purl?"

"Nope," Scottie said, glancing up shyly. "I also don't know what you do when you get to the end."

"Binding off," Alice provided with an encouraging nod.

"Okay, that," Scottie said. "And what about these other blues? When I knit those parts, how do I attach them to my first part?"

"You know, I think it's fate that you came in here at just this moment," Alice said, glancing at an old school clock on the wall. "It's Tuesday and it's five-ten. In five minutes, I've got a class starting. It's for beginning and intermediate knitters."

Scottie had been right—this was a classroom.

And Alice was the teacher.

Of course.

Alice had that easy-in-her-skin, "I know what I'm doing" presence of a teacher. She also had the crow's-feet and strands of gray hair that said she'd been around long enough to know a thing or two.

But Alice didn't seem at all old to Scottie. She had a lightness to her, an ease that Scottie rarely saw in her parents, or those commuters who frowned at newspapers on the "L," or come to think of it, most of Scottie's teachers at Stark.

"So, this class?" Scottie said as Alice went back to bustling around the room, pulling a bunch of knitting needles and yarn skeins out of various receptacles.

"Don't worry, it's nothing like school," Alice said, still puttering. "I don't loom before you, lecturing. People come, they knit, and I slink around behind them, throwing out tips. Very free-form. Oh, and speaking of, the class is also free. Believe me, you'll be shelling out enough money for this yarn. I'm warning you, Scottie, knitting is *addictive*."

That's what Greenie had said just before she'd sailed out of KnitWit, looking happier than Scottie had felt in a long time.

Scottie hugged her three skeins of yarn to her chest and glanced out the window. The indigo evening was growing darker by the minute, but instead of getting anxious about getting home, Scottie felt free. She was already late. It made no difference now how long she stayed here.

I need this more than I need to make curfew, she told herself. Then she flopped onto the shiny peach love seat.

"Alice," she announced with a grin, "I'm in."

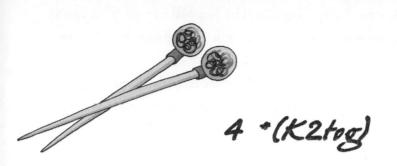

4 *(K2tog)

Okay, Scottie had to admit it. She cringed when she heard the wind chime on KnitWit's door tinkle. The class's first student was arriving and, Greenie aside, Scottie was bracing herself for stereotype central: a Stepford wife or goofy Pippi Longstocking type.

And let's not forget our location, location, location, Scottie reminded herself. *Andersonville.*

Everybody knew what kind of neighborhood Andersonville was. People here wore sandals with socks and dream-catcher earrings. All the food was made out of whole grains, and patchouli was the perfume of choice.

But, once again, Scottie was surprised. The knitter walking in was supernormal, with wavy blond hair, cool, high-heeled boots, and a butterscotch-colored boatneck sweater that fit her perfectly. She smiled at Scottie, plopped into one of the easy chairs, and announced, "I'm making a vow that I'm going to finish two baby hats tonight. Man, my friends are fertile. I haven't been able to make anything for myself in months."

While Scottie laughed, Alice perched on the arm of the woman's chair and said, "Always the bridesmaid, never the mom, huh, Becca?"

"Whatever," Becca said, waving her hand. "At this point in my life, knitting for babies is much more appealing than having 'em."

Alice clapped her hands together and hopped off the chair arm. "You're in luck, sweetie. I just saw a new baby hat pattern. The tiniest little bucket hat."

"Is it easy?" Becca said, raising a perfectly plucked eyebrow.

"Cinchy," Alice said, hustling into the dining room and grabbing a magazine out of a big, tin pot stashed under the table. "You'll be back to Squeezikhstan in no time."

"Squeezikhstan!?" Scottie burst out. "*What* is that? Do I need to learn a foreign language on top of purling?"

"Only if you're Becca," Alice said, tossing the magazine into the woman's lap. "She doesn't like the names you usually find on sweater patterns."

"Of course I don't," Becca said as she flipped through the magazine. "So bland and girlie."

She looked at Scottie.

"I mean, would you wear a sweater called Melissa? Or—oh, here's a clever one—Cable Car."

"Becca's getting her Ph.D. in English," Alice explained to Scottie as Becca went back to page flipping. "She takes names very seriously."

"Because names are important! For instance, this magazine calls its pattern Baby Bucket," Becca declared. She'd found the page with the hat pattern and was giving it a disdainful glance. "Now don't you think, um, Little Bunny Foo Foo would be much better? Maybe I'll even put little ears on it!"

"Not bad," Alice said. "But I much prefer the name you gave that yellow sweater, the one you made for your grandmother."

"The Cardimum," Becca said with a happy sigh. "A classic."

"And Squeezikhstan?" Scottie ventured.

"Oh, it's a fabulous sweater," Becca said. "It's got this tapestry pattern—very Central Asia. But instead of scratchy wool from one of those 'stans,' it calls for angora, which is so fuzzy and soft, you just want to squeeze whoever's wearing it. Thus . . . Squeezikhstan!"

"What was it originally called?" Scottie asked.

"The Betty!" Becca sputtered, rolling her eyes.

"*So* wrong," Scottie agreed with a grin.

As she and Becca chatted, a few other students straggled in. The first was a milky-skinned guy who sat himself stiffly in a straight-backed chair. He carefully extracted from his messenger bag a complicated contraption of thread-thin yarn strung onto four short needles. His forehead furrowed into a field of wrinkles as he looked at it.

"Alice, help," he whimpered.

While Alice rushed to his side, saying, "Now, Michael, you can do this. . . ." two women walked in.

Ah, here we go. Scottie cringed again as she took in the ladies' matching frowsy brown hair and suede Birkenstocks. One wore baggy silk pants and the other, an earthy linen maternity jumper over a basketball-size belly.

Becca wasn't kidding about all that fertility! Scottie mused, sizing up the pregnant woman. She and her friend weren't wearing dream catchers, but they did have on lots of bangle bracelets.

They also had wide welcoming smiles for Scottie, which made her feel guilty for judging them. As they slipped into what were obviously their usual seats in two nicely sagging chairs, they chatted easily. The woman in the silky pants made a joke, which sent the pregnant one into peals of easy laughter.

They looked like they'd been friends forever.

"Scottie?"

Scottie jumped as Alice put a warm hand on her shoulder.

"Ready for purling?"

Scottie nodded, and Alice sat next to her.

"It's basically the knit stitch done backwards, see?" she said, whipping out a pair of her own needles to demonstrate. She did a quick row of the purls before passing the needles on to Scottie so she could practice.

Having done so many knits, Scottie hated purl's backwardness at first. But after doing several rows of the stitches, she was hungry for more information. As soon as Alice was done cajoling Michael into something called a sleeve expansion, Scottie motioned her over.

Alice smiled and leaned over the back of the love seat. She began whispering about things like gauge and seaming. She named seductive stitches like reverse stockinette and double rib and seed stitch, all of which were basically different combos of knit and purl.

"You mean I know all I need to know with knit and purl?" Scottie whispered.

"Basically," Alice said with a shrug. "It's like a little poem, knitting. Short and sweet, but very complicated underneath."

As she said this, she shot a pointed glance at Michael. Scottie threw her head back and laughed. Across the room, the brown-haired girl-friends—named Jane and Patricia, Scottie had learned—looked up from the socks they were knitting. Jane started laughing with Scottie. It didn't matter that she didn't know the joke. She was here, which meant she *did* get the loose easiness Scottie was feeling. Scottie felt like she was embarking upon an adventure with these people, weaving her supersoft knits and purls and sitting on this couch with Alice, who already felt like a friend—

"Scottie!"

Scottie felt a strange lurch in her stomach as a voice made all the rightness of the evening suddenly veer off the road. She looked up.

Amanda was standing in the classroom's open doorway. *Amanda!* Amanda was *here,* and looking seven different kinds of stricken. While Scottie tried to wrap her brain around this development, Amanda glanced furtively around the room. Scottie followed her gaze and noticed for the first time that the lime-green paint on the classroom walls was chipped. The rag rug was matted, and the coffee table was lop-sided and needle-gouged.

Looking back at Amanda, Scottie braced herself for a curled lip. But when Amanda returned her gaze to Scottie, she only looked urgent. Her brown eyes broadcasted, *We need to talk.*

Sorry, Amanda, Scottie thought. *I seem to recall you telling me to go knit or something. Well, here I am, doing just that.*

Her easy smile had poofed away. She knew her already-thin lips were disappearing into a pale line, and her dark blue eyes were going glowery. Her face was tightening into a mask.

Quickly, she looked down at her knitting and began purling like her life depended on it. She urged herself to get lost in the stitches, like she'd done on the Brown Line, like she'd done last night, her toes sunk into fluffy shag.

Yeah, right.

What is she doing *here?* Scottie wondered, barely conscious of her fingers knitting, purling, and dropping stitches right and left. *How on earth did she know where to find me? And* why *did she find me? What? Watching me lose it in school wasn't enough?*

Scottie felt a shift on the love seat next to her. Alice had slipped away, and now Amanda was sitting by her side. Scottie refused to lift her head. All she could see were Amanda's long legs, her orange suede boots, and her wrecked pink nails, clasped nervously in her lap.

Scottie shifted slightly so her shoulder jutted into the space between them. She kept up her purl stitches, wondering if maybe she wanted to go bigger than a scarf. How about a whole damn blanket? She pictured herself underneath a blue-striped afghan, nothing but a lump.

Unfortunately, you could hear through a blanket.

"Listen," Amanda whispered. "I know, Scottie."

Know what?

"I know about your Aunt Roz," she said.

Scottie froze. Finally, she stopped knitting.

(It's a purl thing) 49

"I saw her picture . . . her obituary in an old copy of the *Trib* at Joe," Amanda said. "Four weeks old, to be exact."

Amanda's voice caught, and Scottie sneaked a glance at her. Amanda's brown eyes looked swimmy.

"And then I went to your place and found this address on a piece of paper on your bedroom floor."

Scottie caught her breath. So *that's* where the address had gone. The bigger question, though, was . . .

"Your folks have no idea," Amanda filled in for her. "Don't worry."

Scottie's shoulders untensed, just a bit—not that she let on to Amanda.

"Whatever," Scottie muttered.

"Oh, Scottie, I'm so sorry," Amanda whispered. "I wish you'd told me but . . . I sorta get why you didn't. Things have changed."

Scottie nodded, just slightly. But she wasn't ready to meet Amanda's eyes yet.

"Okay, *I* changed," Amanda blurted. "And you *didn't*, so . . ."

Okay, *now* Scottie was ready. She slammed her knitting to the couch cushion and full-on glared at Amanda. Could Amanda possibly be clueless enough to think that *she* was the only one who'd evolved, just because she'd gotten beautiful and grown boobs?

Come to think of it, Amanda wasn't looking so beautiful to Scottie at the moment.

It is supposed to be just skin-deep, after all, Scottie thought.

She snatched her knitting back, twisted around again, ducked her head, and—

Click-swish-click-swish.

"Oh my God, okay, I guess that was the wrong thing to say," Amanda whispered, the words tumbling out of her mouth. "That's the thing with you, Scottie. I can never come up with the right thing to say. It's like I'm afraid to talk to you anymore."

Click-swish-click-swish.

"Remember how we used to talk *all* the time?" Amanda asked, her voice going high and reedy. "We were just . . . connected, you know? I wish, somehow, that could come back."

Yeah, well I did, too, Scottie answered in her head, *but last night, I made a vow to stop wishing.*

She felt cold, despite the steamy heat whistling out of KnitWit's many clunky radiators. What she really wanted to do—okay, *wished* she could do—was give Amanda a hug, one of the impulsive, gleeful squeezes that used to pass so easily between them.

But those hugs were as far away as the new Amanda, the one who shopped her days away with Maryn and Tiff and went to bars at night. The one who was one step away from getting a boyfriend.

The one who didn't need Scottie anymore.

Of course, if that was the case, why was Amanda here?

Before she could puzzle that one out, Scottie felt Alice glide up beside her. Guiltily, she ducked deeper into her knitting. She was seized with a sudden worry that Alice would think she'd misjudged her when she'd thought of Scottie as some kindred knitting spirit.

She wanted to explain it all to her: *Usually, I'm not this mean, but you've got to understand, things have gotten so bad between me and Amanda. When someone was your best friend once, and then they aren't anymore, it's almost worse than if they'd never been your best friend at all, y'know?*

Scottie felt sure that Alice *would* know.

But of course she couldn't say anything. Not when all the other knitters were *so* listening to her and Amanda's little soap opera. And not when . . . Alice was squeezing onto the love seat on the other side of Amanda!

Wait a minute, what's going on?

Scottie kept purling—*click-swish-click-swish*—but she kept a furtive eye on her friend and her teacher. They looked weird together. Alice was all cardiganed and curly and *right* here. While lithe, glossy Amanda looked tremendously out of place on the antique love seat.

Scottie leaned in slightly to hear what Alice had to say.

But Alice didn't say anything. She just reached over the couch's arm to pluck a twist of whiskery yarn out of a nearby milk crate. The yarn was purple with little glints of gold in it. The needles she grabbed from the coffee table were made of yellowish green aluminum and capped with swirls of black-and-white glass.

Scottie's eyes widened. Those funky sticks had Amanda written all over them.

How could Alice tell?

Alice unfurled some of the purple yarn and quickly cast on a string of loops. Then, still not saying a word, she began to show Amanda how to knit, just as Aunt Lucille had showed Scottie.

Little does Alice know, there's no way Amanda's going to submit to the knit, Scottie thought smugly. *Not only is it too uncool for her, she's totally gonna balk at the math. Counting stitches and counting rows? Measuring inches for a gauge? She's gonna think that's about as fun as getting her teeth drilled.*

She held her breath and waited for Amanda to roll her eyes or sigh deeply or start fidgeting in her seat.

Amanda wasn't *that* rude, but she did give Alice an apologetic smile. She shook her head and shrugged.

Scottie couldn't help but snort.

That's my Amanda, she thought. *Why would she try something challenging when she can squirm—or buy—her way out of it?*

Amanda's pigtails almost whistled through the air as she turned to shoot Scottie a look. Her glare was both resentful and guilty. Maybe it was the guilt that made her act more receptive when she turned back to Alice. She leaned over Alice's steadily working needles and stared at them intensely.

A moment later, she reached out to take the yarn and needles from Alice. In fact, she looked like she couldn't wait to get her hands on the

•• *Chicks with Sticks*

purple yarn and glinty sticks. As she handed them over, Alice introduced herself.

"Amanda," Amanda replied, already staring wide-eyed at the needles in her hand.

Scottie found herself holding her breath as Amanda tried her first stitch. She poked the needle way too far through the loop, and when she wrapped the yarn around it, it got twisted up around the glass needle cap. She exhaled in frustration but she didn't give up. On her next try, she got it.

She got it!

Amanda jumped in her seat and flashed Scottie a huge, spontaneous grin.

Scottie couldn't help it. She grinned back and motioned at Amanda's needles.

Wrapping her yarn around her index finger with more confidence, Amanda did another knit stitch. And then another. Knit, knit, *click-swish*—she definitely had some garter stitch going on.

"I don't think you will, but let me know if you need any more help with this," Alice whispered before sliding off the couch and heading over to another student.

With each stitch, Amanda's cheeks went pinker and her eyes went wider. This was huge!

As the anguish left Amanda's face, Scottie felt her own face relaxing into an old expression: a big, fat, easy grin. No guardrails, no mask.

I bet Amanda feels like a superhero! Scottie thought.

And that was all she felt. No resentment, no *Oh, marvy, Amanda is rich and gorgeous, sexy and popular, and now she's* also *this knitting savant?*

All Scottie could feel was happy. Happy for Amanda and happy for herself! Her wooden needles began to feel warm and pliable in her cupped hands. Her yarn was flowing like water. She drank in the quiet of the room. The vibe was cozy. Weighty. Full.

Scottie and Amanda's *clicks* and *clacks* became synchronized. Their elbows knocked each other occasionally, but neither of them flinched, or scooched away to make more space. In fact, Scottie found herself leaning toward Amanda and felt Amanda angling at her.

They didn't have to say anything. They were back.

And just in time. Amanda and Scottie's syncopated knitting had just reached a perfect hum when KnitWit's door flew open—so hard the wind chimes rattled. Two heavy feet stomped across the foyer, and a girl appeared. She looked a little younger than Scottie and Amanda. She had wildly spiked dark hair, an eyebrow ring, and cargo pants the exact color of mud. Her tattooed arms were crossed across her chest, and her eyes were heavy-lidded.

She assessed the knitting circle for a long, squinty moment before she blew out an exasperated breath and flopped, boy-style, into a corduroy recliner.

"Sorry I'm late," she said to the group. "But I'm here under duress."

Scottie glanced at Amanda, her eyebrows raised.

"I wonder who 'tude girl is," she whispered.

"She's a Starker, that's who!" Amanda hissed back.

"Really?" Scottie looked at the girl again.

"Yeah, I've seen her," Amanda said. "She's in my 'math for 'tards' class.'"

"Amanda," Scottie said. "Don't call it that."

She gave the girl another shifty look as Alice began to make her way over. The girl regarded Alice lazily but made no move to get up or introduce herself.

"So, you think she's got an LD, too?" Scottie said.

"No, she's no dummy," Amanda said. "She's just pissed off about something. You can tell she can do whatever she wants. She just doesn't *want* to do math, I guess."

"You're no dummy, either, by the way," Scottie said. She couldn't believe how easily they were falling back into this friendship thing. Why had it been so hard only a few hours ago?

"Whatever," Amanda whispered, though she flashed a quick smile. "The real question is, what is Alice gonna make of her?"

What Alice did was cross her legs at the ankle and sink to the floor next to the girl's chair.

"Alice Chilton," she said, holding out her hand.

"Tay Cooper," the girl said, just as bluntly. She began to bounce her knee vigorously as she slid deeper into the worn-to-shininess rust corduroy of the recliner. A moment later, she glanced at her bobbing leg, scowled, and made it stop.

"Under duress, huh?" Alice said drily. "That's one I haven't heard before. What? Is your mother trying to deprogram you? She's thinking"—Alice made her voice go squeaky—"*If Tay just knits herself some pretty sweaters, maybe she'll change. Maybe she'll get rid of that crazy eyebrow ring and grow out her hair in time for the prom!*"

Tay stared.

"Brazen," Amanda breathed, sounding impressed.

Well, it worked. Tay smiled.

"It's more like, my guidance counselor thinks I'm hyper and prescribed yarn in lieu of Ritalin," she told Alice. "Look, I'll be straight with you. I'm a one-timer. I'm looking for a revenge project, and that's it."

"No need to explain," Alice said, waving Tay off. "This isn't church. How about a hat? Scarves are a little easier, but hats are smaller and quicker. Especially if you use circular needles."

"Perfect," Tay said. "Got anything in black?"

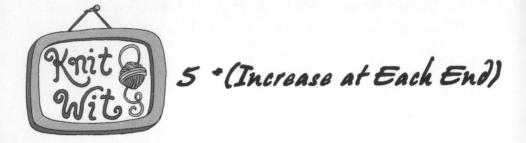

5 + (Increase at Each End)

An hour later, the class was over. Not that Alice kicked anyone out. Instead, the group seemed to reach an unspoken decision—signaled by a collective sigh—that it was time go. The clicks of their sticks finally buzzed to a halt, and everyone began stretching out of their chairs, yawning loudly.

It was late, and Scottie really needed to hightail it home, but she didn't want to. Not yet. As she packed up her newly two-toned scarf, her skeins of blue and copper yarn, and a fat new pair of casein needles that looked like petrified honey, she somehow wanted to preserve this moment, too.

She glanced at Amanda sitting next to her, gazing at the strip of purple fabric she'd just made.

"I can't believe I'm *knitting*," Amanda said.

Scottie stiffened and looked quickly at the floor. Okay, clearly she'd been wrong. She and Amanda had been under some sort of spell as they'd knitted, but now it was time to go back to their usual roles. Scottie—dork. Amanda—princess.

Scottie looked up in surprise when Amanda laughed.

"You're thinking about how evil I am right now," Amanda said.

"I'm just wondering who you are," Scottie said carefully. "The new Amanda or the old one?"

"Let's call her the enlightened Amanda," Amanda replied, giving her swatch an affectionate stroke. "A perfect match for the new Scottie. We've both got some secrets now, don't we."

"Hey, not me," Scottie said with a laugh. "I came out already, in the cafeteria. Remember?"

"Oh yeah," Amanda said. "I forgot that very special episode of *Stark World*."

"We laughed, we cried," Scottie said. "We restrained ourselves from stabbing our best friend with a knitting needle."

Amanda threw her head back and laughed—guffawed so loud, in fact, that all the other knitters stopped what they were doing and stared.

That's right, Scottie thought giddily. *It's a teen invasion. Things are about to get a little noisier around here.*

Well, on Scottie and Amanda's side of the room, that was. Tay was so quiet Scottie had almost forgotten she was there. Only when she slithered out of her corduroy chair and rubbed her eyes roughly did she become too striking to miss. Scottie stared at her with bald-faced interest.

There was a reason Scottie didn't know Tay. It wasn't just that she was a grade younger or that their lockers might have been on opposite sides of the H-shaped Olivia Stark School.

The fact was, Scottie tended to avert her eyes when girls like Tay walked by. They made her nervous. Not the way they scared adults, who thought tattoos and piercings were just gateways to gang tags and meth binges. *Please.*

No, Scottie was freaked by their bravery; that rocker grrrl ability to scream out their rage, to yowl it into microphones or carve it into poetry or cut off their hair and pierce their eyebrows.

She was freaked by that badassness because she wished she had it, too.

Of course, she *so* didn't.

Come on, I can barely bring myself to sing along with Avril Lavigne, Scottie thought with a scornful huff.

And even if her long, straight hair sometimes struck her as way too blah—red highlights or no—she'd never have the courage to chop it short the way Tay had. Or dye it some outrageous color, like her Mom's cherry-red 'do. She couldn't stand the idea of all those eyes on her in the aftermath, trying to probe out, "Why did she do it? What's her damage?"

One thing you could say about blah. It blended. And that was pretty much Scottie's MO these days.

At KnitWit, though, her rules seemed to have changed. Scottie found herself calling across the room, "Hey, Tay! Did you know you go to the same school as us?"

Tay, who'd been moving stealthily toward the foyer, froze. She glanced longingly at the door before she shrugged and said, "Yeah, I'm Starkers all right. Can't you tell?"

She waggled her circular knitting needle, which already had an impressive ring of spongy, black yarn woven upon it.

"Join the club," Amanda said, crossing the room with Scottie. "I'm—"

"Amanda Scott," Tay said. "Yeah, I know about you. How's that campaign for homecoming queen going?"

"What's that supposed to mean?" Amanda asked, suddenly going squinty. Scottie noticed her hiding her chipped nails in her palms before propping her fists on her hips.

"Hey, don't get huffy," Tay said. "I'm just calling what I see."

"And what do you see, in the one class we have together a day?" Amanda challenged.

"I see someone who's figured out that being pretty gets you more popular points than a good math grade," Tay said with a lazy shrug. "Someone who spends a *lot* of mental energy on, y'know, lip gloss."

"Oh, thanks for the sum-up," Amanda snapped. "I feel so deep now."

Tay opened her mouth for another snappy retort when, suddenly, she paused. She glanced around the room and fingered her swatch of chunky black stitches. When she looked back at Amanda, all the fight had flamed out of her eyes.

"Well, maybe you *should* feel deep," she said. "You're here, after all. Knitting's not exactly sanctioned by your crowd, is it?"

"Yours, either," Amanda said.

Okay, how did this catfight suddenly turn into a respect fest? Scottie thought.

"No worries about me," Tay said. "I don't really have a crowd. I mean, beyond Jo—"

She paused. Frowned. And rebooted.

"I'm just me," she said bluntly.

"Tay," Amanda said.

Scottie watched the girls size each other up. Tay towered over Amanda, who was sitcom-star tiny. For every glossy, pearly surface on Amanda, Tay had a boyish angle. They could *not* have been more different.

At least, that's how it seemed at first,

But now that she was free to take a closer look at Tay, Scottie realized that she wasn't nearly as rough-hewn as she'd have you believe. In the steamy heat of the knitting shop, Tay had stripped off her baggy sweatshirt. In nothing but a ribbed tank top, her arms looked muscley and sinewy, especially at the spot on her bicep tattooed with a cuff of interlocking, black waves. But the skin around that angry imprint? It was as smooth and soft as ivory silk.

Tay's eyes, too, were way too pretty to be boyish. They were so dark, they were almost black, and underneath her supershort haircut, they looked huge. Her nose was small and delicate and dusted with freckles.

Most intriguing of all was Tay's circular knitting needle. On her, it should have seemed about as appropriate an accessory as an oven mitt. But in truth, she held her knitting so comfortably, so *affectionately,* it looked like it belonged in her hands—chewed fingernails, frayed cuticles, and all.

This girl, Scottie realized, *may be a badass, but I think she also may be a big softie underneath.* Though she knew little more about Tay than her last name, she already knew her well enough to *not* call her attention to this.

She didn't have the chance, anyway. Amanda was turning the spotlight on *her.* She jabbed a finger in Scottie's direction and told Tay, "That's Scottie, by the way, who sort of dragged me here."

"Oh, really," Scottie retorted. She was back to grinning—grinning goofily—but she didn't care. "Tay, she's a liar. Knitting is Amanda's destiny. Mine, too, I guess. Who knew?"

"Well, you guys are on your own there," Tay said. "This is my first and last visit to KnitWit. I only came here on sort of a dare."

"Guidance counselor issues," Scottie commiserated, flashing back on that pink pamphlet.

"Yeah, well . . . uh, what can you do," Tay said lamely. Clearly, she was dying to make an exit. As Tay shrugged herself back into her sweatshirt, Amanda glanced at Scottie. Amanda's eyes were glinty, and her mouth was twisted into an off-center smirk.

Scottie remembered that expression. It was the look that used to make them sneak into R-rated movies or eavesdrop on couples stumbling through their first dates at Joe.

She wants to be friends with Tay! Scottie realized.

Maybe Amanda, too, saw the smooth under Tay's sandpapery shell. Maybe she, too, wanted a little of that indie action to rub off on her.

Or maybe, Scottie thought, that thing that Alice had said—"I think it's fate that you came in here at just this moment"—applied to all three of them. It was too big a coincidence, wasn't it? Three mismatched Starkers landing in this most random of places on a Tuesday night.

And Amanda must be feeling it, too, she realized.

As Tay put her jacket on over her sweatshirt, Amanda told her, "We're leaving, too. We'll walk out with you."

Tay shrugged and headed for the door. Before she got there, though, she stopped and glanced over her shoulder.

"Thanks, Alice," she said. Alice was scooping stray needles off the coffee table. Instead of replacing them into their coffee can on the bookshelf, though, she planted them in the dirt of an ailing houseplant instead. Then she looked up and cocked her head at the three girls. That sly smile flashed for an instant before she answered.

"You're welcome, Tay," she said. "If you want to stop by and show me the hat when you're done, I'd love to see it."

Tay shrugged again and yanked the door open, traumatizing the wind chimes once again.

Amanda and Scottie gave Alice quick waves before grabbing their coats and bags and dashing after Tay. She'd made it halfway down the stairs before they caught up with her.

"Any particular reason you're following me?" Tay said, still thumping methodically down the steep steps.

"No," Scottie said quickly. She and Amanda exchanged a quick glance.

"Yes!" Scottie corrected herself as they all landed out on the sidewalk. "I mean, don't you think it's weird that we're all here? What are the odds of three girls who know one another all ending up in the same, random knitting class?"

"We don't know one another," Tay said. "Going to the same school doesn't mean we know one another. Would you have ever just walked up to me at school and said hello?"

"Well, probably not," Scottie said, "but that's because—"

"Okay, so we didn't know you," Amanda cut in, burrowing her bare hands into her yarn and needles to keep them warm. "But we do now."

"Oh yeah," Tay said. "We sat on opposite sides of a room for an hour without making any eye contact or speaking to one another. I feel so close to you now, Amanda."

Suddenly Scottie found her courage and broke in.

"Listen, all we were saying was, you know, we're all knitters—"

"Wait a second, I'm not a knitter," Tay said, holding up her hand and taking a step back. Unfortunately, that hand was still clutching her knitting project. Muttering to herself, Tay stuffed the yarn and bouncy wire into the biggest pocket on her cargo pants and began again. "I'm not 'a knitter.' I learned how to do this thing to get back at my counselor. In two weeks, I'll have a hat made for him. And then I'm going to put this whole little episode behind me."

"Okay, then, for the next *two weeks,* you're a knitter," Scottie said with a shrug. "Which means, for the next two weeks, you should eat lunch with us."

"Lunch?" Tay and Amanda said together.

"Yeah . . . lunch!" Scottie said. Her belly did a roller-coaster somersault.

Did I really just say that?

This afternoon, knitting in the cafeteria had felt like a failure—giving up the fight and totally succumbing to dweebdom. Now . . . well, it felt about as dangerous as spiking your hair or piercing your face.

"As if!" Tay snorted.

Scottie's cheeks went hot.

Okay, attempt to be a badass has failed miserably. Must knit myself a Cardimum.

"Scottie," Amanda said, crossing her arms over her chest and tucking her yarn and sticks beneath them. "Lunch? I mean, we have to eat and everything."

"And we have to impress Matt, right?" Scottie blurted back. She turned to Tay, who was gazing up at the black sky, looking bored. "And whoever you're worried about, Tay. Jo— Hmm, is it John? Jocelyn?"

"The Jolly Green Giant?" Amanda chimed in drily. "We get it, Scottie."

"What are you guys afraid of?" Scottie went on. She knew she sounded shrill and was talking a mile a minute. "Dudes, it's knitting, not bomb assembly. What do you think, we'll suddenly be pariahs?"

"Yeah," Amanda and Tay said, again in perfect unison.

"Hey, Amanda!"

The squeaky voice came from across the street, almost lost in the gusts of wind and rush of cars. Instinctively, Amanda tucked her knitting farther beneath the X of her forearms before glancing over her shoulder.

"Speaking of pariahs," she muttered.

It was Bella Brearley. She was perched on the curb, waving wildly.

"Okay, another Starker?" Tay said. "Now this *is* getting weird."

It went without saying that all three girls knew who Bella was. If Scottie was as blendable as beige paint, Bella was like a wildly plumed bird. In the halls of the Stark School, you could *not* miss her.

Her mane of honey-gold dreadlocks was usually tied up so that the coils of hair spouted like a fountain spray. Her celery-green eyes and dark-amber skin made a stunning combination. And her long, thin, gangly limbs had a strange, jerky grace to them. Bella was crazy beautiful, emphasis on the word *crazy*.

For starters, she was nice to *everybody*. Somehow, she knew almost every kid she passed in the hall and called out hellos to all of them. In return, she got cursory waves at best, and snorts of laughter at worst, but she never seemed to care.

Before winter break, she always brought a big basket of carob brownies and wheaty minimuffins to school, passing them out at lunchtime. And on Valentine's Day, she actually gave homemade cards to all the kids in her classes. The boys gagged, and the girls gave Bella those uncomfortable smiles usually reserved for kids on the short bus. But again, Bella seemed to have no idea how oddly she came off.

Home school will do that to a kid, Scottie thought, watching Bella lope across the street. She'd come to Stark sometime in middle school, announcing with no shame at all that she'd never been to school before. Her dad had taught her at home.

And now we all know what happens when you shelter your kid from dodgeball and science fairs and Sadie Hawkins dances, Scottie thought. *You become weirdly happy.*

Over her shoulder, in a burlap bag, Bella carried a pistachio-green yoga mat. Her silk skirt—fluttering over a pair of peach leg warmers—tinkled softly. Tiny bells were sewn to the hem.

"I thought that was you, Amanda!" Bella said. Her voice was still squeaky, but it was loud and confident now. Bella was always confident.

Amanda usually was, too, but now she seemed to shrink into herself.

"Hi," she blurted. "Um, we were just heading home."

"Me, too!" Bella tinkled, bouncing on the balls of her feet. "Where are you coming from?"

"Um, y'know . . ." Amanda was the one acting weird now. Scottie hadn't seen her so shuffly and shy since her preboob days. What was the big deal? It was only Bella.

Tay jumped on the opportunity. Shooting Amanda a mischievous little smile, she told Bella, "We were just at knitting class."

Amanda tightened her grip on her poor purple swatch—while Bella's eyes lit up.

"Knitting!" she exclaimed. She clapped her hands together. Then her fingers fluttered to her wrist, where she wore a bracelet of twisted, red string.

"You know Madonna—I mean Esther—knits!" Bella said excitedly.

"You mean she has time to make bad records, become a Kabbalah queen, *and* knit sweaters?" Amanda said.

"Yeah!" Bella said. Apparently, sarcasm was another subject her dad had skipped at home school. "Is it hard? It looks hard."

"Yes!" Amanda said.

"No way," Scottie overlapped.

"They'll be knitting at lunchtime tomorrow," Tay offered, pointing at Amanda and Scottie gleefully. "You should come."

"Oh!" Bella said. "I have second lunch. When do you have it?"

"Um," Amanda said, "second, but—"

"What a coincidence," Tay said. "You all have second lunch period. Too bad I have first! Well, *ladies,* it's been real, but I've gotta motor. See ya!"

"Tay," Scottie started to protest, but Tay just waved good-bye and jumped off the curb, jaywalking in a lazy arc to the other side of the street. She didn't look back as she disappeared around the coffeehouse on the corner and headed north on Clark.

Leaving Scottie and Amanda with Bella.

"So is this where you knit?" Bella said, gazing up at the KW window.

"Not really," Amanda said. "I mean, we just had a lesson. I was trying to track Scottie down and . . ."

"Do they sell yarn and stuff?" Bella wondered, still gazing. She put a hand to her forehead to shield her eyes from the glare of the street-lamps.

"Um . . . I think they're closed," Amanda said.

"Oh," Bella said again.

And finally, she deflated. Literally deflated. Her long, skinny arms fell to her sides, her head—heavy with dreads—drooped until her chin almost hit her chest, and her glowing smile disappeared.

"I see what you mean."

Scottie felt like she'd just witnessed a historic event: the moment Bella Brearley got a clue and realized that not everyone dug her Patchouli Pollyanna thing. Scottie felt horrible—and sort of horrified.

"They might be closing, but I know the owner's still up there," she said suddenly. She took a step toward Bella and willfully averted her eyes from Amanda, who she *knew* was thinking, *No, no, no!*

(It's a purl thing)   65

"Her name's Alice," Scottie continued, gently placing a hand on Bella's shoulder. Even through Bella's quilted orange coat, Scottie could feel her delicate bones. "She's supercool. Tell her we sent you."

Bella looked up at her, the easy, wide smile coming back. Bella had dimples, Scottie noticed for the first time ever. And a little mole just below her left eye. It disappeared into a crease when Bella's smile reached its full—and usual—magnitude.

"Scottie, right?" Bella said, putting her feathery hand on top of Scottie's. "You have the locker next to Amanda's."

"Yup," Scottie said, glancing at Amanda. "Ever since we first got lockers, in sixth grade."

Amanda still looked sullen, but she nodded. She and Scottie were still okay.

And Bella was back to bouncy. She glanced at the sky, as if she was asking one of her yoga goddesses a question, then walked to KnitWit's glass door.

"So, I'll tell Alice you sent me," she said, giving Scottie a graceful good-bye wave.

"Not just me," Scottie insisted. "Me and Amanda."

Scottie ignored Amanda's small grunt of protest.

"*And* Tay," Scottie added, pointing over her shoulder to the corner across that street. "*That*, Bella, was Tay."

And that, she thought, Alice's comment about fate still reverberating in her mind, *makes four*.

6 · (Add Fringe)

The next morning, Scottie woke up with a zit starting on her chin. Not some little molehill either. This was a big, red mountain.

Fabulous, she thought as she piled on the benzoyl peroxide, followed by a dab of concealer that concealed about as well as Saran Wrap. Now the zit not only looked red, it wore a halo of crusty beige.

So much for wearing my red sweater. It'll make my zit look like Rudolph's nose.

Actually, the sweater wasn't hers. It was a hand-me-down from Aunt Roz. Scottie had been hanging at Aunt Roz and Uncle Alex's cozy little house in Evanston about a month before Aunt Roz's death. They'd been sitting around, chatting and chowing on cookies, when Aunt Roz had beckoned Scottie into her bedroom and pulled the slither of cherry-colored chenille out of her closet. She'd thrust it beneath Scottie's chin.

"Uh-huh, I thought so," she'd said.

"Thought what?" Scottie had mumbled. She'd had a mouth full of Mallomar and hadn't wanted to spew chocolate crumbs. Not that Aunt Roz would have minded. She was not the kind of person who worried about crumbs.

"I thought, when I put this sweater on last week, that it would look a lot better on you," Aunt Roz had said. She'd plucked the last bite of Mallomar from Scottie's fingers and popped it into her own mouth. Then she'd plunked the sweater into Scottie's hands.

The color had been so bright, it seemed to make everything else in her aunt and uncle's peach-and-blue bedroom go a shade paler.

"Whoa!" Scottie had said. "It's *really* red."

"Exactly," her aunt had said. "What's with all the pink and pale blue and ivory you wear? Are you trying to disappear?"

"Hello?" Scottie said. "I'm in high school, remember? High school kids are all about disappearing acts."

"Not the popular kids," Aunt Roz said. "The popular kids in my high school were always so . . . bright. I mean, they didn't need clothes to stand out. The rest of us, well, we dressed up to get attention. Who had the swingiest bell-bottoms? The patchiest patchwork blazer? The biggest hair?"

"Okay, I'm not even going to comment on the patchwork blazer," Scottie had said. "Suffice to say, I'm not a popular kid, Aunt Roz. And wearing a red sweater isn't gonna make me one."

Aunt Roz had blinked at her for a moment before she'd laughed.

"Honey, you misunderstood me," she'd protested. "I wouldn't wish popular-girl status on you for the world. Kids who are popular in high school grow up to be booooring. And statistically, they are the very first ones to put on the freshman fifteen."

"Uh-huh," Scottie had said skeptically.

"I mean it!" Aunt Roz said. "How could *my* niece be a cheerleader, boppy girl? It's not in your genes. But you *will* make a statement, Scottie."

"A statement?"

"You'll say something," Aunt Roz had insisted. "Something interesting and important. When you muster up the guts."

"I think Mom took all the guts and threw 'em onto her last canvas," Scottie had said morosely. "I'm not sure there's any left for me."

"To that, I will say two things," Aunt Roz had said. "One, perhaps this statement you're going to make should *not* be made in the field of art criticism. And, two, there are plenty of guts to go around. Maybe you should start small, with a red sweater."

Scottie had shrugged and looked at her hands, but the words had meant something to her.

She just wished she knew what on earth this mysterious "statement" was going to be. Whatever it was, it was clearly a long way off, when she was no longer a high school mouse but someone she couldn't even imagine yet.

That someone wouldn't have to pump herself up to wear a bright red sweater to school—but the current Scottie did.

And last night, after coming home from KnitWit, she *had*. She'd walked through the door at 9:30, an elaborate and false excuse on the tip of her tongue, only to find that she didn't have to use it. Nothing was waiting for her except a note on the kitchen island and a twenty-dollar bill.

S, her dad had written. *Had to wine and dine some clients tonight. Their request—SushiSambaRio! Oy. Will be late. Order some Thai food and call the cell if you need anything. XO, D.*

Suddenly ravenous, Scottie had ordered up some late-night grub. And while she'd waited for her Pad Thai and Rama Chicken, she'd pulled the red sweater off her closet shelf.

I'm going to knit in the cafeteria, dammit, she'd thought, *and I'll do it in a bright red sweater.*

Yeah, well, Scottie thought now, *that was last night.* In the harsh light of morning, she had an enormous zit and her giddiness had evaporated. The last thing she wanted to say was, "Look at me! I'm making a statement."

"Please," Scottie muttered as she pulled on a long-sleeved T-shirt from The Gap. It was sage green—the same color as the scuffed-up paint on her locker. Perfect.

Except that it wasn't. Because even without the red sweater, Scottie felt painfully conspicuous all morning.

It wasn't her zit (so much) that was making her jumpy. It was her sticks. And her yarn. They were tucked into her backpack, but somehow Scottie was certain they were going to leap out at the first opportunity. She'd reach for her history notebook only to find her blue yarn snaked through its spiral. Or she'd yank out her Spanish book and send her knitting flying into the lap of, say, Tim Gold, the snarkiest guy in the tenth grade. Or even worse, it might land on Maryn, who would scream and toss it off her lap as if it were a diseased rat.

As each prelunch hour passed, Scottie got more and more edgy. By the time she arrived in the cafeteria, she was a wreck. Carefully keeping her sight line above the dead bunny, she selected the most challenging lunch she could find: chicken fajitas with chips and salsa on the side.

When she joined Amanda at their usual table, Amanda was giving her a funny look. Scottie plowed over it by asking, "Where're Maryn and Tiff?"

"Over by the Coke machines with Keller and Sean," Amanda said. "It's a flirt fest. I wouldn't get near them. Maryn's eyelashes are fluttering so hard, you might get hurt."

"Don't worry," Scottie said, heaving her heavy lunch tray onto the table. Amanda eyed it with her best curled lip.

"Hungry today?" she said.

"Oh yeah, famished," Scottie lied.

She began piling her tortilla with bits of chicken, onions, and peppers, as well as sour cream, salsa, and a pile of grated cheese. With great effort, she wrapped the whole mess up and took a big bite. Of course, half the filling fell out of the fajita's back end onto the tray. Scottie frowned at the greasy pile of fajita innards and stuffed a few fingerfuls back into her tortilla, leaving her hands sticky with salsa and oil.

"Okay, Ms. Binge," Amanda said. "I have one question. Do you think salsa washes out of blue wool? If not, I think your lunch is gonna pose a problem to your little knitting scheme."

"Oh, that," Scottie said, widening her eyes as if this was the first time knitting had occurred to her all day. "Well, I guess I'll do some knitting after I've eaten. Y'know, if I have time."

*• Chicks with Sticks

"You are so full of it!" Amanda cried with an incredulous laugh. "You're caving!"

"I don't know what you're talking about," Scottie mumbled through a mouthful of rubbery chicken.

"You were *so* superior! 'What are you guys afraid of?'" Amanda mocked. "'It's knitting, not Bible study!'"

"Bomb assembly," Scottie muttered as she finally managed to down the mouthful of Mexican food. "Make me feel like *more* of a wimp, why don't you?"

"Okay, I will," Amanda said. "What *is* the big deal, Scottie? You knitted here yesterday."

"Yeah, but I didn't *plan* to do it," Scottie retorted. "I didn't have an entire morning to imagine what people would think. And say. This is premeditated geekery."

"Knitting in the first degree," Amanda agreed. Then she leaned forward and whispered, "I don't think you can get arrested for that, you know."

"Well, if you're so brave, then *you* do it," Scottie said.

"What if I told you I didn't bring my stuff?" Amanda retorted. Suddenly she seemed very interested in her own lunch.

"I'd say I didn't believe you," Scottie said, narrowing her eyes and pointing at Amanda's bag. "You are queen of the tiny clutch purse, yet today you just coincidentally bring a giant Kate Spade to school? And what's with the pizza puffs on your lunch tray there? You *always* get salad, Amanda. Yet today you go for finger food."

"Okay, Nancy Drew," Amanda said. "So maybe I considered working on my knit stitch a little."

"But . . ."

"Well, now you've got *me* freaked out," Amanda said. "I mean, we're not just at any high school, Scottie. We're at Stark!"

Scottie frowned. Amanda had a point. For all it's alterna-righteousness, Stark still had a social code. Yeah, conformity was uncool and self-expression was the only true ticket onto the A-list. But you couldn't just express yourself any which way.

For instance, Scottie thought, playing a little game with herself. *Soccer is cool and so is hockey, but football is dumb. Shooting broody black-and-white photographs? Very acceptable. Musical theater? Un. Cutting holes in Mom's old Chanel suit for a little DIY fashion* is cool. *Sewing, cooking, or anything else that smacks of home ec* isn't.

Scottie knew where that left knitting and anybody who did it in public—in the same category as those kids who spent the whole school year preparing for the Math Bowl. Or the Goth chicks whose lunch hour consisted of black coffee, snack cakes, and smokes in the courtyard outside. Or the band geeks who always seemed to be cleaning out their spit valves. *Ew.*

These folks were on the fringe of Stark society. Amanda was used to being in the center of it.

Do I have the right to ask her to risk losing Maryn and Tiff and their clubby crowd? Scottie thought. *And then there's Matt.*

Even though her view into Amanda's life had been limited lately, Scottie knew that Amanda's crush on Matt was major. First of all, the guy was an undisputed hottie, one of the few fifteen-year-olds in school who could match Amanda's beauty. His hair, all gold-and-yellow streaks, was always flopping over his forehead, and his eyes were bright, clear blue. They had a glint in them that was always laughing and teasing and just . . . *perceptive.* Of Amanda in particular.

When Matt stole looks at Amanda during his many forays past her locker, it was as if some sort of promise had already hatched between them, and they were just waiting for the right moment to act upon it.

What would happen to that promise if Amanda pulled her yarn out of her tote?

It looked like Amanda was thinking exactly the same thing. She was gazing over Scottie's shoulder at a table of guffawing guys. In the middle of the throng was Matt, sneaking looks Amanda's way, too.

And the Kate Spade remained firmly closed.

Maybe that's how it should be, Scottie thought. *We can take our KnitWit classes and even knit together after school. But we don't have to be all in everyone's face about it. . . .*

"Hi, you guys!"

Bella had just bounced up to their table. Scottie jumped at the sight of her, then stifled a groan.

Cradled in Bella's long, bare arms was a stash of yarn as out there as the girl herself. She had fuzzy, fuchsia chenille and lime-green mohair, spidery chocolate eyelash, and some ice-blue papery stuff. She had some big fat needles tucked under one arm and a measuring tape on a cord around her neck.

"Scottie, you were right!" Bella said, loping to the other side of the table and plopping into the chair next to Amanda. Her skein of mohair went flying and barely missed Scottie's tray of fajitas. "Alice *was* super-cool. Look at all this stuff! I couldn't decide what I wanted, so she said I could take these home and return what I don't use. But then my parents thought I should just keep it all, because, y'know, you never know what the muse is going to tell you to knit."

"Well, that's really . . . uh, you've really embraced knitting," Scottie said lamely. She noticed that Amanda had again gone into a state of shrink-wrap—her arms were folded across her middle, her shoulders were hunched, and she had slid as far down in her chair as her miniskirt would allow.

It didn't help when Bella turned her full wattage right on her.

"Hi, Amanda!" she said.

"Hey," Amanda mumbled. She picked apart one of her pizza puffs, nibbling at a bit of crust and keeping her eyes downcast.

"I'm *so* glad you invited me to have lunch with you," Bella said, to which Amanda cleared her throat mightily. "Because the one part I didn't get to at KnitWit last night was the *knitting* part."

"You got all this stuff, but you didn't learn how to knit?" Scottie said, poking at the paper yarn. "Wow, Bella, you didn't want to start small? See if you like it?"

"Oh, I know I'll like it," Bella said with a smile. "I mean, it's kind of fate, isn't it?"

A shiver skittered over Scottie's shoulders. There was that word again!

"What are the odds of me running into you guys on the street like that?" Bella said, her big eyes getting bigger. Her eyelashes were so long and golden, they reminded Scottie of feathers.

"It was like the goddess telling us, 'You girls have got some weaving together to do,'" Bella added.

"Weaving together?" Amanda blurted.

"Goddess?" Scottie said at the same time. "What goddess?"

"Oh, you name her," Bella said, crinkling her nose at her.

Ohhhhkay, I'm just not getting this girl, Scottie thought.

Which was fine, because Bella was back to being all about Amanda.

"Remember in tutoring two years ago?" she said. "When I was just coming into Stark from being home schooled and I needed to play catch-up?"

If possible, Amanda stiffened up even more.

Uh-oh, nerve hit, Scottie thought. *No wonder Amanda's been treating Bella like a virus.*

Amanda always hated references to her tutoring. Scottie knew that she'd told the Maryn and Tiff types that her after-school sessions were about PSAT prep. She'd die before she let them know that she actually spent all those hours running through reading and math drills with a boring LD expert.

"It sucks," Scottie had heard Amanda tell them. "My parents are completely demanding. I mean, if I don't get in the ninetieth percentile at least, they're definitely going to snip my AmEx."

Even with Scottie, who *did* know about her learning problems, Amanda hardly ever brought them up. Her motto? Out of chat, out of mind.

• • Chicks with Sticks

Nothing, of course, seemed to embarrass Bella. And besides, as soon as she'd gotten into the Stark groove, she'd quickly graduated from those tutoring sessions. Scottie knew Bella now took honors English and a senior-level philosophy class.

"Remember how I told you my secret code for pi?" Bella said. She started singing that song from *The Sound of Music:* "Trina is fourteen, going on fifteen . . ."

". . . bo-orn in '92," Amanda finished.

"3.141592!" Bella cried.

Amanda destroyed another pizza puff. "I still hum that little song every time I have to use stupid pi," she admitted. "It actually really helps."

"See!" Bella said. "And now I need *your* help. Will you teach me to knit?"

Amanda looked up sharply.

This was new. Scottie knew Amanda *never* felt like the wiser one, who could teach instead of being taught.

And Bella, Scottie realized incredulously, clearly got that! Maybe she wasn't as oblivious as Scottie had always thought.

Amanda searched Bella's earnest gaze, then reached slowly for the needles Bella had plunked onto the table. They were wood—a creamy caramel color. Size 12.

Amanda held the needles under the table so nobody could see her studying their satiny weight. Then she glanced again at Matt, who was stuffing a handful of french fries into his mouth yet still managing to look cute. She sought out Maryn and Tiff, too. They were still in flirt mode at the Coke machine, but they would probably arrive at their table any minute.

She's gonna choke, Scottie thought.

Bella gently handed Amanda the chenille. Amanda almost jumped. She put down the knitting needles and cupped the yarn in both hands, digging her fingers into the silky-shiny bundle.

(It's a purl thing)

"This is *really* pretty," Amanda said, staring into the deep pinky purple. "Can't you see it as a shrug? Maybe with some cutouts in the back . . ."

"In the shape of stars!" Bella breathed.

"Or hearts," Amanda said. "I wonder if I could ever make something like that."

"Amanda, you've been knitting for one day, and you can already do a perfect garter stitch," Scottie said. She shoved aside her fajita and reached across the table to grab the loose tail of the skein. Handing the squiggly bit of yarn to Amanda, she said, "Go ahead, show Bella how it's done."

Amanda looked around again, and Scottie looked with her. At first, she saw the usual blur of boys playing with their food, girls screeching and giggling their way through midday gossip updates, jocks stuffing their faces with triple-decker burgers, and brainiacs poring over their homework.

But when she took a closer look, she noticed that Ben Thomson and Isaac Cartland were drawing comics together. Betsy Reinhart was inking loopy, green flowers onto her jeans. Nathaniel Byrne had just started juggling some apples. Rose Dabney, T'angela Smith, and Angie Watson were singing low and sweet, practicing harmonies for their *American Idol* audition.

And at our table, there's knitting, Scottie thought simply. *Really, it's no big deal.*

Amanda worked the chenille into a slipknot and looped it around one of the needles.

"First," she told Bella, "you have to cast on. . . ."

No big deal at all, Scottie thought, reaching to pull her own knitting out of her backpack. *We're just chicks with sticks, doing lunch.*

7 *(Weave in Ends)

"Amanda, check it out."

The final, Friday bell had just rung, and Scottie and Amanda were doing their last locker dig of the week. While Amanda tossed her books into her locker with a mixture of hostility and relief, Scottie thrust a computer printout in her direction. Amanda gave it a suspicious stare and curled her lip.

"Dude, it's three o'clock on Friday." She sighed. "I've just been released from torture. The last thing I want to do is read some assignment of yours."

"It's not an assignment," Scottie said.

"Okay, then some math quiz you got an A-plus-plus on," Amanda said.

"Well, actually," Scottie backtracked, letting her sticks-heavy backpack fall to the floor, "I guess it *is* sort of an assignment. For us. It's a pattern for this amazing webby poncho with *lots* of fringe."

Amanda raised one eyebrow.

"I downloaded it in study session," Scottie said. "I mean, eventually, we're gonna get sick of making scarves, right?"

Amanda took a closer look at the pattern.

"Yeah, but this looks complicated," she said. "More than complicated. What does all this mean?" She frowned at the first line and read slowly, "CO 120. Work 6 rows in St st, then k2, p1 for 10 rows? St? CO? What the—?"

"Cast on 120 stitches," Scottie said. "Do 6 rows in stockinette stitch, then knit two, purl one. . . ."

Amanda was staring at Scottie as if she'd just spoken Chinese.

"I got a glossary," Scottie explained. "Once you get the hang of it, it's easy."

"For some of us," Amanda muttered.

"Listen," Scottie said, "I've got three words for you. Candy corn. Lakefront. Me teaching you how to read a pattern."

There was a pause.

"Okay, that was a lot more than three words," Scottie said nervously.

Because she *was* nervous.

Back before Maryn and Tiff, before Amanda had started hanging at the Eight Bar and getting fifty-dollar pedicures, a sunny afternoon on the lakefront and a sugar rush had been their idea of a perfect afternoon.

They'd meet at Fullerton Avenue in Lincoln Park, about halfway between Amanda's condo in the Gold Coast and Scottie's place in Ravenswood. Scottie would provide the gossipy magazines; Amanda, the iPod. They'd stop at this funky sweet shop on Broadway and buy a bag of candy—sour, gummy things or nubbly faux raspberries or their favorite, candy corn. Anything went, as long as it was artificially flavored and garishly colored.

Then they'd spend a good fifteen minutes choosing the perfect bit of lakefront lawn, with a view of the skyline to the south and a thicket of trees behind them to buffer them from the roar of Lake Shore Drive. They'd flop onto the grass and spend the day chowing, snoozing, and cringing at the old Ukrainian men who insisted on wearing Speedos into the frigid lake, no matter what the season.

It was all your basic blissed-out bonding.

And that was why Scottie was so edgy now. Deep down, she knew she wasn't just asking Amanda for a sugary, lakefront lounge. What she *really* wanted was to go back in time. It made her feel greedy and totally immature, but Scottie couldn't help it—now that she and Amanda were friends again, Scottie wanted *everything* back the way it used to be.

Plus a few skeins of yarn and a pattern for a webby poncho with lots of fringe.

One look at Amanda's face, though, made her kick herself for even considering it.

"Candy corn? Ugh," Amanda said. "Remember how sick we used to get on that stuff? I can't even look at candy corn anymore."

Candy corn, Scottie berated herself. *What a stupid, little-kid thing to suggest.*

"Of course I *could* go for some chocolate," Amanda said, giving Scottie a sly look. "Have you had Vosges truffles? *So* amazing. They're made with, like, wasabi and lavender. You've gotta try 'em."

Scottie was so relieved, she actually wiped her brow.

"I thought you were going to suggest mojitos or something," she said.

"Oh, really," Amanda said drily. "I told you, we didn't drink that night at the Eight Bar! What other theories do you have about me? Let's see, I have boobs now, so I must be a slut, right? And hmm, what else—"

"Stop it!" Scottie hissed, turning bright red.

Amanda leaned over and cupped her hand behind Scottie's ear.

"A lot's changed," she whispered, "but not *everything's* changed."

Scottie exhaled audibly. Somehow that had been just what she'd wanted to hear.

Amanda went back to pawing through her locker. Now she was extracting a few books from it.

"For example," she continued, "I've got to go to tutoring this afternoon, like I do every Friday afternoon."

"Oh, right," Scottie said. "I forgot."

"Wish I could," Amanda said. "Anyway, what are you up to tonight? Want to check out that new bubble-tea place with me and Maryn and Tiff?"

"Maryn and Tiff? Really?" Scottie said, raising *her* eyebrows now. "They've totally ditched us at lunch the past few days. I thought maybe they'd moved on, y'know, now that you're a yarn girl."

"Nobody's moved on," Amanda said, just a tad defensively. "I think they're just not interested in spending their lunch hour talking about yarn and gauges and stuff."

"So, they're still your friends," Scottie said, hearing a hint of sullenness in her voice.

"Friendship isn't *that* easy to kill off," Amanda said. After a shy glance at the floor, she grabbed Scottie's hand and gave it a quick squeeze.

"You're right," Scottie said quietly.

Her insides felt like warm syrup . . . until Amanda added, "I mean *our* friendship survived even after you became a depresso freak!"

"Amanda!" Scottie screamed. Amanda giggled uncontrollably as Scottie bopped her on the arm.

"You're one to talk," Scottie said through her own laughter. "While I was going all depresso, you were morphing into the Paris Hilton of the Midwest."

Amanda threw her long hair over her shoulders and did a couple exaggerated hip swivels.

Which only made Scottie laugh harder. Tears started streaming from her eyes. Meanwhile, Amanda was laughing so hard, she was clutching her middle and making squeaky little snorts.

When they'd finally caught their breath—and Amanda had stuck her tongue out at the Starkers staring at them as they made their way out of school—Scottie flopped against the lockers. She felt a little weak and light-headed. She didn't know if she should blame the pig-snort-fabulous laugh attack or the gratitude she was feeling.

• Chicks with Sticks

So maybe Amanda's gonna make me forsake candy corn for overpriced chocolate, she thought. *And maybe I can handle that. I mean . . . I like chocolate as much as the next girl.*

She looked at Amanda, who was carefully blotting the laugh tears from the corners of her eyes. In her pink shimmery silk sweater and mocha leather pants, Amanda looked impossibly glam.

Scottie cocked her head. "Maybe we were both just looking for something, y'know?" she said.

"Do you think we found it?" Amanda said, sobering up, too.

"I don't know," Scottie said. She stuffed the pattern into her backpack, shut her locker, and started walking down the hall. "I don't know yet. But it feels like we're on our way."

"I wish I wasn't on my way to tutoring," Amanda said, falling into step next to Scottie. They headed for the stairs. "What are you gonna do?"

"You mean between now and the bubble tea?"

"You're coming?" Amanda squealed. She hopped down the steps to the first landing and did another Paris Hilton shimmy to celebrate.

"Yeah, I'll try it," Scottie said. "But if Maryn makes me be her wingman with some old guy with hairy ears, I'm outtie."

This only brought on a fresh round of pig-snort laughs from Amanda. As the girls left the Stark School, she barely managed to choke out, "See you at seven."

Now Scottie had three and a half hours to kill. She looked up at the sun. The day was cloudless and, for October, almost warm. It was one of the last days this fall that the chilly lakefront would even be approachable.

Scottie decided she couldn't let it go to waste.

So, the afternoon was turning out differently than she'd expected, but Scottie was still exhilarated.

She was at the lakefront. She had her copper yarn and her new poncho pattern. And she had a bag of . . . chocolate. Which meant that even if Amanda wasn't there in person, she was there in spirit. Well, partly. Instead of fancy truffles, Scottie had bought peanut butter M&M's.

At least they're artificially colored, she thought, grabbing a handful to munch as she made her way through the lakefront park.

Now she just had to find the perfect spot. She needed enough sun to cut through the crisp breeze, no view of any Ukrainian Speedo-wearers, and a curvy tree to lean upon.

She tromped across the wide ribbon of grass, loving the sound of the lake, churning as loudly as ocean waves. With each shift of the light, the water turned from icy blue to pea green to slate gray.

The trees dotted the lawn randomly, as if someone had just tossed a bunch of seeds into the air a hundred years ago and let the wind have its way with them. Scottie meandered from tree to tree, rejecting one for being too shady, the next for being too spindly, and the one after that for being dangerously close to a big, rude pile of dog poo.

As she headed to the next tree, about two hundred feet off, it suddenly occurred to Scottie that Bella would probably make a great tree spotter. The girl was way in touch with the earth. She even had the Earth shoes to prove it.

Why didn't I invite her to come knit with me this afternoon? Scottie thought suddenly.

It wasn't like she didn't enjoy hanging with Bella. That first day in the cafeteria, when Amanda had taught her the knit stitch, Bella's giddiness had been infectious. Just as she'd somehow known she would, she'd taken to the yarn immediately.

"It's like music," she'd exclaimed when the chenille started flowing through her spidery fingers. "But silent music! You can't hear it, but you can still dance to it, you know?"

Scottie had nodded enthusiastically. She *did* know. Everything else Bella Brearley had ever said to her sounded like New Age gibberish, but *this* she'd gotten.

Should I be worried? she'd asked herself.

•• *Chicks with Sticks*

By Thursday's lunch hour, complete with mini groat muffins Bella had baked for them, Scottie had her answer: No!

She'd decided to ignore the disdainful looks of Stark's heavy-lidded, black-clad artsy set. She'd also shrugged off Maryn and Tiff's defection to a lunch table where makeup and movie stars still topped the chat menu. She didn't even worry about Matt and Amanda. Matt had stopped by their table to get the scoop on this knitting thing; Amanda had given him her usual haughty/flirty routine. Matt had smiled at her blushy cheeks and given her yarn ball a playful tweak before he'd ambled back to his table of guys.

Scottie had assumed this was Matt-speak for, "Okay, you're a little weird, but you're still in the running."

After that, all three girls had begun to really relax and get their knit on. Amanda buried herself in her knitting, laboriously counting her stitches under her breath. Scottie zoned to her *click-swishy* knitting music. And Bella cheerfully chatted and chatted and chatted as she practiced her purls.

Bella's favorite color, she'd informed Scottie and Amanda, was red. Purple made her nervous, and black was just wrong. When it came to yoga, she was fabulous at downward dog but awful at balance poses. Her theories behind her bad balance ranged from seismic earth shifts to mischievous fairies to the heaviness (but unfortunate irresistibility) of groat muffins. Bella also talked about her favorite bus driver on the number 22 route, the best bookstore in Andersonville, and why they should all boycott eucalyptus. (Apparently, the Australian koala population was suffering from a eucalyptus shortage.)

But mostly, Bella talked about her parents, who seemed to be as prominent in her world as her fabulous crown of hair. Her dad was black, her mom was white, and all three of them were a self-concocted combo of Buddhist, Jewish, and Grateful Dead-ish. They lived in a Victorian two-flat near Wrigley Field, but instead of planting Cubs banners and bleachers on their roof like most of their neighbors, they'd put

(It's a purl thing)

in an organic kitchen garden. Every morning, the three Brearleys did yoga together, and every evening, they did Kabbalah study together.

The operative word was *together*. The Brearleys were totally tight, which explained Bella's earnest-geeky thing.

But it also seemed to be behind her utter openness. *Her* parents knew all about her new knitting thing, whereas Scottie's and Amanda's hadn't heard a word about the Chicks with Sticks.

Scottie had to admit, Bella being all free to be you and me was refreshing. By lunchtime on Friday, she'd realized that she was looking forward to Bella's sunny, awk-weird company.

Which meant that now, as she cruised for the perfect tree, she felt a stab in her stomach—part peanut-butter-M&M-induced cramp, part guilt.

It didn't even occur to me to ask Bella to knit with me this afternoon, she thought.

Instinctively, she swung her backpack around to reach for her cell. But before she could dial Bella up, she arrived at her destination tree.

"Oh!" she cried, dropping her phone in the grass.

Another girl had beaten her to the spot.

The girl's back was slumped against the perfectly curvy tree trunk and her knees were propped up. In the sun that broke perfectly through the half-yellow leaves, her eyebrow ring glinted.

And her knitting needles were *click-swish-click-swishing* with a jerky, badass beat.

"Tay!" Scottie gasped.

With a couple of iPod buds jammed into her ears and her eyes intent on the black-and-brown-striped scarf she was knitting, Tay seemed totally unaware of Scottie's presence.

Finally, Scottie shifted to make her shadow fall over Tay's face. Tay looked up, her long-lashed eyes wide with alarm. When she recognized Scottie, she sprang to her feet and yanked out her earbuds so hard, Scottie winced. Tay scowled.

"You scared the crap out of me," she complained.

"Sorry," Scottie said, still processing what she was seeing here. "Did you think I was a mugger or something?"

"No!" Tay scoffed. "I just—"

She stopped herself and blew out a breath of frustration.

"You were just afraid that somebody might see you knitting," Scottie said.

She wasn't judging, though. She knew just how Tay felt because she'd felt the very same way a few days ago.

Tay didn't answer. She just went all slouchy and made to stuff the needles into her cargo pants. They were just like the ones she'd been wearing at KnitWit on Tuesday, only in army green.

And just as *she* had on Tuesday, Scottie got inexplicably brave.

"Wait," she said, reaching down to stop Tay's hand. "Can I see?"

Tay only hesitated an instant before she shrugged and handed Scottie her length of fabric. Its scratchy wool made Scottie think of hay.

Without thinking, she held the stripes to her face and took a big whiff.

"Dude," Tay said, swiping the scarf back. "It's a scarf, not a bunch of flowers. Don't be gross."

Scottie gritted her teeth to hold back her flush of humiliation, but she failed completely. She could feel her face go bright pink.

Purely in self-defense, she said, "It's not gross. Smell it yourself. That yarn is yummy. It smells like a clean sheep."

Tay emitted another blast of scornful CO_2, but then she surprised Scottie by using her next breath to take a sniff.

She looked impressed.

"Not bad," she admitted.

"Back at ya," Scottie said, pointing at the narrow scarf. "I like the double ribs. Plus, it'll match your black hat. I guess you finished that?"

"Yeaaaahh," Tay said, rolling her eyes.

"And you decided to knit some more?"

"Okay, so I might have liked doing it," Tay spat. "You happy?"

"By 'it,' you mean *knitting*, right?" Scottie said, a smile tickling the edges of her mouth. She could feel her flush receding. In fact, she was starting to enjoy herself very much. "You've become a *knitter*."

Scottie stifled a giggle as she waited for a sputtery explosion from Tay. To her surprise, though, Tay's lips were looking pretty ticklish, too.

"All right, all right," she burst out. "I like to *knit*, all right? You caught me."

The sandpaper was being scraped away. Feeling a thrill, Scottie responded with her own gesture of friendship, the only one she *knew* Tay would receive with respect—mockery.

"Oh, man, you are so yarn-whipped!" Scottie crowed.

"Like you aren't?" Tay shot back. Her smile was big and unguarded now.

Scottie felt the syrupy sensation come back to her. She unzipped her backpack and pulled out her half-empty bag of M&M's, along with her own stripes of blue, sky, and indigo.

"Listen," she said to Tay, "I'll keep your secret safe on one condition."

"Oh?" Tay said, smoothly grabbing a palmful of candies from the bag and crunching them quick. "And what's that?"

"Give me a little space under this tree," Scottie proposed, "and knit with me."

Tay looked down at her feet suddenly, swallowing hard.

Scottie went shifty and uncomfortable.

Okay, I overdid it, she thought. *I mean, most loners are loners for a reason, right? As in, they prefer to be alone. And* definitely *prefer to knit alone.*

When Tay looked up, though, she surprised Scottie again. Her face was glowing with sheepish pleasure.

And some loners, Scottie realized with a jolt, *are just lonely.*

"Well, what are you waiting for?" Tay asked. "Sit down."

With a grateful laugh, Scottie plopped onto the grass. As she kicked her backpack out of the way and settled herself into half of the tree trunk's perfect slouchy curve, she gave Tay a sidelong glance.

"Hey, how do you feel about bubble tea?" she asked.

Tay didn't even look up as she resumed her *click-swish-click-swishing*.

"Don't push it, Shearer," she growled.

"Okay, okay," Scottie said with another laugh. "Forget it. Let's just knit."

8 ✴ (Join Yarn)

After that, nobody was left out. All of them—Scottie, Amanda, Bella, and Tay—had a standing date. Time: Tuesdays at 5:15 P.M. Location: KnitWit.

By the third Tuesday, KnitWit was starting to feel familiar to Scottie. When she alighted on the dusky landing, she grabbed the purple glass doorknob firmly and wind-chimed into the foyer as if she belonged there. Still, her stomach fluttered as she closed the door—a little less firmly—and peeked into the shop.

The dining room's golden glow was as welcoming as always, but tonight, there was no Greenie or other regulars. No Alice. No one at all.

"Hello?" Scottie called out.

Silence.

Okay, so Alice is in the bathroom or something, Scottie told herself. But deep in her gut, she was getting more nervous by the minute. She knew it was crazy, but part of her worried that this was where the other knitting needle was finally going to drop. Her friends would bail. Someone else would take Scottie's spot on the peach love seat. Alice would treat her like a stranger and shower her fullness onto some other newbie. Nobody would exclaim over Scottie's blue scarf, which she'd finally finished. . . .

And the woolly magic of the past few weeks would fade away. It would become distant and difficult to grasp, like a beach vacation you're trying to remember during a bone-rattling Chicago February.

Not seeing anyone in the dining room or classroom, Scottie peeked into the back room. She'd only gotten a glimpse of it in previous weeks, and when she surveyed it now, she found herself wrapping her arms around her ribs in a cozy self-hug. This was the best KnitWit nook yet.

A couch and two chairs were arranged in a tight half circle. They faced a wall-length kitchenette with a white, enameled countertop and a deep gardener's sink. From that sink cascaded a giant, viny plant. Above it, cabinets painted ice blue had mismatched glass knobs. The corrugated metal countertop was cluttered with tea boxes and cookie jars. And in a nook underneath, where a dishwasher might have been, a fluffy gray cat was sprawled on a red-and-purple bed—hand-knit and felted, of course. The cat's name, MONKEY, was embroidered on the bed's lip. Below that, in smaller script, was an addendum: *Beware of Cat.*

Well, no wonder, Scottie thought, giving the cat a second glance. Her belly was so swollen, the skin beneath her silvery fur shone. *Monkey puts Jane to shame. There must be a* lot *of kittens in there. Ouch.*

Monkey gazed at her irritably and echoed the thought.

No, really.

Eow, she mewled. *Eow, ow, ow!*

The *m*-less meows sounded a lot like, "Out! Out! Out!"

Scottie jumped back into the dining room, where the fuzzy things were much more approachable. Still feeling awkward, she began poking through the baskets on the table, scanning for perfect yarn.

She quickly got overwhelmed, though. The yarn was all amazing. The sunflower-yellow alpaca and squiggly aqua bouclé and dusty pink Manos all called out to her. A little poof of gray angora made her think of just-hatched baby birds. She couldn't even begin to name all the colors in a certain skein of iridescent ribbon.

But which yarn was right? Which yarn was *her?*

I don't know, Scottie thought plaintively.

(It's a purl thing)

Alice was the one who had the knack for that yarn-to-girl match-making. Scottie needed her. Where *was* she?

Click.

Behind Scottie, a door in the classroom opened.

Maybe Alice isn't just a yarn yenta, Scottie thought. *Maybe she's psychic.* Because there she was, emerging from a tiny bedroom—another mystery room that Scottie hadn't noticed before. She was beginning to think of KnitWit as a sort of fun house, with lots of little hiding spaces and no clear beginning or end.

Alice stepped through the door, her hair looking—if possible—even sproingier than it had before. When she spotted Scottie, she blinked at her through a sleepy smile.

"Would you believe me if I told you I *never* nap but that I just had the best nap of my life?" she said, motioning to a disheveled daybed in the little room. The bed was a little island of quilts among a sea of boxes containing what Scottie could only assume was yarn, needles, and other knit-stuff.

"I'm just storing that daybed here because we don't have room for it in our apartment," Alice continued, loping over to Scottie and giving her an absentminded hello hug. "The 'we' being me and my husband, Elliott. Anyway, it never occurred to me to actually *use* it. But today, the air was just the right kind of cold and the sky was just the right kind of gray and I was just the right kind of tired and poof—nap! Aaah, it was the best."

Scottie felt her own smile growing goofier with each sentence of this monologue. She could still feel Alice's hug. It was the sort of perfunctory squeeze you give to a friend you see every day. To a familiar.

"I *wish* I could nap," Scottie said. "I have insomnia issues."

She hated the nervous giggle—a wobbly period—that ended her sentence.

Alice paused halfway through an elaborate stretch and looked at her.

"Maybe you need to learn to knit yourself to sleep," she suggested. "This might help."

She plucked a skein of yarn from an old washtub sitting just outside the bedroom door.

The yarn was orange. A deep squashy orange with shoots of chocolate and cinnamon twining through it. Way chunky and impossibly soft, it was a pile of leaves that Scottie wanted to burrow into. It was perfect. It was *her*.

Scottie was shocked to feel a lump rise in her throat as she took the yarn from Alice. She turned it over and over in her hands, marveling at its glinting color and warm, sinewy texture. She loved the slight weight of it, the way the yarn seemed to fit so perfectly in her palms.

She was still studying the fiber when the front door chimed, and in walked Tay and Bella. As usual, Bella looked like a wafty fairy, all fluttery skirt, fuzzy leg warmers, and wild dreads. In comparison, Tay looked like discomfort incarnate. Her head seemed to be at odds with her body. The latter was all off center—hips slouching one way, legs angled another, arms crossed over her sunken-down chest, flat belly pooched out. It was a body staging a protest.

But Tay's face wore an expression of guilty glee that Scottie had begun to recognize. And tucked beneath her chin was her brown-and-black scarf, bluntly bound off and fringeless.

"Where's your black hat?" Scottie said, nodding with a grin at Tay's glossy, superspiky hair.

"I told you," Tay said. "It was a 'present' for my guidance counselor."

While Alice wrapped Bella in the same lazy hug she'd given Scottie, Tay loped into the classroom. She eyed the smushy corduroy recliner she usually sat in. Scottie could practically feel Tay yearning to flop into that big old La-Z-Boy.

But she didn't. Instead, she walked to the other side of the room and plunked herself down in the not-nearly-as-plush wing chair next to

Scottie and Amanda's peach love seat. Hunching forward, she planted her feet far apart and propped her elbows on her knees.

"Wanna get this show on the road?" she said, raising her eyebrows.

Scottie had to bite her lip to keep a big, sloppy, totally relieved grin from taking over her face.

"My ears were stinging on the way over here, Alice," Tay said. "I need to make another hat."

"And *I* need you to use this yarn," Alice said. She bustled over to the big table and pulled a skein of the most fabulous mustard merino out of one of the big, chipped pottery bowls. She tossed it through the two rooms, and Tay snatched it easily out of the air. As she held the yarn up for closer inspection, Scottie gasped softly. The yarn was making Tay change colors! The dark yellow burnished her pale, freckly face so that it looked sun-kissed. Meanwhile, the dark intensity of her eyes melted into soft caramel.

Bella gripped Scottie's elbow.

"You know," she whispered, "the purest form of beauty is beauty one doesn't know as beauty."

And *again,* Scottie got what Bella meant. Tay had no idea that she was pretty. She seemed to make every effort to *not* be pretty. And that made her prettier than ever. Especially in the glow of Alice's perfect yarn.

Oblivious to the way her friends were staring at her, Tay shrugged.

"It's definitely not itchy," she told Alice, "so why not."

"Cool," Alice said casually. "You'll need some number nine circulars for those. Metal or plastic?"

Tay started to answer, but stopped herself.

"You choose," she said, smiling at Alice.

Bella's hand on Scottie's elbow tightened some more.

"I know," Scottie whispered. "That was big."

Tinkle-tinkle-tinkle.

That was Amanda, clutching a *Vogue* magazine that reeked of at least four different perfume samples. As she walked through the foyer,

• • Chicks with Sticks

she pulled a box of Godiva chocolates out of her Spade. She practically skipped over to Alice at the big table.

"I found this silver shawl in here that you've *got* to see," she announced.

Only then did Scottie realize she'd been taking shallow breaths and cinching her shoulders up until they were grazing her earlobes.

But now they were all here, and Scottie felt positively bubbly. She grabbed Amanda's hand and dragged her over to their love seat. Bella loped along behind them and flopped herself into an orange-checked beanbag chair at their feet.

By the time Becca, Michael, Patricia, and Jane tromped in a few minutes later, the girls were already hitting their groove. Their *click-swishes* were beginning to sing, and they were starting to talk.

"No *way!*" Scottie found herself squealing a half hour later. "Amanda, you *did* not buy a thousand yards of Lobster Pot cashmere on the Internet. How much did it cost?"

Amanda went pink and shrugged.

"I don't know," she said. "About two-fifty?"

"Two hundred and fifty dollars?" Bella gasped. "Whoa."

"Well, I wanted to get enough for all of us," she said defensively. "I mean, don't you want some?"

"Oh my God, are you kidding?" Scottie said. "I read on this blog that working with cashmere is like knitting a cloud. It's better than eating Nutella out of the jar. Better than getting straight A's."

"Better than . . . boys?" Amanda asked.

Bella threw the green-orange-gold shawl she was making over her face and emitted a high-pitched giggle.

"Amanda, you're supposed to knit with it," Scottie said, "not *make out* with it."

Scottie couldn't help it. The moment she said "make out," her face went bright red. She felt the color wash over her in one fell swoop.

"Scottie, just *referring* to kissing shouldn't make you blush," Amanda said mischievously. "*Doing* it, on the other hand . . ."

"Oh really?" Scottie said. Bella was still giggling, and Tay was rolling her eyes madly. Scottie had to deflect this humiliation—somehow. "Tell us more, Amanda. Tell us what *you* know about kissing."

Amanda grimaced as if she were struggling with something. Then . . . her face turned bright red!

"Gee, Amanda," Tay mocked. "I thought *referring* to kissing shouldn't make you blush! Maybe you've been *doing* too much of it!"

That's when all of them began laughing so hard that the out-of-control snorts and squeaks started to kick in.

As Scottie gasped for breath, she caught a glimpse of Patricia and Jane, gazing at them curiously.

"Oh, sorry," she gasped, covering her mouth. "Are we being totally loud and obnoxious?"

Jane smiled and nudged Patricia with her elbow.

"We could *so* outgiggle you girls," she said. "We've been friends since college. Just imagine all the private jokes."

"And the knitting disasters," Patricia chimed.

"Oh, my God," Jane cried. "Remember your shrug?"

Patricia slapped her hands on her cheeks and made her mouth gape. She was either doing Munch's *Scream* or that kid from *Home Alone*. Either way, it made Jane dissolve completely. She wrapped her arms around her pregnant belly and *screamed* with laughter.

"Poor Michael," Jane gasped after several guffaws. "He has to contend with our madness every week."

"What? Huh?"

Michael glanced up blearily. His WIP looked like a needle farm. His eyes were shadowed and his skin was milkier than ever.

"Never mind, honey," Patricia said, reaching over to pat Michael's knee. "You go back to your doggie sweater."

So that's *what it is*, Scottie thought.

And then she just knew she was going to burst out laughing again. She slapped her hand over her mouth.

Quick! Must sober up.

One look at Tay did the trick. In the aftermath of their boy-crazy hysterics, she was looking seriously wistful.

Apparently, Scottie wasn't the only one who'd noticed. Amanda was giving her a curious look. After glancing over her shoulder at Jane, Patricia, and Becca to make sure they were reimmersed in their own knit worlds, she leaned into the center of the girls' little circle.

"Tay," she said quietly, "who's Jo—?"

"Josh?" Tay said automatically. Scottie gasped. So there *was* a boy.

The moment the name left her mouth, Tay's mustard-yarn glow disappeared. She looked down quickly and began knitting as if her life depended on it. Her stitching style—always rough and impatient—became more herky-jerky than ever.

"Josh is nobody," she said. Then she shook her head violently. "I mean, he's not *nobody*. He's a friend. Just a friend."

Scottie glanced at Amanda, who was giving Tay a probing look. Tay refused to look up, but she must have felt Amanda's scrutiny.

"Okay, he's not *just* a friend," she admitted.

Scottie held her breath. Tay was actually going to tell them that she had a boyfriend!

"He's my *best* friend," Tay said.

Oh. Scottie exhaled.

"Has been since third grade," Tay continued. "We do everything together."

Okay, so he's not a boyfriend, Scottie thought. *He's just a friend. Who's a boy. Which makes sense, I guess, since Tay's, like, half boy herself.*

Scottie resumed her knitting and tried to hide her disappointment.

So, there'll be no juicy dirt about Tay's love life, she told herself. *Oh well. On to the next sub—*

"I mean, it makes total sense because we were next-door neighbors for years," Tay blurted, furrowing her brow as she hit a tricky turn in her mustard hat.

Scottie glanced at Amanda once more, a questioning look in her eyes.

Is Tay actually *confiding in us?* she wondered.

Amanda put a finger to her lips and turned her attention back to Tay.

"Josh was basically the only refuge I had while my parents were doing everything short of killing each other," Tay said.

"Oh no," Bella gasped. "Is there domestic violence in your home, Tay? Because you could go talk to a counselor at Stark about that."

Tay actually laughed.

"You're more with it than you seem, you know that, B?"

Bella looked confused until Tay assured her that, no, there was "no domestic violence in my house."

"It was just the verbal kind," Tay said. "My parents fought like you wouldn't believe. Over money. Over what to have for dinner. Over taking out the garbage. And once they started divorce proceedings, over me."

"Oh, yuck," Amanda said. "Custody battle? I've heard those suck. Were you twelve, at least?"

"Nah," Tay said. "Ten."

Amanda explained to Scottie and Bella. "If you're twelve, you usually get to choose which parent you go with. But if you're younger than that, they choose for you."

"How do you know so much, Miss Golden Child with the perfect family of four?" Scottie said.

"Please," Amanda scoffed, "I live in the Gold Coast. Where *everybody* signs prenups because *everybody* gets divorced eventually."

"Yup," Tay said. "Money and happy marriages don't seem to mix."

"Well, I guess *my* parents are safe," Bella said cheerfully, looping her pale yarn around her needle. "They are SO not rich. Mom's an acupuncturist and Dad's a holistic therapist. I'm paying for this yarn with my job at the yoga studio!"

"Why does none of that surprise me?" Scottie said with a giggle.

But Amanda was back on Tay.

"So, what happened?" she said. "With the whole divorce thing."

"Joint custody," Tay said.

"Ouch!" Amanda said.

"Yeah, it pretty much bites," Tay admitted. "I'm at my mom's in Andersonville four nights a week and at my dad's in the Ukrainian Village the other three. Unless, of course, it's a holiday week, in which case Dad gets four days and Mom gets three."

"How do you keep track of it?" Bella cried.

"Oh, Dad bought me a Palm Pilot, and Mom bought me a Black-Berry," Tay said drily. "Let's just say their communication skills have *not* improved with divorce. Doesn't really matter, though, because I ditched both of them."

"You threw *away* a Palm Pilot and a BlackBerry?" Scottie cried.

"Here's what you learn in your first year of joint custody," Tay said. She slouched deeper into her chair. "Don't get attached to stuff. Don't get weighed down by stuff. Because if you come to care about stuff, then you'll find that that *stuff* is never where *you* are when you want it. It's *always* at the other apartment. Trust me on this one."

"Okay," Amanda said, "your cargo-pants-every-day wardrobe is starting to make sense to me."

"And the wash-and-wear hair," Bella said, pointing at Tay's almost crew cut.

"Okay, okay," Tay said, waving the girls off with her mustard swatch. "If I need psychoanalyzing, I can go to Mr. Adrian."

"*He's* your guidance counselor?" Bella said. "I love him! Whenever you say something he doesn't get, his bushy red eyebrows get all scrunchy. They look just like a caterpillar."

"That's him!" Tay cried, laughing as she did a quick stitch count. "Let's just say, it's all caterpillar, all the time, when I'm with Mr. A. I guess I give him a hard time."

"Why?" Bella asked.

"Because I don't even want to be seeing the guy," Tay sputtered. "The Starkers that be make me talk to him once a month. You know, to make sure the divorce doesn't drive me to smoking or drinking or writing dirty words on the bathroom walls."

"Anger management," Amanda said, making mocking quote marks in the air with her fingers. "They *so* love to manage us."

"Totally condescending," Tay agreed. "Just like my last meeting with Mr. A."

"What happened?" Scottie asked. She loved how it was getting easier and easier to chat-and-purl at the same time. Her coppery poncho was totally coming along, *and* Tay was totally opening up!

"Well, first of all," Tay said, "he called me Taylor, even though he knows I hate it."

"Taylor!" Bella said, looking up from her knitting with sparkly eyes. "I love that name. I have this biracial doll that I named Taylor. . . ."

Bella's voice trailed off when she realized everyone was staring at her.

"What?" she said.

"A biracial doll?" Amanda said.

"Well, I don't play with her any*more*," Bella said with a laugh. "She's just something my parents gave me when I was a kid. You know, a little 'It's okay to be different' self-esteem booster."

"Looks like it was *wildly* successful," Tay said with a kind laugh.

"Oh yeah," Bella agreed. "I mean, my doll Taylor and my Martin Luther King Junior board game were, like, my *favorite* things when I was little."

"See? That proves my point," Tay said drily. "*Taylor* is a name for a baby doll. Or for some girlie girl with friends named Ashley, Britney, and Meghan. It's *so* not me."

"So, why did Mr. A call you that?" Scottie said.

"Oh, he had some theory," Tay said, propping one leg on the arm of her chair and bouncing her other knee up and down with a nervous *rat-a-tat-tat*. "He thinks I'm cutting *too* much stuff out of my life. I've shortened my name, shortened my hair, and as for the list of friends on speed dial in my cell phone—"

"Let me guess," Scottie cut in. "It's pretty short?"

"It's pretty much just Josh," Tay admitted.

Scottie felt terrible for Tay. Not that her *own* cell phone was brimming with names, but at least her social circle was more than a one-stop shop.

Where Scottie went sympathetically quiet, though, it seemed Bella came up with solutions.

"I have an idea! Mr. Adrian will *love* this," Bella exclaimed. She was so excited, she fluttered her shawl in progress through the air. "*We'll* be your friends, Tay. And Josh can be your boyfriend!"

"What?!" Amanda and Scottie cried.

The funny thing was, Tay didn't protest at all—probably because, from the looks of her, she'd suddenly lost the ability to breathe. She stared at Bella for a moment, openmouthed. Then she quickly ducked her head and focused on her yarn.

Not that she could knit, with her fingers trembling and all.

Looks like Bella just called it big-time, Scottie thought. *Tay wants to stop guying around with this Josh and start swapping spit with him.*

She was also seriously in need of a topic rescue. They all were. An awkward silence was hanging over the girls' heads.

"So, why did Mr. A dare you?" Scottie blurted desperately.

"W-what?" Tay said. She looked up in confusion.

"To come here," Scottie said. "You said he dared you."

"Oh yeah," Tay said, coming slowly out of her Josh-induced freakout. "I don't know, it was more of his dumb psychoanalysis. His niece started knitting, and it, like, changed her life, so he thought he had all the answers, suddenly. He gave me a flyer about this KnitWit class and said, and I quote Mr. Caterpillar Head himself, 'Look at all this restless energy you've got. I guarantee, knitting will calm you down in more ways than one. Step out of your comfort zone just once. Try to relax and do something nice for yourself. I dare you.'"

"He dared you?" Amanda said. "Is that even allowed?"

"That's what I said!" Tay exclaimed. "He didn't seem too worried about it. So, just to show him, I came. I knitted."

"And you got yarn-whipped," Scottie said with a giggle in her voice.

"Yeah," Tay said with a dejected sigh. "That's the part I didn't plan on. This is . . . so weird."

"I know how you feel," Amanda said. "I mean, me? A knitter?"

"Yeah, that was pretty much my take on it, too," Scottie said.

"I don't know *what* you guys are talking about," Bella said. "Knitting's the perfect thing for me! I think my parents are kicking themselves for not coming up with it first!"

Scottie's laugh spewed out of her—a torrent of giggles. Amanda launched straight into her pig snorts, and Tay laughed so hard, she just wheezed—no sound at all. Bella joined in with her high-pitched giggles, even if she didn't *really* know what was so funny.

Their laughter was loud enough to rouse Michael from his doggie sweater and make Becca, Patricia, and Jane lapse into their own nostalgic chuckles.

For Scottie, it was more than just a hilarious moment. Somehow all that laughter finally set her free from the fear that she'd brought to KnitWit. Now she only felt glad to have these three friends to knit with. She felt grateful to Tay for confiding in them. And she felt mighty lucky that none of them was named Ashley, Meghan, or Britney.

Part of her wanted to ask more.

What was so magical about Josh?

What was it like to be so close to your parents?

Did the tattoo hurt?

What the heck *was* a groat?

But Scottie swallowed back her flood of questions.

•• *Chicks with Sticks*

What's the rush? she thought as Alice—smelling faintly of vanilla and wool—sat down next to her to show her how to work dropped stitches into her webby poncho. *Winter's just about to start.*

Scottie had always hated Chicago's winter. The sun set at 4:30 in the afternoon, and the sidewalks became a series of treacherous ice rinks. Scottie shivered all the time, constantly craving fuzzy fleeces, down duvets, and loads of hot chocolate. Every time she left her (drafty) loft, she had to wrap herself in so many layers, she looked like a Thinsulate-clad potato. By February, she was always feeling shrivelly and despondent.

This winter, though, Scottie thought with a deep sigh, *is going to be different.*

Instead of filling her with dread, the deepening chill outside made her hopeful. Winter was now a time—and a reason—to knit.

To knit together.

9 ✴ (Knit in the Round)

Scottie didn't even notice it until the class was almost over. But now she saw it—each girl had twisted in her seat so that she touched the next one, just slightly. From her beanbag chair, Bella had tipped one knobby knee onto Amanda's shin. Amanda's other leg, tucked underneath her as she knitted, grazed Scottie's thigh. Scottie's fuzzy-socked foot, propped on the arm of Tay's chair, just dinged Tay's elbow. And Tay's booted toe brushed against Bella's Birkenstocked one.

Scottie pictured the electrical circuits she'd learned about in physics class. As her teacher had explained it, energy could flow through the tiniest points of contact.

Tell me about it.

Scottie sighed contentedly and sank deeper into her seat. The noise of all the girls' needles didn't exactly make music, but they coexisted comfortably. Tay's *click-swishes* were almost violent, tugging and snapping loudly. Bella's stitches were feathery whispers. Amanda's flowed in fits and starts, faltering when she overthought it and recommencing when she took a deep breath and put her trust in her fingers.

And Scottie's own knitting music? That was like asking her what her face looked like when she wasn't looking in the mirror. Her knitting was already a part of her. She felt like she knew it as well as she knew her own body. But like her body, it had its mysterious side.

That must be, Scottie thought with a glance at the yarn tail looped lightly around her index finger, *why my tension was so loose a few days ago that I might as well have been weaving a fishnet, and the next day, it went so tight I lost three inches of width.*

But tonight, everything had flowed. After several botched attempts, Scottie had mastered the double-looped-then-dropped stitches at the heart of her poncho. Then she'd hooked her heels on the edge of the love-seat cushion, hunkered down, and knitted herself into a zone—a zone so comfortable, she forgot about time and barely noticed when the other students began to trickle out of KnitWit, their fingers exhausted. Tay had to give Scottie's toe, still propped on the chair arm, a little nudge to jolt her back to reality. When Scottie blinked the yarn out of her eyes, her friends were standing up to stretch. They smiled at her sleepily.

"Zoned?" Amanda asked.

"Totally zoned," Scottie answered, unfurling herself from the love seat with a happy sigh. "I was just thinking about what a better place Stark would be if we could set up a little knitting lounge on every floor."

"And they made the break between classes longer," Bella chimed in as she squirmed herself out of her beanbag chair. "Then we could stop there and have a little knit during breaks."

"Exactly!" Scottie said.

This time, she forgot to feel weird about that electric info-current that seemed to be flowing between her brain and Bella's.

"Can't you see it?" Scottie went on. "If we all knit our way through the day, we'd be a lot more happy."

"And productive," Amanda pointed out. "I swear, my head just works better after some time on the sticks."

"We could put herbal tea in each lounge," Bella said, dreamily rewrapping her ball of fluffy, green-orange yarn. "And we should bring in some little lamps, too. Fluorescent lights are murder on your electrolytes. I read it on the Web."

Tay was rolling her eyes again.

"You guys aren't serious, are you?" she said. "I mean, this does seem to be the kind of student initiative that the Head Starkers have wild fantasies about. But no *kids* would show up at a knitters' lounge! It's too lame and weird."

"But *you* knit," Bella said. "Why wouldn't other people come, too?"

"Well, you might not have noticed, B," Tay said, softening her voice for Bella's sake, "but I'm not exactly an average girl."

"Got that right," Bella said, grinning big and wide. "Neither am I."

"None of us are," Tay admitted, "even prom queen Amanda."

"You know, that's just what I was thinking."

That was Alice, piping up from behind them. The girls widened their tight little circle to let her in. As she stepped in to make a snug fit between Scottie and Bella, Alice said, "There's something I want to say."

Oh no, Scottie thought, bracing herself for a lecture. *We were too obnoxious for the class. And then Amanda had to go and make that kissing comment.*

Alice looked each of the girls briefly in the eyes and said, "I saw something special happening here tonight. A circle being woven."

What? Scottie thought. *Wait a minute. So instead of a lecture, we're getting some sort of New Agey sermon?*

Scottie shifted uncomfortably. She wasn't sure if this was much better than a lecture.

Tay was looking just as freaked as Scottie felt. And Amanda's face was going plastic and polite. Scottie recognized the expression. It was Amanda's party face, the one she rode like a raft through boring parental functions, amusing herself with snarky thoughts that she hid behind her pretty mask.

But Scottie didn't want Alice to be one of those adults to be tolerated with a fake smile. She didn't want her to be goofy or oblivious. She'd thought Alice was different.

"Okay, I know what you're thinking," Alice said. "This hippie lady is going all New Age on us."

The girls gave one another sidelong looks, then dissolved into relieved laughter. Their masks fell away as Alice continued.

"Listen," she said. "I do have something I want to do with you guys. And on the surface, yeah, it *is* pretty New Agey. But beneath those trappings, I find meaning and . . . well, I just want to open that door for you, too."

"What are we talking about here?" Tay said.

"A smudge ceremony," Alice said simply. She reached into the pocket of her cardigan (today it was a long, nubbly duster, the same blue-gray as her cat). She pulled out a bundle of leaves, bound tightly by crisscrosses of waxy string.

Bella was nodding enthusiastically, but the rest of the girls looked blank.

"It's a Native American thing," Bella jumped in to explain. "You light the sage and swirl the smoke around your home or your body to get rid of negative energy."

Alice pulled a tuft of silvery green grass out of her other cardi pocket.

"And then smudging with this sweetgrass," she said, "brings the positivity in."

"Um, listen," Tay said, launching into a protest without a second thought, "one of the things my parents fought about in their divorce was my religion. Was I going to be Presbyterian like my dad or Catholic like my mom? I mean, we're talking a *lot* of billable hours in lawyers' offices over this, which basically resulted in me being very, *very* anti this kind of thing."

"That's why we'll make this ceremony our own," Alice said. "The smudge can be what you want it to be."

"Well, I want it to be a little less, uh, ceremonial," Tay said, crossing her arms over her chest.

Scottie was pretty much going in that direction, too. To her, knitting felt sacred enough without any ritual looming over it.

But not just knitting, she realized. *Knitting with my friends. The four of us doing this together.*

And suddenly she blurted, "I know what we should do."

"What?" Tay said.

"We can make a circle of smoke," Scottie said. "Tying us together."

It was the corniest thing Scottie had ever said. But at the same time, it felt right. It wasn't like she wanted to do a rain dance every time she felt like making a pair of socks, but she realized she agreed with Alice. The Chicks with Sticks should do *something* to recognize their strange, *click-swishy* quartet. It seemed important.

"Great idea, Scottie," Bella said. "Let's use just the sweetgrass. It totally reeks of good vibes. Smell it!"

Alice nodded and held out the tuft of frizzled grass. The girls all leaned in and gave it a little whiff.

"Mooooo," Amanda said.

"Amanda!" Scottie whispered, shooting Bella and Alice a nervous glance. She didn't want them to think Amanda was making fun of this sweetgrass thing, even if it *was* kind of goofy.

Luckily, Alice and Bella were the first ones to crack up.

And then they looked to Scottie. Clearly, they were expecting her to follow up her little suggestion with more of 'em.

And to Scottie's surprise, she actually had one ready.

"Each of us should make a circle with the smudge," she said. "While you're doing it, say something about our group."

"What are we supposed to say?" Amanda asked, just a tad whinily. She hated any and all assignments.

"Whatever you want," Scottie said with a shrug. "Talk about knitting. Talk about us. Talk about Monkey the cat."

"Just say what you're feeling," Bella suggested, clasping her hands. "Let the smoke speak to you, and let it move you to speak."

"Y'know," Alice said, handing Bella the sweetgrass and some matches, "I think it's best not to overthink these things. Like knitting. It flows best when you just *do* it."

Szzzzzz.

Bella struck the match and lit the sweetgrass. Scottie was mesmerized as the tuft flamed up, then quickly died into a flickery smolder. It smelled delicious, like a combo of burning leaves and just-mown lawn.

Alice stepped out of the circle, and instinctively, the four girls stepped inward, closing the gap in their ring until they were shoulder to shoulder.

Bella held the smoldering tuft out to Scottie.

"You start," she whispered.

"Me?" Scottie squeaked. "I don't really know what I'm doing."

"Oh yes, you do," Tay said. Scottie looked at her, wary of a curled lip or Tay's typical sarcastic slouch.

It wasn't there. Tay actually looked impressed.

Maybe she's just glad I was the one who came up with this ridiculous idea, and not her.

But deep down, Scottie felt support from Tay. From all the girls. Which made the smoke circle seem superfluous, but Scottie gingerly took the sweetgrass from Bella anyway.

As she wafted a wobbly ring around her friends' heads, she said, "I used to have my aunt's kitchen, and then I discovered knitting. These were the only places I really felt like me. Like myself. Like . . . I was at home."

Scottie felt like she was babbling and her face was hot with . . . she didn't know. Embarrassment? Emotion? Estrogen?!

She couldn't worry about that now. She had one more thing to say.

"Now I have one more home," she said simply. "You guys."

Abruptly, she thrust the tuft into Amanda's fist. While Amanda drew her circle around the girls, Bella grabbed Scottie's hand. Scottie smiled at her gratefully.

"Knitting brought me back to Scottie," Amanda said, "but it's also giving me something new. Let's just say, I'm not used to the feeling of really *knowing* something. And I like it."

Only Scottie knew exactly what Amanda meant, and she couldn't help it—she got choked up, especially when Amanda looked straight at her with calm, proud eyes before passing the tuft on to Tay.

Scottie swallowed hard. She couldn't let herself tear up. If she did, she *knew* Tay would throw in the towel.

"I didn't want to like this," Tay said while she waved the sweetgrass vaguely in the air. "Any of this: knitting, yarn, sitting around gabbing with a bunch of girls. But I do. Like it, I mean. And, as my guidance counselor so smugly pointed out while wearing the black hat I made him—which was way too small by the way . . ."

The other girls burst out laughing.

". . . knitting *does,* I don't know, calm me. It makes me want to stay put for more than five minutes. And that's . . . new. And I guess it's good. And . . . that's all."

Tay clamped her mouth shut and shoved the tuft at Bella.

Bella's waft, of course, was the most wafty of them all. She made a little crown of smoke over the head of each of her friends and capped it off with a swirly pirouette for herself.

"There's something we say at the end of every yoga class," she said. "*Namaste.* It means 'The Perfection within me salutes the Perfection within you.'"

Scottie grimaced.

I guess, she thought, *we should have expected some hearts and flowers from Bell—*

"Y'know, I always hated that saying!" Bella blurted.

Um, never mind, Scottie thought as she, Tay, and Amanda cackled again.

"Don't tell my mom and dad," Bella said, picking up steam as her friends' giggles died down, "but yoga makes me feel anything but perfect. Anything but enlightened. I mean, I'm striving, that's the whole point, right? But sometimes I think I'll strive forever and never get there, wherever 'there' is.

"But here," Bella went on, "I can finish a scarf in a few days. I can make a sweater with arms long enough for *my* arms. Maybe, with you guys, I can achieve perfection after all. My kind of perfection, anyway."

Scottie blinked.

That was the most gettable thing she'd ever heard Bella say.

As the swirls of sweetgrass smoke dissipated, it was clear that it was time to break up their little circle, gather their gear, and head home.

But nobody moved.

Silently, they all seemed to agree to stay here, holding one another's hands, until the smoke was swept out the window that Alice had quietly opened.

Scottie didn't know if it was two minutes later or ten when the room filled up with cold, exhaust-scented air and the warm, sweet smoke finally disappeared.

She gave Amanda and Bella's hands a squeeze before she let them go.

It was Alice who broke the spell—in a good way. As the girls silently stuffed their Works in Progress into their bags, she said, "You know, you guys, I just got this progressive blanket in the mail that's right up your alley."

"What's that?" Bella said.

"Oh, it's fun," Alice said. "It's a great big communal project started on a knitting blog. Everybody in the chain makes a square out of whatever yarn you want, whatever stitch you want. The only rules are, it has to be four inches by four inches."

"Okay, and then what?" Tay said.

"Then you sew your block onto the blanket," Alice explained, "and send it on to the next knitter."

"That sounds cool!" Scottie said.

"I wonder who gets to keep the blanket," Amanda said.

"The blogger who started it," Alice said as she ducked into the little bedroom off the classroom. She emerged with a large, padded envelope. Pulling a piece of paper out of it, she read, "Annie LeRoi, Joliet, Illinois."

"How random," Tay said. "Let's see the blanket!"

Alice pulled out a rectangle about the size of a baby's blanket. It only had about two dozen squares to it so far. There was a basic garter-stitched square of fuzzy, royal blue angora, a rainbow-striped one knitted in seed stitch, a red square with an embroidered star, and a lacy square of wire-thin pink silk.

"It's beautiful," Bella exclaimed. "We should *so* do this."

"We could collaborate," Scottie said, "and do the squares together."

"Nah, that's boring," Tay said. "We should do the squares in secret, then get together to sew them up."

"Deal!" Scottie cried. "Let's make a date now so we don't forget it."

"Well, actually there's a deadline," Alice said, looking at the blanket's info sheet. "You need to send it on to the next knitter by November sixteenth."

"What day of the week is that?" Amanda said.

"Wednesday."

"Perfect!" Amanda said. "The night before, we can sew our squares together in class and then send it on."

"Scottie, why don't you hang on to the blanket until then," Alice said, handing her the big envelope.

"Why me?" Scottie said, somewhere between shy and proud.

"Duh, because you have the biggest backpack," Tay said. "Don't think you're *too* much of a knit goddess, Shearer."

Of all of them, Scottie laughed the hardest at this. Then they all hugged Alice good-bye and walked out the door. Before clomping down the steep stairwell, Scottie said, "Wait, I have one more thing to say."

She grabbed a bit of purple chalk out of the cup next to the door and found some space in the corner of KnitWit's blackboard. Grinning madly, she scratched out: THE CHICKS WITH STICKS ROCK!

"Oooh, check out the badass knitter." Tay laughed. "Keep her away from any spray-paint cans, you guys. She's gonna start leaving tags in alleys."

Scottie straightened up suddenly.

"You just gave me another idea," she said.

"Oh no," Tay said, flinging her stripy scarf around her neck. "No more! I've had all the bonding I can handle for one night."

"Even if it involves hot chocolate?"

Within ten minutes, Scottie and her friends were stepping out of a cab in front of Joe, just across the street from the Stark School.

Joe was most Starkers' caffeine station of choice. Once upon a time, it had been an Irish pub. Dark, woody, and redolent of megastrong coffee, it was the perfect place to burrow or brood. Joe's booths were deep enough to hide in for hours with a book or laptop. The espresso was served in shot glasses and the mochas in pint glasses. The fireplace in the back roared all year round, even during summer heat waves.

The best part about Joe, for Scottie's current purposes, was the coffee table in the back. Not only did it sit between the fireplace and a cluster of beautifully tattered easy chairs, but it was a site for sanctioned defacing. Over the years, Starkers had carved so many messages into the table, there were now carvings on top of carvings. They included the usual lovers' initials in hearts and a couple brilliant caricatures of Stark teachers. There were antiwar statements and items of gossip. But mostly the scrawls were just initials and names—people using their fork tines and butter knives to make their marks.

Amanda and Bella staked out a spot by the coffee table while Scottie and Tay picked up four Irish-coffee mugs of hot chocolate, with extra whipped cream.

For about five minutes, the girls slurped in silence. Without asking, Scottie knew that her friends were mulling over the smudge ceremony they'd just completed at KnitWit.

Amanda was the first one to speak. And when she did, she was still back there, in that weirdly profound place.

"There's something else I want you to know," she said. "Especially you, Tay. You shouldn't be the only one to tell a secret tonight."

And that's when Amanda began to tell her new friends the things that hardly anybody—save Scottie—knew about her.

She told them about being pulled out of her second-grade classroom to spend an afternoon in "testing." After that, her parents had been called in for a meeting with Stark's learning specialist. Even her dad had shown up, and he *never* left his office at the brokerage house unless it was an emergency. Amanda's mother had emerged from the meeting teary-eyed, her father incredibly stern.

"It's not like it was a surprise, though," Amanda said, looking into her lap and chipping at her nail polish—now a frosty lavender. "I mean, I think that's why they sent me to Stark in the first place, instead of some plaid-skirt-and-kneesock school in the Gold Coast, with all their friends' kids. They knew I was a slow reader. They saw me get my numbers backwards. They knew *something* was up, and I'm sure they didn't want word to get around."

Scottie's eyes widened. She'd never heard Amanda put it quite like that. Not that she was surprised. Amanda's parents were all about appearances. Her dad's client dinners and her mother's charity teas hinged on the illusion of perfection: the perfect home, the perfect clothes (as in Chanel, Chanel, and more Chanel), the perfect vacation plans, and, of course, the perfect children. Amanda's precocious little brother fit the bill. Trey had come back from their summer in Europe reading French *and* Italian.

Meanwhile, Amanda was still struggling with her mother tongue.

Scottie had a feeling that was why Amanda had kept her knitting a secret from her parents. In the Scotts' world, knitting just would *not* do. They were the sort of people who rode horses but never groomed them. They threw dinner parties, but never cooked. They wore three-hundred-dollar sweaters from Neiman's, but never, ever knitted them.

Amanda didn't mention her parents again, but she did tell her friends about her head-against-a-brick-wall tutoring sessions, her Scotch-tape-in-the-locker trick, and her breezy way of ordering at restaurants: "I'll have what she's having."

She told them about the frayed-electrical-wire feeling in her head.

She told them that she always held the boys who liked her at arm's length, lest they find out her secret.

"And now," she said quietly, still chipping at her nails, "you know what I meant when I said that stuff, during the smudge ceremony."

"Yeah," Tay said, so quickly that the lump returned to Scottie's throat. "I think I sort of know how you feel, even. Not the part about boys crushing on me. As if."

Amanda smiled, even if she wasn't ready to meet her friends' eyes yet.

"But the part about keeping secrets," Tay said, "keeping your real self safe. Yeah, I get that."

Bella didn't say anything. She just sidled out of her chair, leaned down, and wrapped her spindly arms around Amanda in a long, sweet hug.

Scottie's contribution? It wasn't eloquent but it was the only thing she had—the idea that had brought them there in the first place.

She dug into her backpack and pulled out a small, metal, double-pointed knitting needle. Then she crouched next to the coffee table and carved:

C

w/

S

(It's a purl thing)

Northwest of this logo, she scratched in her initial.

When she was done with her *S*, Tay took the needle. She didn't say a word as she made her own mark on the coffee table.

Bella went next and finally, with tears bobbling at the ends of her mascara'd lashes, Amanda.

The four girls stood around the table then, gazing down at their creation:

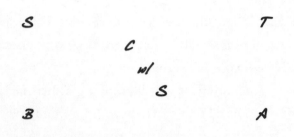

"You know it'll be gone in a few weeks," Tay pointed out. "Covered over with other carvings."

"It doesn't matter," Scottie said. "We'll know it's there, even if we can't see it anymore. We'll know we made a statement."

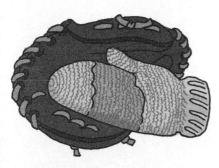

10 *(Continue as Established)

After that night, the Chicks with Sticks were an Entity. It was as simple as that.

Scottie wouldn't allow herself to completely believe that there had been actual magic in those swirls of smoke. Or that needling their initials into the coffee table at Joe had somehow solidified their sisterhood. But she did let herself relax a little bit. As long as she was knitting with her buds, she no longer worried that they might poof away at any moment.

Luckily, they were knitting a *lot*.

They knitted on the "L" and at the library.

They knitted their way through study session and their finger-foodie lunch hours. They knitted in the booths at Joe and over frozen yogurt at Windy's. Their favorite place to knit, of course, was at KnitWit, where Alice had told them they could stitch and bitch whenever they wanted.

When Scottie woke up a couple Saturdays after the smudge ceremony, her first impulse was to do just that: spend the gloomy, fall day curled up in KnitWit's kitchen, purling away at the sweater she was making from the squash-colored yarn Alice had found for her.

Still semi-groggy in bed, Scottie was just reaching for the phone when her bedroom door opened and Amanda popped in.

(It's a purl thing)

"I was just calling you!" Scottie cried.

"Were you calling to order up Plotinsky's bagels?" Amanda said. Tucked beneath her arm was a steamy paper bag.

"Oh man, Plotinsky's!" Scottie breathed. She sat up and held out her arms. "Toss one over!"

"What are you still doing in bed?" Amanda asked, withholding the bagels in a most momlike fashion. "It's almost eleven."

"Which must be why I'm so hungry," Scottie teased.

Since she'd started knitting, her insomnia had disappeared. No, that was too weak a word for it. It had left the building so emphatically that now Scottie didn't just sleep—she conked. Her nights were all about dreamless, unmoving, never-get-up-to-pee, oblivious-to-all-train-whistles, *wonderful* sleep.

She must have been catching up.

But upon the arrival of Amanda plus bagels, she was happy to shake the last of the wooze from her eyes. She hopped out of bed and plucked a poppy-seed bagel from Amanda's bag, sticking her tongue out at her before she took her first bite.

"These were Aunt Roz's favorite," she said after she'd swallowed.

It had just popped out, and she wasn't sure why. The fun factor in the room instantly plummeted. Amanda blinked and looked at the floor uncomfortably, but Scottie actually felt all right. Better than all right. She took the paper bag out of Amanda's arms and whispered, "It's okay, really. It doesn't hurt so much anymore, to be reminded of her. It's actually kind of nice."

"What would she think of your knitting? I wonder," Amanda said.

Scottie cocked her head as she put the bagel bag on her desk.

"I think . . ." She glanced into her open closet, where her aunt's red sweater made a garish slash in the middle of an otherwise muted pile of clothes. "I think she'd say I was making a statement," she said.

She took another big bite of bagel and smiled.

"You'll make another one when you finish your sweater," Amanda said. "Let's go to KnitWit. We'll bring Alice a bagel."

"Oh! Okay!" Scottie said. "Yeah, let's go."

She jumped into her Pumas and headed to the bathroom to brush her teeth.

"Hello?" Amanda said, tailing her through the echoey hallway. "Any interest in putting on some, oh, I don't know, *clothes* before we leave?"

Scottie looked down at her pink-and-red-striped flannel pj's. They were a lot more comfortable than jeans. *And* more interesting.

I wonder what knitted pajama bottoms would feel like, she thought. As she started brushing her teeth, she pictured a pair of fuzzy, felted capris with baggy legs and scalloped cuffs. She could use that Debbie Bliss Soho Alice had shown her a few days ago, if it wasn't too expensive.

"Are you thinking about yarn?" Amanda said, butting into Scottie's daydream.

"No!" Scottie said through a mouthful of foam.

"You were," Amanda insisted. "Do you know, you have a yarn face? Your eyes get all melty and you rub your fingertips together."

"You're lying!" Scottie squealed as she spit her suds into the sink.

Amanda squinched up her face and rubbed her fingertips together.

"Ooh," she mocked. "Meunch Fabu! R2 Paper! Yummy, yummy!"

"Oh. My. God," Scottie said, tossing her toothbrush onto the bathroom vanity. "Just for that, I'm *not* getting dressed. Your stylish self is going out with a girl in her jammies. Besides, if you brought Plotinsky's, I need the elastic waist."

"If anyone asks, I'll tell them those are the newest thing from Juicy Couture," Amanda said, pointing at Scottie's pink-and-red stripes. She herself was wearing fuzzy gray drawstring pants flared over silver sneaks with a gorgeous, off-the-shoulder ivory top and the skinny scarf she'd made from that first skein of purple-gold wool.

"Whatever," Scottie tossed off as she twisted her hair into a quick plait and slapped on some lip gloss. On impulse, she also grabbed a bobby pin with a rhinestone butterfly out of the depths of her bathroom drawer and planted it just above her braid.

"Doesn't matter what you're wearing—you look beautiful, sweetie," Amanda said, patting Scottie's cheeks impatiently. "Now let's *go*. The bagels are getting cold."

Somehow Scottie wasn't surprised when she and Amanda walked into KnitWit fifteen minutes later to find that Bella had beaten them there. If Scottie was addicted to knitting, Bella was obsessed! She'd probably arrived at KnitWit early that morning, and now she was knitting away in the kitchen, tucked away from the Saturday shoppers milling about the dining room and classroom.

"Hi!" she gasped as Scottie and Amanda walked through the door.

Why was she out of breath? Because Alice's still-pregnant cat was sitting on her lap. Monkey was pinning the poor girl to her chair, pressing her enormous belly into Bella's flat one. Bella was breathing in shallow pants and holding her knitting up beneath her chin so as not to disturb the kitty.

"Um, Bella?" Amanda said, tiptoeing up to stroke Bella's voluminous hair. "Wouldn't that stockinette stitch go a little smoother without an enormous cat on your lap?"

"But she's purring," Bella whispered, glancing down at Monkey with a mixture of affection and fear. "This might be the only comfortable moment she's had for days. It'd be selfish to ditch her."

"You're a better soul than me," Amanda said with a shudder. "I can't stand cats."

Scottie, meanwhile, was examining Bella's work.

"A sweater?" she said, when she'd identified the supersoft swatch, a sweater front the color of a tiger's eye. "You're already up to a sweater? What about that green-and-orange shawl you were working on?"

"I finished it," Bella said. "I gave it to my mom, and she was so

　　　•• *Chicks with Sticks*

thrilled, she's been wearing it every day. I mean, she *won't* take it off."

Amanda's and Scottie's eyes met.

I wonder what it's like, Scottie thought, *not to have any secrets from your parents. To just . . . to not have the need.*

Scottie was getting ready to ask Bella this very thing when Amanda's cell phone started ringing. Before she could answer it, Tay burst into the room, her own cell phone clamped to her ear. She skidded to a halt as she took in the other three Chicks with Sticks. Slapping her phone shut, she told Amanda, "Don't bother to answer. That was me calling you!"

"*You* were calling *me?*"

"All of you, actually," Tay said. She shook her head in wonder. "And here you all are. Weird. Maybe it's not BS, the way you guys go on about fate and bonds between us and stuff."

"Gee, thanks for the vote of confidence," Bella said drily.

"Oh, my God," Scottie screamed. "I think Bella is being *sarcastic!*"

"What?" Bella said, clutching her throat dramatically.

"I was waiting for this moment," Amanda said proudly. "We are *such* bad influences."

"I didn't mean it!" Bella cried.

Eow.

Monkey had roused herself. Sitting up in Bella's lap, she glared at all the girls accusingly. With another *eow*, she heaved herself to the floor and waddled grumpily over to her bed.

"You've even offended Monkey," Amanda scolded.

"Ohhhhh," Bella sighed, with either regret or relief. Though she waved a bit of yarn in Monkey's direction, trying to lure her back into her lap, Scottie could tell that she was enjoying having her full lung capacity back.

"So, Tay," Scottie said. "Why are you believing in fate all of a sudden?"

"My dad," Tay said, taking a deep breath and pulling a sheaf of tickets out of her front pocket, "just got me four tickets to the Cubs game. *Today's* Cubs game."

Scottie, Amanda, and Bella looked at her blankly.

"Hello?" Tay said. "It's the play-offs? Tickets like these don't even *exist*, and yet I hold them in my hand! They're even bleacher seats, which is where all the fun is."

"Wow," Amanda said flatly. "So, uh, thanks for sharing, but why bother telling us? You're totally taking Josh."

"Are you kidding?" Tay sputtered. "Josh is a Sox fan. He wouldn't go to Wrigley Field if you paid him. Which is why *I* never get to go there, unless it's with my dad doing his divorced-daddy-day-care thing. Blech."

"Wait a minute, let me get this straight," Scottie said. "Just because Josh doesn't like Wrigley Field, *you* don't get to go to Wrigley Field?"

"Well, it's easier to get tickets to Comiskey anyway," Tay said sullenly. "Since the Sox suck."

Amanda frowned.

"What I want to know is why does *Josh* get to decide what you guys are gonna do? What about *you?*"

"Listen, do you want to go or not?" Tay spat back. "Because the game starts in less than an hour."

Okay, I guess we're not going down the Josh route, Scottie thought.

"Um, we'd sorta planned on hanging out here and knitting," Scottie said, pointing at her flappy, flannel pj's.

"We got bagels and everything," Amanda added.

"Are you guys actually telling me that you have *no* interest in this game?" Tay shouted. "The Cubbies make the play-offs, and you just . . . just don't care?!"

"Didn't they do that last year, too?" Bella wondered aloud. She was back to her knitting. Scottie couldn't believe how fast her fingers were flying. She was one with the wool. Scottie felt a twinge of jealousy, but tried to tamp it down quickly.

Thou shalt not envy another Chick's sticks, she admonished herself.

Then she glanced at Tay, and added, *Or ditch a Chick in her time of need.*

"Okay, so let's just take our knitting to go," she suggested. To Tay she said, "Are we allowed to knit in the stands, or do we have to wave foam fingers and stuff?"

Tay went all scoffy.

"Ah, bring your yarn," she said, "if you insist."

"What about you?" Scottie said.

Tay grinned slyly and pulled back one flap of her puffy blue jacket. Poking out of the deep inner pocket was her mustard yarn, a crumpled printout of a pattern, and a few short needles.

"I'm making mittens to match my hat and scarf," she said. "But I'm only knitting between innings!"

While the girls dissolved in laughter, Bella popped out of her chair.

"I'm going to go find Alice in the other room and give her my bagel," she said.

"Aren't you hungry?" Amanda asked.

"Oh, I don't really do white flour," Bella said. "Terrible for the colon."

"Well, guess what, B?" Tay said, grabbing an everything bagel out of the bag and taking a big bite. "Those clothes are terrible for a baseball game. It's *cold* out!"

She was pointing at Bella's frowsy skirt, her almost sheer tights, and her thin, boatneck sweater.

"Yeah, I have some wardrobe issues, too," Scottie said, glancing wistfully at her jammies. "I better stop at home and change."

"Me, too," Bella said.

"There's *no time,*" Tay said, looking at the ceiling impatiently. "Dudes, you live in Chicago. It didn't occur to you that you might have to deal with some weather today?"

"That's what cabs are for," Amanda said with a shrug.

Tay's toe began tapping, and her face went bright red.

Uh-oh, Scottie thought. *Must intercept!*

She ran up to Tay and grabbed her shoulders.

"Don't freak," she ordered her. "Yes, we're having a fashion emergency, but you've forgotten who is in our midst."

With a flourish, Scottie pointed at Amanda.

"Say hello to our resident diva," Scottie announced, "owner of approximately nine hundred and fifty pairs of shoes, holder of her own American Express platinum card since she was eleven . . . Amanda Scott!"

"Whoo-hoo!" Bella said, jumping up and down and clapping.

Amanda scowled and aimed a number 15 needle at Scottie.

"What?" Scottie protested. "You have a talent, darling, don't hide it!"

"Har, har," Amanda said sulkily.

Of course, a moment later, she actually did hatch a plan.

"Trixie's Attic!" she declared. "It's cheap, it's fun, and it's on Belmont, a five-minute walk from Wrigley. There's a Red Line stop right there, so we won't get caught in traffic. We can load up on cheap duds and be at the game before they've even started singing 'America, the Beautiful.'"

"Uh, I think it's, 'Oh, say can you see,'" Scottie pointed out gently.

"She can sing whatever she wants as long as we get there on time," Tay said, yanking her hat down low over her eyebrows.

Bella grabbed Scottie by the elbow. The two of them darted through the dining room to find Alice, who was chatting with some customers.

"Thanks for letting us hang here," Bella said to Alice, "but we wanted to go somewhere a little more private, more intimate, y'know?"

"Oh?" Alice said, looking surprised.

"We thought Wrigley Field was the perfect choice," she said with a giggle.

Alice threw her head back and laughed. "Bella, I think that's the first sarcastic thing I've ever heard you say!"

"The second!" Bella said. She looked torn between being freaked and proud.

"So," Alice said, still chuckling, "how on earth did you get tickets to the play-offs?"

"Tay did," Scottie said. "So you'll have to eat all the bagels without us. But see you Tuesday?"

"See you Tuesday, sweetie."

When Alice hugged her, Scottie found herself sinking into her arms. The warm, vanilla-woolly scent of Alice's hair was already irresistibly familiar. Scottie had to tear herself away to run with Bella down the stairs. Tay and Amanda were already waiting for them on the sidewalk. They had forty minutes to get to Wrigley Field.

"Oh my God, Tay, it's *so* you."

Scottie had just plucked a pink sequined bustier edged in black lace from one of the trashiest racks in Trixie's Attic.

From several clothes racks away, Tay squinted at the little number and gave Scottie a sneer. She fought back by grabbing a black, conical, skaterboy's hat and racing across the scuffed-up linoleum to force it onto Scottie's head.

Scottie ran to a mirror to check herself out.

"I am hid-ee-ous!" she screamed while Tay busted out in wheezy giggles behind her.

So far, most of what Scottie had seen here pretty much fell into two categories—trashy or ugly. That was the thing at Trixie's Attic. It was all about cheap, in-your-face party gear or cheap, in-your-face bum wear.

The only thing that kept people coming was the knowledge that there were treasures to be found if you pawed through enough of Trixie's trash. And as she whipped off her ridiculous hat, Scottie spotted one. It was another hat, over in the vintage (okay, *used*) section, just past the marabou-trimmed thongs.

The hat was a twenties-style cloche made of felted pink wool and decorated with a smattering of burgundy suede flowers. The little blossoms reminded Scottie of the pins that had danced across Alice's cardigan on the day they'd first met.

Scottie almost ran through the crowded racks to pluck the cloche off its stand. She found another mirror and slipped on the hat. It fit perfectly, settling around her face like a picture frame. The hat's shape made the angles in her face sing, and its pink rosied up her cheeks nicely. All she needed now was a bee sting of red lipstick.

And . . . that coat!

Talk about fate. The very first thing Scottie's eyes fell upon after she tore herself away from the mirror was a belted camel coat with a collar of faux fur. It was retro glam with a funky beat. It was the kind of look-at-me getup Scottie *never* wore. It didn't really go with her blue-striped scarf—which she'd been wearing every day since she'd finished it, but Scottie didn't care. The ensemble still felt completely perfect to her.

And when she added some five-dollar bell bottoms and a pair of brown pleather gloves, it only set her back a total of forty-two dollars.

After slipping on all her new duds, Scottie marched up to Tay and declared herself Cubs ready.

"You're wearing that?" Tay said. Her mouth hung open as she looked Scottie up and down. "To a baseball game?"

"I was just trying to make a statement," Scottie said. She had a sudden spasm of regret as she looked down at her nonreturnable clothes.

"Yeah, I think Dorothy Parker made the same one, like, eighty years ago," Tay said. "Seriously, Scottie. Just grab one of those ten-buck fleeces over there."

"Sorry," Scottie said. She tried to reel in her worries and recapture the glee of her impulse buy. "I already bought this stuff. It's too late."

"Okay, I'll let you get away with that outfit if you help me find Amanda and Bella." Tay sighed. "Where *are* they?"

"Right here!" Amanda announced proudly from right behind them. As Scottie and Tay glanced over their shoulders, they both gasped.

Amanda had added a hot-pink pea coat and a tangerine-colored watch cap to her outfit, but that's not what had floored her fellow Chicks.

It was Bella. Her hippie-dippie look was *gone*. Outfitted by Amanda, she looked like a cross between Tyra Banks and, well, Amanda.

She was wearing jeans. The longest, skinniest, flariest, navel-baring jeans in Trixie's Attic. On top of that, she had on a crisscrossed halter top and a little black jacket. Bella's dreads coiled out of a black beret that made her green eyes pop, and on her feet, she wobbled (just a bit) in spiky-sexy boots. Now Amanda was helping her into a puffy silver coat and fuzzy white gloves.

"You did all this in the last ten minutes?" Tay asked. She seemed impressed.

"Bella!" Scottie said. "You're so . . . not you!"

"I know!" Bella said, bending at the waist to check out her pointy toes. "This is so weird."

"But fun, right?" Amanda said. "Playing dress-up is always fun."

"I guess," Bella replied, looking up with a crooked smile. "I've never really thought about it. My parents will freak when they see me."

"Never really thought about *that* before, either, huh?" Tay said. "Freaking out your parents?"

"No," Bella said, blinking widely. "Why would I?"

Scottie, Amanda, and Tay looked at one another and laughed. Amanda gave Bella a sympathetic squeeze.

"Welcome to our world," she said.

Scottie stared at Bella, feeling a twinge of guilt.

Okay, playing with yarn is one thing, but this is an extreme makeover. Could this possibly be what flower-girlie Bella wants?

Bella was still gazing down at her outfit. Her hands fluttered nervously over her middle, buttoning, then unbuttoning, her jacket and skimming across the slice of belly exposed by her jeans' superlow waist.

Scottie braced herself for anguish. But when Bella looked up? She was grinning uncontrollably.

"Come on, you guys," she said. "What are we waiting for? We have a game to go to!"

Scottie let out a howl of laughter while Amanda gave Bella another bear hug. Bella giggled, too, as she zipped up her puffy silver coat and headed for the door.

She was still Bella, all right. Even with her spiky heels, her gait was as lanky and lopey as ever. She was still wearing her red Kabbalah bracelet. And, of course, she still carried her burlap bag, overflowing with needles and yarn.

"So, tell me again which guys we're rooting for?" Amanda asked Tay. "The white-and-blue or the white-and-red?"

"Oh my God," Tay said, unburrowing one hand from her mitten in progress to slap her forehead. "Questions like that pretty much ruin baseball for me."

Scottie rolled her eyes as she flipped her needle around and started another row of her sweater front.

"It's the white-and-blue," she said to Amanda. "That's Moises Alou batting. He hit .325 with 85 RBIs this season."

Tay dropped her mitten. Without missing a beat, Bella grabbed it from beneath the bleacher, dusted a few peanut shells off it, and handed it back to Tay. Tay took it without looking at Bella. She was too busy staring at Scottie.

"Scottie?" Tay said. "You're like this baseball geek. How did I not know about this?"

"Not all girlie girls are alike, you know," Scottie said smugly. "Before my dad became Mr. All-Art-All-the-Time, we used to go to Cubs games. Of course that was when the Cubs sucked, so you could basically walk up and buy a ticket whenever you felt like it."

"Yeah, but remember that time a couple years ago when they almost made it?"

Since Amanda was sitting between them, working on her hot-pink chenille miniskirt, Tay and Scottie leaned backward to dish.

"I was *there* the day that guy reached out and caught the foul ball," Scottie gushed.

"The one that should have been an out?" Tay yelled. "Oh man, I wish I'd been there. Wasn't there a huge fight on Sheffield Avenue after?"

"You know," Amanda said, getting to her feet suddenly, "why don't I let you boys talk while I go sit with Bella over here."

Bella shifted to make room for Amanda. Her long legs—even longer with her three-inch heels—didn't quite fit into her bleacher seat. She looked a bit like a stranded jellyfish with long squiggles of yarn trailing all around her.

But she also looked like she was having the time of her life. As she knitted nonstop, she checked out the game and ogled the fans sitting nearby.

One of them, a tubby guy sitting right next to Bella, was messily gnawing on a loaded Chicago hot dog. With every bite, he dripped mustard and relish down his hand. Even from a few seats down, Scottie could smell the Vienna beef dog.

Oh, gross. Scottie's nostrils flared.

Bella twisted in her seat, turning her back on the offensive meat eater.

This is the part where she runs screaming back to her yoga studio, Scottie thought, feeling Bella's pain.

"Hey!" Bella cried out, waving her hands (and her yarn) over her head. *"Hey!"*

Well, I didn't mean literally. . . . Alarmed, Scottie, twisted in her own seat to see what Bella was shouting about. Tromping up the stairs, and just about to pass their row of seats, was a hot dog vendor.

"RED-hots! HOT dogs," he shouted from deep within his royal-blue hoodie. "Get 'em right here!"

"Yeah! I want one!" Bella screamed. She pulled a couple bucks out of her knitting bag and passed them down the row to the hot dog guy. A few seconds later, she was cradling the silver-wrapped, forbidden dog in her hands.

"No. Way," Amanda cried. "Bella, an hour ago, you didn't even eat white flour. If you're going to eat meat, start with a chicken breast, for God's sake. Even some steak. Step away from the hot dog if you know what's good for you."

"I'm trying new things," Bella said. Her eyes were gleaming as she began to unwrap the dog. "I just want to taste it. I've never had one. . . ."

Bella's voice trailed off as she finished opening the wrapper. The hot dog stared up at her. It was pre-dressed in Chicago dog excess—mustard, tomatoes, a pickle spear, a few peppers, and some other gloppy condiments. But all that gunk couldn't mask the meat.

Bella opened her mouth.

"No!" Tay whispered.

She raised the thing—white flour and all—to her lips.

"Oh my God!" Amanda cried.

Bella bit.

"She's gonna hurl!" Scottie said. "Quick, grab her knitting."

Amanda whisked Bella's shawl in progress out of her lap as Bella swallowed.

"Oh," she muttered. "Oh . . . oh, wow."

"What?!" Amanda shrieked. "Do you need some air? Do you want to go to the bathroom? Clear the way, folks!"

Bella gave her friends a bewildered look, then took another joyful chomp out of the hot dog.

"It'sh good!" she slurred with her mouth full.

"Ugh, I think *I'm* gonna be sick," Amanda said.

"What have you done to Bella?" Scottie said to Amanda. "You've created this carnivorous babe!"

"Hello, I'm right here!" Bella said, looking up from her dog. "I'm fine. I'm great, in fact. Wow. Hot dogs . . . who knew?"

"She's right, you know," Tay said. Since the players were switching sides on the field, she'd been consulting her mitten pattern and counting stitches. "I could use a dog myself."

When she'd finished counting, she stood up and waved her mustard mitten in the air.

"Hey there," she called to the vendor, who was still working their section. "Another hot dog! With everything! Over here!"

But before the vendor could toss her her own foil-wrapped bundle of nitrates, Tay suddenly plopped back in her seat. In fact, she hunched over, clutching her mitten in panic.

"What is it?" Scottie said, putting her hand on Tay's back.

"It? Not it! He! Josh!" Tay hissed. "He's here!"

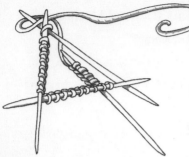

11 *(Change to Double-Pointed Needles)

Ducking, of course, did no good. Josh had spotted Tay. He hollered her name, waved wildly, then began making his way over to their section.

"I thought you'd have to pay him to go to Wrigley Field," Scottie said as Tay frantically fumbled at her jacket zipper, evidently desperate to stash her knitting inside her coat before Josh arrived.

Of course the zipper stuck. And then Josh was very, um, expedient about working his way through the crowd. He hopped up onto one of the bleachers and began stepping from bench to bench, tiptoeing between the butts of several annoyed Cubs fans.

One squashed pizza slice and one spilled beer later, Josh was standing on the Chicks' bench right next to Tay, who was still sitting. As she peered up at him, she squashed her mitten and double-pointed needles into her fist. Meanwhile, Josh reached down and snatched her yellow hat off her head.

"I must be seeing things," he announced. "Color? Tay Cooper is wearing a color that's not gray or brown or black? I think she's gone girl."

"Shut up," Tay said, bringing her free hand down onto Josh's foot.

"Ow!" he said, hopping easily off the bench to face Tay. That's when, for the first time, he noticed Tay's friends.

Gaped at her friends was more like it.

• • *Chicks with Sticks*

Suddenly Scottie remembered that she wasn't as invisible as she usually was. In her pink cloche and faux-fur collar, she felt like she was wearing a Halloween costume on Valentine's Day. Her hands flew to her head, sending her own WIP clattering to the cement.

Josh scooped her sticks and yarn off the dirty cement.

"Thanks," Scottie said, holding out her hand and avoiding his eyes. Josh, however, didn't return her stuff. Instead, he turned it over in his hands.

"What *is* this?" he said, sneering.

Scottie shot Amanda an imploring look.

Amanda will know what to say, she thought. *She'll do one of her withering, WB-ish zingers, and Josh will slink back to where he came from.*

"We're knitting," Amanda said simply.

Or not.

To make matters worse, Amanda gave Josh a demonstration, holding up her pink-miniskirt-in-the-making and doing a bit of *click-swish* action.

Josh went even more gapey. Then he went snide.

"So, Tay," he said, "you're hanging at Wrigley with *knitters!*"

"Well . . . what are *you* doing here?" Tay sputtered. "What about your beloved Sox?"

Pretending she was simply stretching, she whisked her arms— including her mitten— behind her back.

"Whatev," Josh said. "Simon had tickets. What was I supposed to do, say no? The Cubs definitely *do* suck, but hey, play-offs are play-offs."

"Now there's a guy you can count on," Amanda grumbled into Scottie's ear.

Meanwhile, Tay was starting to act a little shifty herself. Inching away from Scottie, ever so slightly, she shrugged and said weakly, "Uh, that was my thinking, too. My dad scored the tickets and . . ."

Tay shrugged in her friends' direction again.

Okay, is it just me, or did Tay just dis us? Scottie thought. *Which couldn't be* more lame. *I mean did she or did she not carve her initials into a table with us? And besides, Josh is not nearly as cute as I pictured. Is he really worth all this fluttering?*

Scottie aimed a squinty stare at her friend.

And don't think Tay didn't feel it. She glanced at Scottie and mouthed, *Sorry.*

Huffing quietly, Scottie resumed her knitting. As she did, *she* inched closer to Amanda and Bella, who were *click-swishing* away, too.

Meanwhile, Josh was leaning sideways to try to get a glimpse of Tay's hands behind her back.

"What's that you're hiding behind you?" he asked.

"What? Nothing," Tay said quickly. "What are you talking about?"

"You've got something back there," Josh said. "Is it food? Can I have a bite? I'm starving!"

"You're always starving," Tay retorted. "When is all that food gonna result in a growth spurt, already?"

"Oh, right," Josh snorted. "You know, growth spurt or not, I'm way taller than you. Five-foot-ten, baby! Ain't you bittah!"

Scottie looked Josh up and down and had to admit that his five feet ten inches were *sort* of cute. Josh was superskinny, especially in his baggy skater's denims, with an impish, pointy-chinned face, soft green eyes, and a thatch of curly hair. If that hair had been dark brown instead of sandy, he would have been a shoo-in for that Chrismukkah kid on *The O.C.*

Clearly, all that cuteness (well, semi-cuteness) was having a *major* effect on Tay. Her face was ruddy, and her eyes were practically flashing smitten sparks. Scottie also blamed the semi-cuteness for Tay's slow reaction time when Josh suddenly pounced on her.

"Lemme see!" he cried, looping his arm behind her back. Before Tay could even open her mouth in protest, Josh had snatched away her mitten.

"Josh!" she bellowed. "Could you respect my privacy, like, even a little bit?"

•• *Chicks with Sticks*

"This," Josh snorted, "coming from someone who used to climb into my bedroom window at night?"

"What?!"

Scottie and Amanda had screamed this simultaneously. Even Bella had dragged herself away from her sweater for a moment.

Tay waved her friends off.

"It's *so* not what you're thinking," she said.

"What *are* you thinking?" Josh said dumbly.

Oy vey, Scottie thought. *I can't believe I'm yearning for a crush on one of . . . those.*

"We just had a little *Dawson's Creek* thing going," Tay explained to the girls, "because we lived next door to each other. I'd sneak over . . ."

"While your parents tore up the kitchen, fighting," Josh volunteered.

"Uh, yeah, thanks for the commentary, dude," Tay said.

Her cheeks were even pinker as she turned back to her friends with the final, crucial part of her explanation.

". . . and we would watch TV," Tay said bluntly. "And that was it."

"No," Josh protested.

Scottie gasped. She was starting to feel like she was *in* a WB show.

"We played video games, too," Josh said. "Tay's a murderer at *Grand Theft Auto*. But not as good as me."

"If you ever let me play you at *Doom*," Tay retorted, "I'd beat the pants off you."

Scottie gasped once more.

"I mean," Tay said, looking at Scottie shiftily, "figuratively speaking."

"Whatev," Josh said again. "Let's get back to the subject you're so desperately trying to get *off*."

Now it was Amanda who gasped. Then she stifled a giggle.

"What?" Bella whispered. "I don't get it."

"I'll explain later!" Amanda squeaked. "Tay's in trouble."

Amanda was right. Their bud was positively squirming as Josh loomed over her.

"So," he said with a belly laugh in his voice, "you're knitting. Tay Cooper is a knitter. Of mittens."

He held up her hat.

"You made this, too?"

"Never you mind," Tay muttered.

"No, really," Josh said, studying Tay's hat and half mitten thoughtfully. "This stuff is actually really cool."

"Really?!"

Tay's eyes went so wide, they seemed to take up her whole, blushing face.

"Well, I *did* make them," she admitted. "I mean, it started as a dare from Mr. A. You know, my guidance counselor."

"The caterpillar guy," Josh said. "Yeah, I remember you telling me about him."

"And then . . . I don't know," Tay said. "I kinda liked it. I mean, it's not as boring as you'd think. Plus, you can make stuff."

"Exactly," Josh said. "In fact, I have an idea for your next project."

"Yeah?" Tay said. She was really loosening up now that Josh was being cool about her secret yarn fetish. Scottie could almost see the tension draining from Tay's shoulders. That is, until Josh's devilish grin returned.

"A tea cozy!" he declared. "Every girl needs a tea cozy in her life. Maybe you could make a pink one."

"Josh!" Tay squeaked. Her face fell for an instant, before she covered up with anger. "Shut up."

"Yes, a tea cozy with little flowers on it," he went on, mincing. "Or . . . an apron! You could knit yourself an apron now that you've gone girl."

"I have *not* gone girl," Tay growled.

"Excuse me?" Bella piped up. "I still don't get it. Tay, if you're having gender identity issues, it's nothing to be ashamed of. Stark even has a club for that. The lesbian-gay-straight-transgendered-and-questioning support group."

"Okay, this conversation is *so* over," Tay shouted. She jumped to her feet and grabbed her knitting away from Josh. Then she began shoving her way down the row, stumbling over several pairs of legs as she went. Scottie felt awful for her.

"What's her damage?" Josh said, looking after Tay. "Damn, Tay's so moody lately."

Scottie stood up, too.

"Hmm, who knows?" she said. "Well, uh, thanks for stopping by, Josh."

"Uh-huh," Josh said. But he seemed in no hurry to go.

"What she means by that is, *see* ya," Amanda added.

Bella gave Josh a little wave.

"Huh, oh yeah," Josh said. He emitted a snorty laugh and pointed up the bank of bleachers. "I'll just come out the way I came in."

"Ohhhhh-kay," Amanda said. "You do that."

Scottie gave her fist a little pump and said, "Go Sox!"

"Sox!" Josh roared, throwing both arms in the air.

Then finally, *finally,* he left.

"*What* was that?" Bella said.

"Bella, honey," Amanda said, turning to Bella and giving her beret an affectionate pat. "Tay doesn't have gender issues. What Tay has is a crush."

"On that!" Scottie said, pointing at the departing Josh disdainfully. "What does she see in him?"

"What do I see in Matt?" Amanda said with a shrug. "It's not really something you can explain."

"Like knitting!" Bella said.

"Speaking of," Scottie said, "was that harsh or what? Tea cozy? Apron!?"

"Apron, my butt," Amanda fumed. "That guy so doesn't get it."

"The problem is," Scottie said, "Tay thinks he does."

She glanced over her shoulder. Tay was still in view, climbing the stadium stairs two at a time. Her head was ducked low, and she looked perfectly willing to plow down anyone in her way. Luckily, people were jumping aside when they saw her coming.

"Do you think she's okay?" Bella said. "She didn't even get her hot dog."

"I think Tay's definitely been more okay than she is at this moment," Amanda said, joining Scottie in gazing worriedly at their retreating friend. "We should go after her."

Scottie glanced around Wrigley's brimming bleachers.

"If we all go, our seats'll be snatched up in a second," she said. "I can go."

Even as she said it, she felt a nervous lurch in her gut. What was she supposed to say to Tay? She knew nothing about crushes.

But she *did* know Tay. Or at least, she was getting to know her. And Scottie had a hunch that—as much as Tay thought she wanted to be alone right now—she didn't *really* want to be alone. She needed a Chick by her side.

The Sticks, though, Scottie wasn't so sure about. She handed her sweater front to Amanda before she began sidling down their row.

"I'm sure she just needs to blow off some steam," she called back to Amanda and Bella. "We'll be back in five."

Well, maybe Scottie had been a bit optimistic. It took a full five minutes for her even to *find* Tay. And when she did, Tay wasn't exactly in the mood for a heart-to-heart. She was tromping up one of the steep ramps that led to the nosebleed seats, her head ducked low, and her eyes decidedly red-rimmed.

"What?" she barked snuffily when Scottie caught up to her.

Scottie jumped.

"I came to see if you were okay," she said.

"Oh yeah," Tay snapped, "I'm great. I've just been humiliated in front of my best friend, *and* my mitten has peanut shells all over it."

• • *Chicks with Sticks*

She uncrunched her fist to show Scottie her abused WIP. Not only was the mustard yarn indeed dotted with shells, the double-pointed needles Tay was using to knit in the round were hanging on to the mitten by their fingernails. One more shake and the needles were going to go flying.

"I can't believe Josh saw my knitting!" Tay yelled, shaking the mitten viciously.

Plink, plink!

There they go. Scottie sighed as the metal needles slid completely out of the mitten's loops and clattered to the cement. She had to scramble to snatch them up before they rolled down the ramp.

"Don't bother," Tay said. "My knitting days are over. This is *so* not me."

She began stomping toward a trash can, already brimming with stinky napkins, crushed beer cups, and dripping hot dog wrappers.

"No!" Scottie screamed. She ran Tay down and intercepted the tangle of yarn before she could trash it.

"I don't get it!" Scottie cried. "Josh was just joking around with you. Who cares what he thinks, anyway?"

"*I* do!" Tay said. "You don't understand. Nobody wants to be friends with someone like me. But Josh always did. He didn't care if I was basically a boy. He *liked* it."

"Well, so do we!" Scottie sputtered. "Me and Amanda and Bella. And we also don't mind if you . . . what did he say? Go girl. *Or* if you don't! Can you say the same thing about Josh?"

That stopped Tay in mid-fume. All her anger seemed to melt, suddenly, into sadness.

"You know what?" she said, sounding stunned. "I don't know the answer to that. I guess we've kinda had a groove going, me and Josh, that I've never tested. Y'know, Comiskey instead of Wrigley."

"*Grand Theft Auto* instead of *Doom*," Scottie suggested with a little smile.

"Al's Italian beef instead of Fluky's hot dogs," Tay said with a little smile of her own. But with one glance down the ramp—toward the bleachers, where Josh was sitting—her angst seemed to return. She slapped her hands over her eyes.

"Ohhh," she groaned. "This was all so much simpler when we were twelve."

"Yeah," Scottie said, leaning heavily on the ramp railing. "I don't speak from a lot of experience here, but it seems like crushing on a guy pretty much sucks."

"It totally sucks!" Tay burst out. "I mean, I thought my parents' divorce was the worst thing I'd ever have to go through."

"And then Josh started smelling like cute boy instead of like dirt," Scottie said, "and life as you knew it was over."

"Uch," Tay groaned again. "Shoot me now."

"Not when there're three innings left," Scottie said, giving Tay a tentative poke in the arm. "Come on, Tay! Come back and finish watching the game with us. You're the only one who cares about this play-off thing anyway."

"But Josh is there," Tay said. Her eyes were going pink and watery again. "I can't face him with that stupid mitten."

Both girls looked down at the needle-free, peanut-littered half mitten in Scottie's hand. It was already beginning to unravel.

"I guess there's not much to save anyway," Scottie admitted. "Maybe you *should* just toss it. I'm not saying you should quit knitting! But this little mitten's just crawling with bad memories now."

"Right," Tay said, grabbing the yellow wool and turning back to the garbage can.

"Hey, wait!" Scottie said, running after her again. "Before you toss— I have an idea."

"What?" Tay sighed.

Grinning wickedly, Scottie found the project's dangling tail and gave it a good pull. An arc of mustard yarn squiggled out of the mitten.

"Alice told me that frogging can be very therapeutic," Scottie announced.

Tay's smile was slowly returning. *"Frogging?"*

"You know, you make a mistake and then you rip it, rip it out. Frogging," Scottie said.

"But I think you have to frog your *own* stuff for it to really work," Tay said. She plucked the yarn tail from Scottie's fingers and tugged, hard.

Zzzzz.

Another arc bobbled out of the mitten.

"How's it feel?" Scottie said.

"Pretty good," Tay admitted. She pulled harder the next time.

Zzzzzzzz!

"Take that," Tay whispered at the mitten. It had been pared down to a finger-length little nub by now.

"Finish her off!" Scottie cried.

"Yah!" Tay roared, giving the yarn a huge yank. She frogged relentlessly, unraveling the rest of the mitten until it was a mitten no more. It was just a frizzled pile at the girls' feet.

Scottie scooped up the yarn and grinned.

"Done!" she said. "Now let's get back to our seats before Bella goes crazy and orders a pepperoni pizza or something."

"Can you *believe* she ate that hot dog?" Tay cried as she and Scottie began tromping back down the ramp.

"What are her parents gonna say?" Scottie howled.

As Tay ticked off a few hilarious scenarios, Scottie felt elated. She'd actually succeeded in talking Tay Cooper off the ledge! She felt like someone should give her a BFF gold star or something.

If only, Scottie thought a bit wistfully, *I were this good at curing my own damage.*

(It's a purl thing)

Scottie and Tay got back to their seats in time to catch the top of the sixth inning. Bella and Amanda, of course, were oblivious. They'd spent the past twenty minutes stitching up a storm and, apparently, earning some gold stars of their own.

Almost as soon as Tay had settled onto the bleacher, Amanda blurted, "Bella had a brainstorm while you guys were gone."

"It didn't have anything to do with pepperoni pizza, did it?" Tay said, smirking at Scottie.

"No, it was about you!" Bella said earnestly. "Here's the thing—that night at KnitWit when I said Josh should be your boyfriend, I totally called it, right?"

Tay scowled. "Okay, I'm just starting to recover from the whole Josh interface," she said. "Do we have to go there again?"

"Well, no, not if you don't want to," Bella said, deflating a bit. She pulled her beret brim down and adjusted her tight jeans before she blurted, "It's just I had an idea about how you could make it happen!"

"Make *what* happen?" Tay said.

"I know a way that you can let Josh know you love him," Bella said.

"I never said I *loved* him," Tay said. "Jeez."

Of course, as she said this, her angular face mushed up, her eyes moistened, and her hands started to shake.

Oh yes you did, Scottie thought.

"Love or like—like or whatever," Amanda said, "this really *is* a good idea. Tell her, Bella."

"You should make Josh a sweater," Bella announced, fluttering her fingers dramatically.

"Are you crazy?" Tay sputtered.

Yeah. Scottie glanced irritably over her shoulder at Josh's section of the bleachers. *No way does that guy deserve a homemade sweater.*

"Seriously, Tay," Amanda said, jumping into the fray. "Think about it. You're in this holding pattern with Josh because you can't figure out how to tell him how you feel, right?"

Tay didn't respond.

"I'll take that to be a yes," Amanda said. "So, you make Josh a sweater, and that's like telling him without having to *tell* him."

"Because he'll see how much work you put into the sweater," Bella explained, clasping her hands dreamily, "and he'll just *know*. I mean, sweaters are *hard*. You only knit a sweater for somebody you *really* care about. Somebody you looooove!"

"Oh, please," Tay retorted. "Josh doesn't know anything about knitting! For all he knows, it's easy. For all he knows, a sweater takes, like, two hours."

"So you make him a sweater that rocks," Scottie blurted. She couldn't help it. She'd warmed to Bella's idea. The more she thought about it, in fact, the more it seemed like a brilliant solution. Anti-chatty Tay could let her sticks do the talking for her!

"Not only will your sweater open the door to a boyfriend–girlfriend thing between you two," Amanda added, "it'll make him respect the craft of knitting."

"It's the perfect solution," Bella cried.

Tay frowned and turned back to the game. Nomar Garciaparra hit a single, Todd Walker struck out, and Aramis Ramirez made it to second base before she finally replied.

"Well, the idea doesn't completely reek," she said. "I'll think about it."

Bella bounced in her seat excitedly, and Scottie and Amanda shot each other wild grins.

"A WIP with a purpose!" Scottie whispered in Amanda's ear.

"It's totally gonna change her life," Amanda replied confidently.

Scottie nodded. And tried to squelch that annoying little voice in the back of her head.

Yup, it was saying. *Hope you know what you're doing!*

(It's a purl thing)

12 ✳ (Slip, Slip, Knit)

By the time the game ended, it was almost dark. The girls' moods had darkened, too. And it wasn't because the Cubs had lost.

"My feet hurt," Bella said as they tromped down the ramp toward Wrigley's exit. She was shuffling painfully in her spiky heels. "Not to mention my belly. What do you think they *put* in hot dogs?"

"Oh, harmless stuff," Scottie said. "You know, like snou—"

But she stopped herself before she could launch into a riff about snouts and ears and other Upton Sinclair horrors. Frankly, her heart wasn't in it. After Tay had finally committed to Josh's love sweater at the bottom of the seventh, Scottie had gotten even more nervous. That was right around the time that Bella's indigestion had kicked in—and Amanda had begun freaking out about Matt.

"I mean," she'd whispered to Scottie, "seeing Josh totally mock Tay's knitting . . . it just makes me wonder what Matt thinks."

"A, who cares what he thinks?" Scottie had replied. "And B, didn't you already pass the Matt test? He came over to our table at lunch and played around with your yarn. In some cultures, I think that means you're already married!"

Amanda had barely cracked a smile.

Whoa. Scottie's grin had faded fast. *Tough audience.*

✳ ✳ *Chicks with Sticks*

"Scottie," Amanda had said, "this is serious. I *really* like this guy. And now I feel like a freak squared! First, I'm dumb—"

"You're not *dumb*," Scottie had interrupted. "You've got a totally established learning disability, which is nothing to be ashamed of."

"Whatev," Amanda had said.

Okay, how *annoying is it that Josh's boy-cabulary is so catchy?* Scottie had asked herself. *Almost as annoying as the fact that Amanda is letting her LD ruin her life!*

"The point is," Amanda'd said, "now I've got another strike against me—this whole knitting thing."

That had stung.

"You didn't think like that before," Scottie had said. "You've been knitting all over town. We're the Chicks with Sticks, remember? We were gonna take back the knit and make it cool?"

Scottie's voice had gone high and squeaky. She took one of her number 8s and poked Amanda with it. The gesture was supposed to be teasing and fun, but Scottie knew it smacked of desperation.

"Ow!" Amanda had said, rubbing at the spot in her arm.

The jolt did seem to do the trick, though. A few minutes later, she'd shaken her head and smiled at Scottie, if weakly.

"Don't listen to me," she'd said in apology. "You know how I can get."

"Gloomy and hopeless and self-defeating?" Scottie prompted.

"Dude!" Amanda had said. "Tell me how you really feel!"

"Sorry," Scottie said with a cringe. "I guess I just get a little tired, sometimes, of you being so down on yourself."

"I know, I know," Amanda said. "Please, my parents have given me so many pep talks, I've got 'em memorized. 'Oh, Amanda, you're so charming. Oh, Amanda, you have such a flair with clothes. Oh, Amanda, your little "learning problems" don't mean a thing because you're pretty. You'll find a nice, wealthy husband to take care of you someday.'"

"They say that?!" Scottie asked, aghast.

"In so many words," Amanda said with a shrug.

Okay, Scottie thought, feeling her blood pressure rise. *Somebody needs to send Amanda's parents a little heads-up about the way things are in the twenty-first century. As in, it's no longer kosher to marry your daughter off to the highest bidder!*

"You know you have a lot more to offer than that stuff, don't you?" Scottie whispered.

Amanda had shrugged again. Then she'd taken what Bella would call a deep, cleansing breath, knocked out a sparkly smile, and picked up her bright pink miniskirt.

"Sorry about the buzzkill," she'd said. "You're right. Let's take back the knit. It totally beats this boring baseball game!"

Even if Amanda had perked up after that, the chat had left Scottie feeling a little weary and more than a little worried. It helped, though, as the Chicks clustered on the corner of Clark and Addison, to catalog the afternoon's knitting. Despite her upset stomach, Bella had finished her entire sweater front. Scottie had finally gotten the hang of the ribbing on *her* sweater front. And Amanda had lengthened her swatch of hot-pink chenille dramatically.

After admiring all the WIPS, they made a date to meet at KnitWit the next afternoon.

"I can't wait to show Alice my front," Bella said. Though she was still clutching her belly, stroking her fuzzy fabric seemed to give her a blast of energy. "I know I'm supposed to do the back now, but I think tonight, over some Stomach Soother tea, I'm gonna start on one of the sleeves. I just can't wait to see what a *sleeve* feels like."

"Aren't you tired?" Tay grumbled. "You've been at it all day."

"Not even close," Bella said. "In fact, I think I'm starting to get what my yogi keeps talking about—the exhilaration of meditation. He's right. It rocks!"

She shifted from foot to foot painfully.

"It's even better when you're barefoot," she pointed out.

•• Chicks with Sticks

"Speaking of," Scottie said. "I think it's time for me to jump back into my jammies. I'm gonna head home, you guys. See you tomorrow."

She hugged each of her buds good-bye and perched herself at the Addison bus stop. The bus would take her to Ravenswood Avenue, a two-block walk from home.

She'd told a little white lie, though. She wasn't quite pajama-ready. In fact, she was feeling agitated with unfinished business.

Something had been nagging at her all day.

I have this whole new life, she thought as she watched her friends meander into the crowd on Clark Street. *New friends,* lots *of new yarn, Alice . . .*

Scottie thought of vanilla-woolly Alice and how different she was from Scottie's mother, who wafted the sharp, citrusy scent of her hair gel everywhere she went. Or the chemical odor of her acrylic paints. Where Alice was soft and easy, Scottie's mom was so angular she was almost sharp. The cords in her neck always seemed to be pulled taut, as if she was straining at something.

Whatever she was reaching for, it wasn't Scottie. She was too busy with her paintings and her art buyers, her glam openings and trendy sushi dinners.

She could have long, animated phone chats with Scottie's sister, Jordan, about cinema vérité and the French New Wave. But between Scottie and her mom lay a blank space, at least lately.

Why was it so hard for Scottie to imagine giving her mother half the hug she'd bestowed upon Alice—so easily!—at KnitWit that morning?

Scottie knew there'd been a time in her life when the smell of paint and turpentine had warmed her up the way the smell of vanilla and grassy wool did now. She just couldn't recapture it. She could barely remember it.

Guilt gnawed at Scottie's stomach. And hunger, too. She was grateful when the bus lumbered up to her stop. She didn't even mind when dozens of other Cubs fans piled onto the bus with her, stealing

(It's a purl thing)

all the seats. She gripped a handrail and stood for the short ride home.

Maybe Mom and Dad don't have plans tonight, she thought. *We could get some takeout or something. (Anything but sushi—gross!) And I can fill them in on my little secret—this scarf I've been wearing every day? I didn't buy it. I made it. I made a poncho, too. And now I'm working on an actual sweater. And by the way, I've got some new friends.*

Scottie gripped the handrail tighter and stood on her tiptoes. Over the heads of the other riders, she could see the freight-train tracks—*her* train tracks—approaching. She was almost home, and suddenly she couldn't wait to get there.

There was only one problem.

Scottie's whole "I can't wait to get home" thing? Apparently, about sixty art collectors felt the same way! Even before she arrived at her door, Scottie could hear the unmistakable hum of one of her parents' art parties going on inside the loft.

No! Scottie thought. *This is seriously the last thing I'm in the mood for tonight.*

In fact, she couldn't even bring herself to open the door. She just stood, frozen, in front of it, wondering where she could go if she fled.

I guess I could take my knitting and go to a movie, she thought. *Alone. On a Saturday night.*

Before she could decide if she had the guts for such an indie act, a shrill voice came at her from the end of the hall.

"Oh, hal-LOO? Hold the door for us, won't you?"

Scottie peered down the hall and saw a couple of familiar figures—two of the art buyers who followed her mom's work as if she was a rock star.

Great! Scottie fumed silently. *I can't blow off regulars. Dad would have a heart attack.*

Scottie couldn't remember the names of the man and woman stalking skinnily down the hall, but oh, she recognized everything else about them. How could she *not* remember the woman's "trademark" kelly-green glasses. Or her honking voice. (Her accent was Welsh, which Scottie only knew because the woman had told her so at another opening.)

Welsh lady's husband was unforgettable, too. He never seemed to say a word. Scottie figured that was because *his* trademark—superbright leather pants—did all the talking for him.

"Oh, it's *Scottie!*" the Welsh woman cried as the couple finally arrived at the door. She turned to her husband, whose leather pants tonight were eggplant. "Dah-ling, you remember Carrie and Shel's little girl, don't you?"

Leather Pants Man grunted and smiled.

Okay, what *does that mean?* Scottie thought.

It didn't matter because Welsh Lady was answering her own question.

"Of course you remember her," Welsh Lady cooed. She kissed the air next to Scottie's cheek. "My dear, you haven't changed a bit. Most teenagers get all gawky and strange-looking when they develop, but not you! Why, you look twelve if you're a day."

She laughed as if she'd just told the funniest joke ever, as if she hadn't just insulted and humiliated Scottie. *Twelve?!*

Since breaking the kelly-green glasses of a devoted collector would probably be a no-no, Scottie just forced a smile. Okay, it was probably more of a grimace. Then she turned to fling open the loft door. Just as Scottie had hoped, Welsh Lady spotted a new victim the moment she walked inside. With another braying "Hal-LOO," Welsh Lady and Leather Pants Man fluttered away.

Scottie sighed with relief. Then she scanned the crowd milling around the loft and the gallery.

There! She spotted her mother over near the assemblage of couches and chairs that made up the loft's "living room." She was whispering into the ear of a server holding a tray of, wouldn't ya know, sushi. Mom was pointing frantically at a corner of the loft. Apparently, a dead spot had developed in the party and the Creator was *not* having it.

Well, guess what, Mom, Scottie thought as she marched up to her mother, *I'm not having* this.

"Mom!" she whispered.

Her mom turned to her with an overbig smile.

Amanda's not the only one who's got a party face, Scottie thought. Mom even glanced at the hepcats in her orbit before she cried out, "Scottie! Look at you in your thrift-store chic! My daughter is *so* cool."

Scottie'd forgotten she was still wearing her Trixie's Attic coat and hat. Going hot with embarrassment (and, well, the fact that she was still wearing her coat and hat), she snatched the cloche off her head and unbuttoned her coat, revealing the half-baked outfit underneath. She'd replaced her pajama bottoms with her new bell-bottoms, but under her faux-fur collar, she'd left on her flannel pj top.

"Whoops," Mom said, reaching over to pull Scottie's coat closed again. "Not very party ready, are you?"

"It would have helped if I'd known we were having a party!" Scottie snapped. "Then I would have made other plans for the night."

"I didn't mention it?" Mom said breezily. "Well, it was sort of a last-minute thing. I've been so prolific since . . . well, lately."

You mean since Aunt Roz died, Scottie thought. *First, you use her funeral for leftovers, then you splash your grieving-sister drama all over your canvases and throw a party.*

"Anyway, your father thought we should give a few people a taste," Scottie's mom continued, "of the latest oeuvre."

My mother did not *just say "oeuvre," did she?*

"Sweetie, I'm sorry I didn't tell you," Mom said. "You've been spending so much time with Amanda lately, I haven't seen much of you!"

Scottie's guilty twinge returned. She'd already forgotten about her plan to fill her parents in on all the stuff that had been going on in her life lately. So, she shrugged and told her mom, "That's okay. It's no biggie."

Mom pointed to a couple of the servers working the enormous room.

"Now, I know how you feel about raw fish," she said, "but I want you to know that I ordered some fried dumplings and spring rolls, too. Just for you, sweetie."

"Thanks," Scottie muttered.

"Why don't you go change your clothes, and then you can come back and join us," Mom said. "And stop in the gallery. You haven't even seen my new paintings!"

Scottie slumped to her room, feeling like a disheveled kid who'd been sent to wash the dirt off her face.

How condescending could she be? Scottie thought. *Not to mention self-absorbed. No, "How was your day, Scottie?" Or, "Hey, Scottie, what's going on in your life?" Or even, "What a pretty blue scarf!"*

Once her bedroom door was shut and locked, Scottie stomped to her closet to look for something to wear.

And then, for the first time since arriving home, she smiled.

Twenty minutes later, Scottie was gliding across the loft to the gallery. She was wearing shiny, black cigarette pants that she'd borrowed from her mom's closet and a shimmery camisole that she'd once bought on a whim from H&M. Her hair was pulled into a loose bun on top of her head. She'd used more rhinestone bobby pins to clip back the fuzzy bits around her face.

The whole business was capped off by her copper poncho.

It was the second item she'd ever knitted, and, well, okay, it looked like it. The neck hole was a little large and lopsided, so it kept sliding off one shoulder. At some places in the poncho, Scottie's dropped stitches had created the webby effect that the pattern had promised. At others, they just looked like squinchy mistakes.

All this was part of the reason Scottie hadn't yet had the courage to wear the thing in public.

But tonight, she told herself, *I'm going to focus on the positives. This yarn brings out the red highlights in my hair, for instance. And my poncho has loads of fringe.*

What's more, when she'd finished the project at KnitWit the previous week, her friends had positively heaped praise upon it. Amanda had squealed, she was so impressed, and Bella had tried it on and twirled around, running her fingers through the fringe.

Then Alice had squinted at the poncho with a teacher's judging eye. Scottie had cringed, knowing Alice could spot every one of her mistakes, and probably a few that Scottie didn't even know about.

But all she'd said was, "For your second project ever, this is remarkable. And because it's your second project ever, you're always going to remember it."

The memory warmed Scottie up, despite the cool air *whooshing* onto her skin through her holey poncho. She grabbed some spring rolls off a passing tray and went into the gallery to view her mother's *oeuvre*.

Maybe, she thought crunching into her snack, *I'll even talk to some people. As long as they aren't Welsh Lady and Leather Pants Man.*

Of course Scottie's confidence dipped a bit as she began to look over her mother's paintings. As usual, she *really* didn't get them. Still, she made an effort, gazing at each of them for several long minutes. She gave up when all the colors crashing together started to make her feel woozy.

Maybe Dad can explain them to me. She felt palpable relief as she looked away from the big, asymmetrical canvases. She spotted her dad at his usual spot—by the front desk of the gallery space. He was meeting and greeting guests, letting everybody know that should the urge to buy come over them, he was ready to handle it.

"Hi, Dad," Scottie said, sneaking up behind him. She tossed her greasy spring-roll napkin into the wastepaper basket behind the desk.

"Hi, sweetie!" her dad said, kissing her cheek absently. "Where have you been all day?"

"I thought you were at the club this morning," Scottie said with a shrug. Scottie's parents usually spent their Saturdays at the East Bank Club, working out, getting massages, and, of course, schmoozing up sweaty commodities traders and architects who might be interested in buying a little modern art.

"Who knew," Scottie added, "that you were actually in party prep mode!"

"What?" her dad said. He dragged his eyes away from the milling guests for the first time to really look at Scottie. "Did we not tell you about this? I'm sorry, honey. Business has just been so crazed lately, it must have slipped my mind."

"No biggie," Scottie said, trying hard to sound convincing. "So these paintings . . . they're different, huh?"

"Uh-huh," her dad answered absently. He was back to scoping out potential clients. Two of them, in fact, were approaching now—a guy with crow's-feet that definitely did *not* match his soul patch and his much younger, bored-looking date.

"Shel!" the guy said heartily. A few bright orange fish eggs were stuck in his soul patch, Scottie noticed. "Stunning work, just stunning. That Carrie—it's like creativity central over here."

Scottie smiled.

"You don't know the half of it," she said.

Then she actually slapped her hand over her mouth, she was so shocked.

What *did I just say?* she asked herself in horror. Two cartoony images popped into her head. In one, she was grabbing the words out of the air and *un*saying them by stuffing them back into her mouth. In the other, the Chicks with Sticks were jumping around, pumping their fists and yelling, "You go, girl."

Scottie groaned quietly, dropped her gaze to the floor, and hoped that her comment would be tossed off as a bit of meaningless banter, one of those party quips that everybody says but nobody really listens to.

Unfortunately, her dad chose *that* moment to suddenly slip into involved-parent mode.

"What do you mean, sweetie?" he said, giving Soul Patch and Girlfriend a shifty glance.

"What I meant, was . . . well. . ." Scottie realized she was fiddling nervously with her poncho's fringe as she fumbled for an explanation.

Ah, what the hell. She thrust the fringe out toward the three adults.

"I made this!" she announced.

Okay, how much did I just sound like a kindergartner showing off her finger painting?

"You . . . you what?" her dad said.

Soul Patch just smiled politely, but the girlfriend actually seemed to perk up. Pursing her vamped lips, she leaned over to inspect Scottie's poncho.

"You knit!" she said. "Knitting's really hot now, y'know?"

"Tscha!" Scottie said enthusiastically. "Do you know KnitWit? Up in Andersonville?"

"Oh, *I* don't knit," Girlfriend said quickly, tugging at the cuff of one of her shiny, thigh-high boots. "Yeah, it's . . . not my thing. But it's really cool that *you* do it."

Was that a compliment or an insult? Scottie thought. *You never can tell with these folks.*

The only reaction she *could* read was her dad's. He was flummoxed as he cocked his head and examined Scottie's poncho—her hippieish, full-of-holes, completely amateurish poncho.

If Scottie hadn't been wearing, basically, underwear underneath, she would have ripped it off right there. As it was, she had no choice but to endure her dad's perplexed appraisal.

"Well," he said, "you're just full of surprises, Scottie. So you're a knit—"

Her dad shot the hepcat couple another glance.

". . . a fiber artist!" he declared.

"A what?" Scottie said.

•• *Chicks with Sticks*

"Of course everybody has to start somewhere," her dad said, patting her on the shoulder. "Even your mother did."

Huh? Scottie thought as her dad returned his attention to Soul Patch and Girlfriend.

"Did you know that Carrie used to be a portraitist?" he said. "She was all about oil paints and pretty lighting. She used to paint pictures of Scottie when she was a little girl."

"No, really?" Soul Patch gasped.

"Just shows how far one can go," Scottie's dad said, slinging his arm around Scottie's woolly shoulders affectionately.

And now I know how low *one can go,* Scottie thought. *I get your message loud and clear, Dad. Knitter is to Lame as "Fiber Artist" is to Cool.*

Scottie suddenly felt very aware of her face. She felt herself struggling to arrange it into a benign expression, even as her throat was closing up. This was not good. She clenched her fists and ordered herself not to make a scene.

If you burst into tears or something, she warned herself, *they're only going to talk about how droll teenage histrionics are. And somehow,* that'll *become all about the Creator, too. "You know,* Carrie *used to be a teenager!"*

So, Scottie forced herself to stand there, stony, until Soul Patch and Girlfriend moved on. When they were finally gone, her dad turned to her.

"So, you're knitting!" he announced. He smiled feebly. He still didn't seem to know quite what to say about Scottie's poncho. That was fine with her. She wasn't exactly feeling chatty, either.

"You know," she said abruptly, pointing through the gallery door into the loft, "I think I just saw some dumplings go by. I'll see you later, Dad."

"Oh, sure, honey," her dad said. "You go nosh."

He waved her away. In a minute, he'd be schmoozing up another potential client, his yarn-dabbling daughter forgotten.

(It's a purl thing)

Especially since she'd totally lied. She wasn't leaving him for a snack. She was ditching this scene altogether! She sped across the loft, feeling like a beleaguered video-game character as she dodged around the black-clad schmoozers, barely avoided barreling into one of the sushi servers, and almost slipped in a puddle of sickly-sweet Chardonnay that someone had spilled on the cement floor.

Finally, though, she made it to her room. She slammed the door and resolved to spend the rest of the night there, in hiding.

It's not like anybody'll miss me, she told herself as she yanked off her poncho. *I'm only a knitter, after all.*

13 + (Cast on 102 (110, 118, 126) Stitches)

"Fiber artist?" Tay said. "What the hell is a fiber artist?"

"Don't know," Scottie muttered. "Don't care."

It was Sunday afternoon, and all the Chicks were sitting around the KnitWit kitchen. Alice was at the little stove, making a pot of Chai tea, and Monkey was sprawled on her bed beneath the counter, snoring loudly.

On the table, at the girls' feet, was a potluck of treats. In the throes of a hot-dog hangover, Bella had brought some edamame and a plateful of groat muffins. The fancy chocolates were, of course, Amanda's contribution, and the BBQ potato chips were Tay's.

As for Scottie, she'd shown up with some badly needed comfort food—a plastic tub of homemade marshmallows from her favorite bakery. She was kneading one of the sticky cubes between her fingertips as she told her friends about the horrible art party and her clueless parents.

"Listen," Alice said over her shoulder, "I got the same thing when I started knitting. From my husband, no less! Well, he wasn't my husband yet. He was my boyfriend. My silly, *silly* boyfriend."

"What did he say?" Amanda said, looking up for a moment from her pink project.

"He said, 'You boycotted home ec. You can't scramble an egg. You did your master's thesis on Gloria Steinem, for God's sake. And now you want to knit? I thought you were a feminist.'"

"You *are* a feminist," Scottie sputtered. "Totally."

"Which is what I told him," Alice said, pouring five cups of Chai. "I told him there's nothing nonfeminist about making pretty things out of yarn. And for that matter, there's nothing nonfeminist about making socks that keep your boyfriend's feet warm. I mean, he does the same for me, right?"

"Elliott *knits*?" Tay said.

"Please," Alice said. "The guy is *so* far gone. The other night, I had to hide the credit cards so he wouldn't go ordering any of that Curious Creek Kilimanjaro off the Web. Thirty-seven bucks a skein!"

"That's almost as bad as Amanda's Lobster Pot," Bella breathed without looking up from her sweater.

"I just wish Elliott would make something useful." Alice sighed. "He's always knitting these little throws that are about as substantial as sea foam. And don't even get me started on the gloves he made me for my birthday. Fingerless! What's up with fingerless gloves?"

"Um"—Amanda giggled—"I think it's called fashion?"

"Whatev," Alice said.

Needless to say, Alice had heard all about the Josh drama, too. That was why, in addition to adding one increasingly annoying term to her lexicon, she'd pulled a fabulous sweater pattern out of her library for Tay. It was a henley with a wide, floppy hem that was perfect for Josh's sharp-shouldered, long-torsoed, urban-sporty vibe. Officially, the pattern was called the Pablo, but about thirty seconds after Alice had produced it, the Chicks had redubbed it the Ollie Cat, in honor of Josh's skateboard fetish *and* Monkey, who was so painfully pregnant by now that they wanted to throw her a bone.

As for yarn, Alice dug up some Brown Sheep superwash, which existed at just the right intersection between baby softness and scratchy durability. The color was Midnight Pine—as murky as Lake Michigan

•• Chicks with Sticks

when you looked at it from one angle, as shimmery as moss from another.

Soon Tay was outfitted with everything she needed: twelve hundred yards of the green yarn rolled into balls with Alice's cool ball-rolling gizmo, a new pair of number 7 bamboo needles, and the Ollie Cat pattern printed out in megabold Arial Black.

Now all she had to do was start casting on.

Which isn't going to ever happen if she just sits there stroking her yarn, Scottie thought.

"Uh, Tay," she said, a smile playing around the corners of her mouth, "you know Josh isn't *in* that yarn yet, right? You've got to actually knit it first!"

While Amanda and Bella unleashed the first round of giggle-snorts of the day, Tay blinked in surprise. Clearly, she'd been lost in a daydream.

"Can I help it if this yarn is the exact same color as Josh's eyes?" Tay said. "It's *distracting*."

"She *has* gone girl," Amanda said, her eyes widening.

"No, I haven't!" Tay yelled reflexively. But then she stopped herself for a moment and revised. "Dudes, I *am* a girl," she said wearily. "I have all the parts and I even have a crush on a boy. Yes, it's all true. But it doesn't mean I'm gonna start wearing eye shadow or skirts."

She gave Amanda's shimmered-up lids a pointed glare before adding, "Any more than Alice is gonna suddenly join the DAR just because she's a knitter."

"DAR?" Scottie said.

"Daughters of the American Revolution," Amanda groaned. "My mother's a member. Bra burners, they're not."

Alice chuckled and put her mug on the counter.

"Must get back to the yarn trawlers," she said, heading for the dining room. "Don't burn any bras while I'm gone. Acrylic scorches like you wouldn't believe."

(It's a purl thing)

Bella was the only one who didn't laugh. She didn't seem to even hear. She was way too busy being one with her sleeve.

"Wow, you're really immersed, B," Tay said.

"Huh?"

Bella's fingers finally stopped flying, and she looked up blearily. "What was that?"

"She said, why don't you drop that sleeve for, like, two minutes," Scottie improvised. "Rest your fingers and chow with us."

She held out her marshmallows.

"They're vegan," she singsonged enticingly. "They're even gelatin-free. I checked."

"No, thanks," Bella said with a frown. "I just want to get to the end of this row. . . ."

"Is something wrong, Bella?" Amanda said. "You were so psyched yesterday. Knitting was, like, your new Kabbalah and yoga, all in one."

"Yeah, it still is," Bella said, but she didn't sound very enthused about it.

"*I* know what's wrong," Tay said. She pointed at Bella's outfit. Other than the puffy silver jacket on the floor next to her chair, Bella's look was completely devoid of yesterday's glam-girl vibe. She was wearing a blowsy flax top, an ankle-skimming skirt, leg warmers on her legs, and arm warmers on her arms. Her dreads cascaded, unadorned, around her skinny shoulders

"Your parents saw your new clothes last night and freaked," Tay said. "Am I right?"

Bella's next few stitches were decidedly nonfeathery as she said, "No, they didn't freak. They thought it was . . . cute!"

"Cute?" Amanda blurted.

Remembering her own dad's patronizing appraisal of her poncho, Scottie breathed, "Ooh, that's harsh."

"Yeah," Bella said. She seemed confused and indignant at the same time. Scottie noticed that Bella was winding a bit of her honey-brown

•• *Chicks with Sticks*

yarn around and around her spidery index finger as she spoke. "My mom was all, 'Oh, I remember when *I* first came home from a Vietnam protest in Earth shoes and a dress made entirely out of hemp. My parents hit the roof.'"

"So why didn't *your* parents hit the roof?" Tay said.

"I don't know!" Bella wailed. "I was wearing sexy clothes. *And* high heels, which, as we all know, are both misogynist and bad for the spine. I even ate a *hot dog*."

She shot Monkey a guilty glance.

"That is the first time I've eaten meat since I was a baby, when my grandmother accidentally gave me a piece of chicken," she admitted.

"So, I don't understand," Amanda said. "You commit this major rebellion and your 'rents just laugh it off? Was that reverse psychology or something?"

"Just psychology," Bella said glumly. "They looked at each other and their eyes got all gooey and my dad said, 'Our little girl's individuating!'"

"Oh man!" Tay said, slapping her forehead. "How is it that people become so clueless when they procreate?"

"My mom actually suggested inviting all their friends over for a 'self-actualization dinner party,'" Bella said, pooching out her bottom lip. "It was bad enough when they threw me a surprise party after I got my period for the first time."

"They didn't!" Tay, Amanda, and Scottie screamed en masse.

"They did!" Bella said. Her yarn was pulled so tight around her finger now, it was going purple. "I mean, at the time I thought it was sweet. A little weird, but definitely nice."

"Well, it wasn't *not* nice," Scottie allowed.

"But now I'm having these strange feelings," Bella said. She unlotused her legs and stomped one of her narrow feet onto the rag rug with a thump. "These totally confusing feelings."

"And these bizarro feelings are—?" Tay prodded. In the heat of the conversation, she'd begun casting on her eighty-eight stitches of Midnight Pine. She *click-swished* as they waited for Bella's answer.

"I sort of . . ." Bella gritted her teeth for a moment before she burst out, "I sort of want them to mind their own business!"

Then she slapped a hand over her mouth and bugged out her eyes. "Oh wow," she whispered through her fingers. "That was so mean!"

"No," Amanda said with a laugh. "That was so *teen*. I've said it before and I'll say it again—"

Tay and Scottie jumped in to utter it with her: "Welcome to our world."

Bella lowered her hand and allowed herself a little smile.

"Thanks, you guys," she squeaked. "This stuff would be twice as scary without you. I mean, I feel like I don't even know who I am all of a sudden. But I also have this incredible urge to figure it out, like, immediately."

"Without your parents *telling* you who you are," Scottie said. She flashed back to the art party, to her mom telling her to go change, to her dad saying, "So, you're a fiber artist!"

"Yeah," Bella said. She shook her head and unwound her finger so she could get back to working on her sleeve. "*Really* confusing."

Amanda grabbed a cream-filled chocolate and squished it angrily between her fingers.

"Parents just think of us as extensions of *them*," she complained. "Like we're just *products* they've made. If they had their way, we'd just fall into line and become exactly what they want us to. God forbid we try to figure things out on our own."

Scottie scooped her WIP off the coffee table, but she couldn't bring herself to start knitting. A memory was blocking her path. She saw herself, age seven, wearing a dress of frothy, white tulle.

She'd been placed by her mother upon a pile of jewel-colored pillows. Her bare legs had been so cold, they were covered with goose bumps. Scottie had shivered and rubbed her hands up and down her shins to warm them up.

"Scottie!" her mother had burst out. It had been the first word she'd spoken in a half hour. She'd slammed her brush down on the table next to her easel and run a paint-smeared hand through her chin-length brown hair.

"Now you've gone and messed up the pose!" she'd scolded.

Scottie warmed herself now by burying her fingers in her squash-colored wool. She glanced up at her friends. Before she could stop to think about it, she was spilling out her thoughts to them.

"I *was* a product," she revealed quietly. "Like my dad said, my mom used to paint me when I was a kid. Before she became 'Carrie Shearer, abstract artist and hepcat,' her oeuvre was . . . well, me."

"I remember that," Amanda said. "You used to hate posing for your mom."

"Yeah, it was totally boring and uncomfortable, not to mention weird," Scottie said with a nod. "I was like this doll she dressed up and scrutinized."

Scottie plucked at her yarn vaguely and sighed.

"But . . ." Amanda prompted.

"But, when she moved on," Scottie said, "I was sort of sorry. I know I hated posing for her, but when my mom stopped painting me, I felt like she stopped seeing me altogether. If I wasn't her subject, I wasn't that interesting anymore."

Bella stopped knitting for a moment.

"Oh, Scottie," she said. "That's so sad."

Scottie swallowed hard and looked at her lap—until Tay spoke up.

"Wait a minute," Tay blurted. "A second ago, everyone was whining about their parents being all suffocating. Now, Scottie, you're upset that your mom doesn't play with you anymore. So which is it? Do you want your parents in or out?"

Scottie blinked at Tay in surprise.

"I—I don't know," she squeaked. "Do I have to choose?"

Tay shrugged and went back to her knitting. Scottie glanced at Bella. Did *she* think things were that black-and-white, too?

From the looks of things, she hadn't heard a word Tay said. She was back in her knitting zone. Her cheeks were sucked in, her eyes were squiny with intense focus, and her body was as still as a statue but for her steadily humming fingers.

Now, she'd *make a great subject for a painting,* Scottie thought. She shook her head and knitted a few stitches. Watching the squash yarn weave itself into neat little waves, exactly as she wanted them, she muttered, "I guess we'd make our parents' lives a lot easier if we really *were* products—a perfectly ribbed scarf or a cardigan that goes with everything."

"You're comparing a cardigan," Tay said drily, "to a kid?"

"Yeah, right," Amanda said. "A *sweater* doesn't change. It doesn't have thoughts or grow up or have problems. It can't control you, you control it!"

"Oh yeah?" Scottie raised her eyebrows and glanced in Bella's direction. If Bella had heard her, she didn't show it. She didn't even glance up from her lightning-fast purls.

"Eek," Amanda responded in a whisper. "You've got a point there. Well, I'll just speak for myself, then. You guys? Look!"

She held up her knitting needles. They were naked. Yarnless.

"I just finished binding off!" Amanda announced. "I'm done with my miniskirt!"

Feeling way grateful for the subject change, Scottie bounced in her chair and clapped her hands.

"Try it on!" she cried.

"Yeah, let's see," Tay said.

Scottie jumped out of her chair and ran to the kitchen door.

"Alice!" she called out. "Come see. Amanda's work in progress is in progress no more."

Amanda, meanwhile, was pulling her skirt over the wide cuffs of her jeans and sidling it up her slender legs.

"I still have to block it and everything," she warned her friends, "so it's not *totally* done. . . ."

Her voice trailed off as she pulled the stretchy pink tube over her hips . . . sort of.

The left half of the skirt's waistband was puckered high up on Amanda's waist, while the other side flopped off her hip with about as much spring as wet hair. The clingy fabric of the skirt was riddled with bulges. And the hem?

"Well . . ." Scottie said, searching desperately for something good to offer, "the asymmetrical look is still in this year!"

Amanda was pawing at her skirt, looking confused.

"How did this happen?" she wailed.

"Don't panic," Tay said. "I'm sure Jane and Patricia have much worse stories to tell than this one. Let's see your pattern. Maybe there was a mistake in it."

"I didn't use a pattern," Amanda spat. "It's just a miniskirt. It's a glorified tube top. So, I just took that scarf that I made before and tried to make it a little wider, and a little shorter, and I did a three-needle bind off to seam the ends together."

"I guess," Scottie said, "I guess it's not that simple."

"No, it's not," Alice said with a sigh. She'd just arrived and was leaning against the kitchen doorjamb. She looked at Amanda's skirt with sympathy, and just a hint of bemusement.

"Oh, sweetie," she said. "This happens to everyone! I swear to you. You make a scarf and it goes really well, and the next step seems so simple. And it is, but it *does* require a little organization. All you need to do is think algebraically. A skirt is all about percentages—a hundred percent around the hips, a little less around the waist and hem. With a few calculations, some counting, and a nice, floppy circular needle, you'll be good to go."

"A few calculations," Amanda said. "Some counting. That's all?"

Amanda's voice was thick with hostility.

"You know, Alice," she said, "it's *not* that simple for everyone."

"Well, I . . . I know," Alice said, taking a few quick steps toward Amanda. "But that's why you have me. And your friends—to help you."

"Oh, really? You can help me?" Amanda sobbed. She was yanking the skirt down, stretching it out even more. "Years of tutoring haven't made a dent in my stupid brain, but *you're* some kind of miracle worker? What? Is your little smudgy plant going to make my head work?"

"Amanda!" Scottie gasped.

"Oh, whatev," Amanda said. But this time, it was anything but funny. Amanda threw her wad of pink chenille on the floor, grabbed her coat and bag, and stalked out of KnitWit.

Scottie's other knitting needle? It looked like it had just dropped.

14 ✦ (Make Bobble)

Later that afternoon at home, over a plate of leftover hors d'oeuvres, Scottie did the only thing a best friend could do at a time like this. She started Googling.

"Learning disability Chicago," she typed into her iBook. The search results consisted mostly of articles defining various types of LDs and doctors offering testing for them.

"Oh, we're way beyond testing," Scottie muttered. Nibbling at a soggy dumpling, she tried a few other permutations. "Learning disability adolescent Chicago," and "help teen LD Chicago" yielded pretty much the same things.

Scottie pondered as she chewed. Then she shrugged and murmured, "Amanda tells it like it is. I will, too."

"Learning disability teen crutch Chicago," she typed.

Before she could bring herself to hit the GOOGLE SEARCH icon, she disabled her IM. If she didn't, she just *knew* Amanda's screen name—Shopprgrrrl—would pop up. It was a Murphy's Law thing. During guilty Googling, the person you were snooping about inevitably IM'ed *at that very moment* with a coincidental "Whassup?"

Not that Amanda ever really writes anything in her IMs, Scottie thought sullenly, *besides "Hi," "Good night," and "Call me."*

That realization was so annoying that Scottie stabbed at the Enter button in frustration. She slumped in her desk chair as the search results cued up on her screen.

She almost couldn't believe it when, down at the bottom of the list, she spotted an item that looked totally clickable.

She went straight to the site and started reading.

"No way," she whispered as the information sank in. "Bingo!"

"The dog or the game?"

Scottie jumped and spun her chair around. Her mom was standing at her bedroom door, an oversize book tucked beneath her arm. She was wearing her favorite, paint-spattered overalls and the comfortable, wire-rimmed glasses she wore in the presence of family only. When she was out in public, playing Carrie Shearer: Artsy Artist, she wore hexagonal specs with yellow plastic frames.

"Um, not the dog *or* the game," Scottie said. "I just found something I was looking for. For . . . a school report."

"Oh," her mom said. She crossed the room and sat on Scottie's bed.

"So, how'd you like the party last night?" Mom said.

Scottie gritted her teeth.

Oh, it was great, Mom, she thought. *Until, of course, Dad made me feel like a total reject, and I fled to spend the rest of the night in my room. Guess ya didn't notice.*

Figuring her mother also wouldn't notice if she didn't really answer, Scottie said, "Did you make any sales?"

"One," her mom said brightly. "And we got a lot of interest about some other ones. A *lot* of interest. Dad's made a stack of appointments for second viewings."

"Cool," Scottie said. She suddenly felt a little queasy. She wanted to blame it on the limp leftovers, but, in truth, it was because she was nervous. She wanted to test Tay's theory. Could she be Carrie Shearer's daughter *and* a knitter (but *not* a fiber artist)? If she told her mom about the wonderful compulsion she felt whenever she got hold of some new yarn or flipped through a pattern book, would she even begin to get it? Or would her mom think the Chicks with Sticks were hopelessly goofy?

And another thing—how was Scottie supposed to start this conversation? It seemed like so long since they'd been on the same wavelength, Scottie didn't even know where to begin.

Maybe I could start by telling her that that soul patch guy's girlfriend thinks knitting is hot. . . .

As it turned out, all Scottie's nervous plotting was moot, because her dad had already spilled.

"So," her mom announced brightly, "I heard about your shawl!"

"Poncho," Scottie corrected her.

"Oh, a poncho. Cool," her mom said. Was it unfair that Scottie found it annoying that her mother always said things like that? "Cool!" and "Excellent!"

She only cribbed them off of me, Scottie snarked, *along with my Avril Lavigne CD.*

"Anyway," Mom continued, "I think I know why you didn't tell us about your. . . ."

"Knitting," Scottie blurted. "It's called *knitting.*"

"Knitting," Mom repeated. The beginnings of a smile twitched at the corners of her thin lips. "I just want you to know, I felt the same way when I first picked up a paintbrush."

"Really?" Scottie said. Something hopeful glimmered in her stomach. "What way was that?"

"I wanted to keep it to myself," her mom said. "I didn't want anybody to know that I wanted to be an artist until I was good enough to have something to show. Until I'd found my place."

"Okay . . ." Scottie said slowly.

"Anyway, I didn't have anyone to help me find my way," her mom said. "I sort of muddled around for a while doing, you know, *crafts* until I found my voice. Then I got some training and began to become a real artist."

An artist with an oeuvre, *no less*. Scottie couldn't squelch the jab. Because as she started to get an inkling of where her mother was going with this little speech, her hope was flaming out fast.

"And now *you're* going down the same path," her mother declared. She squeezed her book tightly to her chest. "Oh, Scottie, I'm so proud of you. And now I want to give you the help I wish I'd had when I was your age—help to find your own artist within. So you can move beyond this . . ."

"Knitting," Scottie almost barked.

"Right," her mom said, "to something that really speaks from you. And fiber, Scottie. Oh, what a cool medium you chose. It's so tactile, so vital. There's so much you can *do*."

I'm thinking she means beyond making hats and mittens.

"Anyway, I don't want to get all gushy on you," Mom said. Scottie's utter silence seemed to be making her edgy. "I just wanted to give you this. You know, to give you a little inspiration." She handed over the heavy book.

Scottie read the title flatly. *"Softness and Surrealism: Women Fiber Artists of the Early Twentieth Century."*

When Scottie flipped the book open, she almost recoiled. Surrealism, indeed. The glossy photos were of strange stretches of fabric threaded through with wire and razors; an abstract image sewn of cloth and what looked like tufts of human hair; several soft sculptures that were pink and ovoid and *way* too Georgia O'Keeffe for Scottie's taste.

"It's sort of a modern history," her mother said eagerly. "Just to get you started. Some of the more recent fiber art out there, now that's *really* mind-blowing. In fact, there's an exhibition coming to the MCA in a few months. Maybe we could go."

Scottie didn't even feel like crying. Instead, she was numb.

I guess I was wrong, she thought. *There's no way my mother could get it.*

But she couldn't say that. She couldn't say, "Guess what, Mom? I'm not a painter like you or a gritty filmmaker like Jordan or a 'fiber artist' like the people in this book. In fact, if you ask me, everything in this book is *beyond ugly*."

She couldn't say that because her mother wouldn't get that, either.

So Scottie just said, "Thanks, Mom. You know, I just remembered that I told Amanda I'd meet her at Joe. We're gonna . . . do our homework for tomorrow."

"I always saved my homework till Sunday night, too," her mother said, winking at her. She and Scottie both stood up at the same time, and after a pause, Mom opened her arms wide.

Scottie felt awkward as she put the giant book down on her desk so she could hug her mother. She tried to sink into the hug, but her mom felt brittle and guarded in her arms. She didn't seem to need softness the way Scottie did. Cashmere yarn and marshmallows and a hug that smelled of vanilla and wool—those just weren't her bag.

Scottie forced a smile as she pulled away from her mother. And she managed to keep that plastic smile pasted on her face until she'd grabbed her backpack, stuffed a couple of notebooks into it for show, and made it out of the loft.

Scottie didn't go to Joe, of course. She headed to KnitWit. That was the first place she'd wanted to run to when her mom had given her that awful book.

But even as Scottie jumped in a cab and directed the driver to the shop, she wondered why she was bothering. It was 5:00 P.M. and already dusky. She knew Alice closed up early on Sundays. She *knew* she'd arrive to find the place locked up and dark. She also knew that standing on Foster Avenue and looking up at KnitWit's not-glowy windows would be utterly depressing.

Still, she couldn't stop herself from just trying, from hoping that some smile of smudgy fate had kept Alice late tonight.

When the cab dropped her off beneath the KW shingle a few

minutes later, Scottie was almost afraid to look up. Finally, she forced herself to peek at the windows. And—even though she'd expected it—she exhaled in a long, disappointed gush to see that the lights were indeed off.

She looked around, feeling wan and aimless. Half the storefronts on the block were dark, but on the corner the coffeehouse was lit up.

Well, I actually do *have homework to do,* Scottie thought. *Might as well get a hot chocolate and do it there.*

Without enthusiasm, she crossed the street and peeked into the coffeehouse's windows. The place had none of Joe's inviting gloom, nor the swank of a trendy Starbucks clone. It was as nondescript as its name: Sally's Coffee & Tea.

Scottie gave KnitWit's windows a last, longing glance as she began to push her way through the revolving door.

Wait a minute!

From this angle, she could see a shred of light inside the store! She kept pushing until she'd landed back on the sidewalk. Then she peered harder at the windows. There *was* a light on—in one of the shop's back rooms.

Scottie hurried across the street and up the stairs. When she tried the purple glass doorknob and found it unlocked, she felt a shiver run down her spine.

I've got to admit, she thought, *I sort of thought all that smudgy fate talk was BS, too. But this is too perfect not to be fate!*

"Hello? Alice?" Scottie called. From the foyer, she could see that the light was coming from the kitchen.

Something else was coming from the kitchen—a strangled squawk that Scottie couldn't identify.

Frozen in the foyer, she called out again. This time her "Hello?" sounded strident.

"What! What is it?"

Scottie sighed with relief at the words, not even caring that Alice's voice sounded rough and irritated.

"It's me," Scottie called, dashing through the dark dining room into the warm light of the kitchen. "Scot—"

She stopped suddenly when she saw what was happening. Alice was crouched below the kitchen counter. She didn't even glance in Scottie's direction. She was too busy attending to Monkey. It was the cat who was making those horrible sounds. She was giving birth to her kittens. Right then! Monkey's swollen belly was heaving. Scottie saw a blur of wet fur and blood. It was like nothing she'd ever seen before.

"Oh, my God!" she screamed.

Monkey let out a moan.

"Scottie," Alice snapped, glancing over her shoulder for the first time. "Don't yell. Monkey's having a hard enough time as it is."

"Sorry," Scottie whispered, taking a few tentative steps forward. "I've just never seen an animal give birth before. I've never seen *anyone* give birth."

Squirming in a heap near Monkey's front legs were three kittens. They were all blue gray like her, but one had white feet and another had a black-tipped tail. They were squeaking like baby birds and nuzzling blindly at the air. Between painful mewls, Monkey gave the kittens a few weak licks.

"Oooooh," Scottie cried. She dropped to her knees next to Alice and reached out to pet one of the adorable kittens.

"Don't, Scottie," Alice snapped. "We need to leave Monkey be. Besides, another one's coming."

Scottie clamped her mouth shut and willed herself not to coo any-more. Then she watched in awe as Monkey straightened her hind legs, screeched loudly, and finally gave birth to a horrible-looking, bloody . . . *something*. It looked more like a piece of liver than a kitten. Scottie slapped her hand over her mouth to keep from crying out again. Then she watched in fascination as Monkey immediately began licking at the strange-looking bundle. In a few minutes, Scottie realized that nothing had gone wrong. The kitten had simply been born in its sac and Monkey was licking the membrane away. It was gross, but sort of beautiful at the same time. And totally mesmerizing.

There was a moment of calm as they waited to see if there would be another kitten, and Alice seemed to return to herself. In fact, when she turned to Scottie, her face was glowing. She wrapped her arms around her and said, "I'm sorry I snapped at you like that. You'd think I was in labor myself! But oh, Scottie, I'm so glad you're here!"

"I'm glad, too," Scottie said with a happy sigh.

She and Alice watched in rapture as Monkey started nudging her first kittens toward her belly so they could eat. Meanwhile, she continued to lick and lick at the newest baby, scouring its skinny, scruffy little body.

But, all too soon, at least to Scottie, it all started again. Monkey squalled and spasmed and another kitten arrived. A fifth!

As Monkey got to work on this one, Scottie laughed. "How many more of these can she put out?"

"I don't know," Alice said. "A normal litter is three to six kittens."

Monkey stiffened and yowled. Another one was coming already!

"Looks like Monkey's quite the overachiever," Scottie said. Within a few minutes, number six had arrived. Monkey licked at it, as she had all the others. But unlike the other kittens, this one didn't begin squirming and mewling when it was clean.

That's when Scottie noticed this baby looked tinier and skinnier than the other kittens, too.

"Oh, my God." She didn't scream it. This time her voice was low and ominous. "Alice? Alice, I think it's—"

Before she could finish her sentence, Alice had a grabbed a dish towel from the counter and scooped the kitten into her hands. Her hair—which had been twisted into a bun and secured with a knitting needle—suddenly came undone and cascaded over her face.

Alice didn't seem to notice. She had started to rub the kitten, using the tips of her thumbs to massage its tiny chest and wiggle its scraggly limbs.

"C'mon, little kitty," she coaxed. "I know those other guys were womb hogs, but we want you here."

The kitten was still motionless. Its mouth was open, and its tongue was hanging out.

"C'mon, little guy," Alice said. As she rubbed and rubbed at the kitten, she kept up a running monologue. "Or girl. I can't really tell what you are. But I know that your mama loves you. Don't make Monkey mad, little kitty. She's got quite a temper. So come on, stay with us."

Suddenly there was a little peep. Scottie jumped. She leaned forward, moving aside Alice's curtain of curls to get a closer look. Only then did Scottie realize that tears had been silently coursing down Alice's cheeks.

As the kitten began to tremble and squirm weakly in Alice's cupped palms, Alice finally gave voice to her tears. Her sob was like a dam breaking. She cried and cried, even as she dried the kitten off with her dish towel and put it on Monkey's belly to give it the easiest access to its mother's milk.

"Oh, I'm sorry, Monkey," Alice choked out, running her hand over the cat's drooping head. Monkey's tongue flickered out to give Alice's hand a little lick. "I thought it would help things, these kittens. But look what I've put you through."

Scottie put her hand on Alice's back.

"Alice, she's fine," she said. "They're all fine. It's okay!"

Alice heaved a final shudder and grabbed a clean dish towel off the counter. She used it to wipe her eyes and blow her nose, before giving Scottie a sheepish, wet smile.

"Whoa, looks like I was due for a good cry," she said. "Sorry about that, sweetie."

"Oh, that's okay," Scottie said. She was pretty sure she meant it, but to tell the truth, she hadn't seen many grown-ups cry, and Alice's big weep had sort of freaked her out. But she also felt honored that Alice had let her see it.

How not *condescending can you be,* Scottie thought, and smiled.

With the drama of the birth behind them, it was safe to start cooing over the kittens. Scottie and Alice spent the next few minutes praising Monkey and stroking the tiny babies with their fingertips. All the kittens were nuzzling at Monkey's belly now, eating noisily. Monkey's head was flopped down on her bed, her eyes closed.

"Six kittens!" Scottie said. "Wow."

"Wow," Alice said, nodding so much her curls bounced.

"Alice?" Scottie said.

"Hmm?" Alice murmured. She didn't look up from Monkey. She was running her hand over the exhausted cat's back in long, soothing strokes.

"What did you mean when you said you thought the kittens would help things?" Scottie said. "Help what?"

Alice stopped stroking the cat and looked down at her hands, fiddling for a moment with her hammered-gold wedding ring.

"I don't know exactly." She sighed. "I guess I thought they might bring new life to KnitWit. I mean, figuratively, not just literally."

Scottie looked around the kitchen, at the crazy glass cabinet knobs, the cozy tea tins, and the fridge door positively wallpapered with photos of KnitWit regulars proudly wearing their woven treasures.

"I don't get it," she said. "You couldn't fit more life into this place if you tried."

Alice shrugged.

"Maybe that's the problem. I'm tired, Scottie." She sighed again.

"You might not believe this, but I started KnitWit nine years ago as a lark. It was either this or the Peace Corps. *Or* culinary school."

"I thought you couldn't scramble an egg," Scottie said. Her nervous laugh had returned.

"Hence, the culinary school," Alice said drily. "Anyway, I guess I never expected this place to become such a *force,* you know? It took on a life of its own."

"Which is what's so great about it!" Scottie insisted.

"Yes. And no," Alice said. She went back to stroking Monkey's back, ruffling the cat's silky, blue-gray fur absently. "Sometimes I feel like its taken over *my* life. So many things I wanted to do, or at least try, have *so* fallen by the wayside. I can barely remember what they were anymore."

"Can you remember just one?" Scottied coaxed.

Alice shrugged and sighed again.

"Well, I always wanted to give writing a shot," she said. "Maybe write a book about knitting. But also about more than knitting, if that makes sense."

Not really.

But Scottie didn't want to say that out loud. She didn't want to admit to Alice that this entire conversation was confusing her. Alice sounded just like *Scottie*—always searching, never certain.

Isn't that supposed to go away? Scottie wondered in a wave of panic. *Y'know, along with acne and flat-chestedness?*

If Alice sensed Scottie's silent freak-out, she didn't show it. She was staring at Monkey as if she was seeing something else.

"More than knitting," she repeated. "Sounds like such a nice concept."

Not to Scottie, but again, she kept quiet. Soon afterward, the kittens finished eating and snuggled into a pile of fuzzy balls against their mother's belly. The entire feline family fell asleep, and Alice and Scottie pulled themselves to their feet. Before they tiptoed out of the kitchen, Alice stopped to look into Scottie's eyes.

"Things are changing," she whispered. "Isn't it great? Thanks for playing midwife with me."

Then she gathered Scottie into a hug—the soft, enveloping hug Scottie had come here for, even if she hadn't realized it until this moment.

But now it was only half-comforting. Perhaps because Alice only felt half as solid as she once had.

I'm not ready for things to start changing, she thought into Alice's shoulder. *I just got here.*

15 *(Yarn Over)*

The following Wednesday, Scottie and Amanda were waiting for the Metra train to Hyde Park. It was November now, and winter was seriously settling in. They stomped their feet on the platform and rubbed their hands together as they waited.

"I might have to trade in the pleather soon," Scottie said, gazing sadly at her funky Trixie's Attic gloves.

"You'll have to knit yourself mittens with some of your new yarn," Amanda said. "I can't believe we're going all the way to Hyde Park for yarn. What's this place called again?"

Scottie had the answer all ready.

"Spin Cycle," she said.

She'd come up with the name a few days ago, and she had to admit, she was kind of proud of it.

"Seems a bit clever for Hyde Park," Amanda said. "They're so *serious* down there."

Scottie froze and turned her back on Amanda so she could wince. Amanda was *so* right. Hyde Park was the home of the University of Chicago, where students were famous for tromping gloomily around their Gothic campus, muttering about Hegel or physics theorems. Its one island of hipness, according to Scottie's ruse, was a little-known yarn mecca called Spin Cycle.

The train saved Scottie by clattering into the station. The girls clambered on board and climbed to the top floor of the double-decker car. They settled into seats that faced each other and gazed out the green-tinted windows at the industrial clutter that surrounded the tracks.

"I wonder what Alice thinks of Spin Cycle," Amanda mused as she gazed. "Do you think she'll be jealous that we've defected?"

"We haven't 'defected,' drama queen!" Scottie teased. "Besides, I'm surprised that you'd care about that, after you ditched knitting class last night. I'm a little surprised that you're here at all, actually. When you ran out of KnitWit on Sunday, I was worried that your knitting days were over."

"No," Amanda said quietly. She was gazing into her lap now, tracing a line back and forth in a groove of her red stretch cords. "No way could I quit altogether. I just needed a little time to, I guess, recover. And I've got to gear myself up to apologize to Alice."

"Don't worry," Scottie said, flashing for about the hundredth time on the night Monkey's kittens were born. "She'll understand, I'm sure of it."

Amanda nodded and looked up. Her cheery smile looked pasted on.

"So, anyway, I'm not quitting *altogether,* but I am quitting *some* knitting," she said. "I love scarves, and scarves I can knit without a pattern. All you have to do is choose a stitch and stop when it's wide enough. You don't even have to count! So, I'm going to be a scarf knitter. I'm cool with that."

"Amanda," Scottie said, propping her elbows on her knees so she could lean in close. "Are you really cool with that?"

Amanda bit her lip as she nodded weakly.

"Why are you lying?" Scottie said. "You don't have to do that whole cover-up thing. Not with me."

Amanda squeezed her eyes shut and two tears trailed slowly down her cheeks.

"Oh, Scottie," she said in a shaky voice. "I'm just . . . well, let's just say I was having some pretty crazy fantasies."

"About what?" Scottie said.

"Okay, well, we both know I was never gonna get into Yale or Princeton or U of C, right?" Amanda said. "But for a minute there, I thought I'd found something I *could* do."

"Knitting," Scottie declared.

"Yeah, but not just knitting," Amanda said. "Designing. I mean, I could see that miniskirt *so* clearly. I could see the angle of the seams and the details I was going to stitch on after I'd finished it. I could see the shape of it. I could see an entire outfit built around it. And the fact that the stitches came to me so easily . . ."

Another two tears fell before Amanda could choke out the rest.

". . . it gave me hope," Amanda said. "A ton of it! But now I don't know. I can't deal with a pattern, Scottie. I just can't. I feel like my head is gonna explode every time I look at one. I actually had a kind of panic attack last night. I was trying to read that poncho pattern you gave me. I was reading it in the cab on the way to KnitWit. Then . . . I sort of freaked out. That's why I didn't show."

Scottie took a deep breath. She was never going to get a better entrée than that one.

"Amanda"—she quavered—"we're not really going to Spin Cycle."

"We're not?" Amanda said with a sniffle.

"Spin Cycle doesn't even exist," Scottie said. "I made it up."

"You what? Scottie," Amanda said wearily. "This doesn't make sense."

"Listen, I want you to meet someone at U of C," Scottie said. "I e-mailed him, and he said you were totally up his alley."

"Wait, what?" Amanda had flicked away the last of her tears. "Slow down and back up. Who's at the university? Some guy?"

"Some professor," Scottie corrected her. "He's a psychiatrist named Cal Anderson."

Scottie unzipped her backpack and pulled out the printout she'd made from the Web site.

"He's doing a study on the 'psychological inhibitors that impede and/or retard learning capabilities.'"

"He's studying retarded people?" Amanda cried. "I'm not retarded!"

"Shhh," Scottie whispered. Other people on the train were starting to stare. "Of course this isn't about retarded people. It's about people with learning disabilities like you. Here's the thing. There are techniques that can help you read and write and do math, even though it's still harder for you."

"I know that," Amanda snapped. "What do you think my tutors have been drilling me with all these years? Those stupid learning techniques. The problem is, I can't get them."

"You can!" Scottie insisted. "*I* think you can, anyway. Like that one tutor told you, you're just psyching yourself out. You get frustrated or scared. The flames start shooting inside your head, and you freak. And then you give up. And *then* you do anything you can to avoid having to deal. It's almost like your LD is a crutch—"

Scottie clamped her mouth shut before she could say anything else. She'd blurted all that stuff without thinking, and now it was out there, hanging in the air, as harsh as scouring powder.

Feeling ashamed and weary herself, Scottie mumbled, "Anyway, that's the 'psychological inhibitor' part."

She braced herself. She was sure the other people on the train were about to get an earful of an even bigger Scene by Amanda.

When, in a minute or two, no wrath came, Scottie looked up. Amanda was just staring out the window again. Scottie had barely noticed that the train had just passed through the tunnel beneath Michigan Avenue. They were emerging back into the light, on the south side of the city. The train would hit Hyde Park in about ten minutes.

"So," Amanda said, "you made up this yarn store because . . ."

"If I told you the truth about this," Scottie said, "I didn't think you'd want to check it out."

"Well, I don't," Amanda said bitterly. "But—"

Amanda pulled the heels of her Uggs up to the edge of her seat and gazed at Scottie over her knees. "But . . . I will."

"You will?" Scottie squealed.

Who's making a scene now? she asked herself. But she didn't care.

"Listen, if this guy tells me that instead of being stupid, I'm a psycho freak," Amanda said with a wry smile, "well, I think that's a step in the right direction, don't you? Having mental issues is almost cool these days."

Scottie laughed, adding, "Just like knitting is cool! I mean, who'da thunk, right?"

That sobered Amanda up.

"I might *not* have gone through with this, if not for the knitting," Amanda said. "I just . . . I don't want to lose it, Scottie. Not when I just found it."

"I know exactly what you mean," Scottie said, looking into Amanda's sad eyes. "It's sort of like that smudge ceremony. I mean, we know it *wasn't* magic, but then again, it sort of was! It was like . . . a healer."

Amanda gave her a pointed look.

"I know that sounds weird," Scottie said with a self-deprecating laugh. "I don't know, maybe I'm channeling Bella or something."

"It's not magic, Scottie," Amanda said. "It's knitting."

"I know that," Scottie said, feeling like a total dork.

"I mean, it's a really cool thing," Amanda said, "and maybe it's leading us to some other pretty cool things. But it's not like knitting can just solve all our problems."

"I *know* that," Scottie repeated impatiently.

She really wanted off of this subject, and lucky for her, it was almost time to get off the train. The brakes were squeaking, and the train was slowing. Without meeting Amanda's eyes, Scottie muttered, "Our stop is coming up." She stood up to sidle her way down the aisle to the steps.

"Are you mad?" Amanda said as she clomped down the steep metal staircase after Scottie.

"No," Scottie said. It took a minute, though, as the train chugga'd to a stop, before she really meant it; before she could say, "I know you're right. I guess we're just always looking for that *one* thing, right? That one magic button."

"Like a Superman headshrinker who can make me all better?" Amanda said, hopping lightly off the train.

"Yeah, just like that," Scottie said with a giggle.

The girls walked in silence through the still streets of Hyde Park. When they hit the campus—as stern and stony as a complex of castles—Scottie consulted her printout to get directions.

"Mandel Hall, room 254," she muttered. They were standing in a quad surrounded by buildings.

"Do you know how to get there?" Amanda said, rubbing her arms vigorously.

Scottie spun around, reading the somberly carved names of each building: "Cobb Hall, Bond Chapel, Swift Hall, Administration Building . . . um, no."

Amanda made a scoffy noise in her throat, then grabbed the nearest passerby by the sleeve of his worn pea coat. The guy, loaded down with books, glared at her.

"Um, hi," Amanda said with a glistening smile. "Can you tell me where Mandel Hall is?"

The guy spun around and motioned with his head at a sidewalk slanting out of the quad.

"Just head down that path. When you see Hutchinson Commons in front of you, Mandel Hall will be on your right," the guy said. "Approximately sixty-one-point-five meters and you're there. "

"Thaaanks," Amanda said in her most bubbly voice. She flashed him a bright, flirty smile, too . . . and got absolutely no reaction.

"Bye," the guy grunted. He turned and continued his tromp down the sidewalk. Scottie glanced over her shoulder. The guy was making a beeline to the library.

"Well," she said as she and Amanda headed in the opposite direction, "I think we may have discovered the only place on earth where boys are oblivious to your charms."

"Maybe if I Velcroed a textbook to my chest," Amanda offered.

Scottie laughed so hard she stumbled. But Amanda just kept walking and rubbing her arms vigorously.

"Are you that cold?" Scottie said.

"I'm that nervous," Amanda said. "I guess I'm glad I didn't know about this earlier. If I'd had a few hours to think about it, I'd really be sweating it by now."

"He just said he was going to ask you some questions and do a few simple tests," Scottie said. "And then you'll just talk."

Amanda skidded to a halt.

"Tests?" she said. "What kind of tests? *Written* tests?"

"I don't think so," Scottie said, her voice rising a half octave. "I mean, I don't know. I didn't think to ask."

"You don't *have* to ask questions like that," Amanda said accusingly. "That's why you didn't think to ask."

"I'm sorry," Scottie said. She was doing her own nervous arm rub now. "This was stupid. I should have just given you the guy's number and let you do what you wanted."

"But you knew I'd never go through with it," Amanda said. "Especially by myself."

Scottie shrugged and Amanda shrugged back, and they resumed their tromp toward Mandel Hall. When they found it, right where the surly student had said it would be, Amanda bit her lip and eyed its

Gothic, arched windows. Like every other building on campus, it was beautiful and intimidating all at once.

Sort of like Amanda, Scottie realized.

Maybe Amanda, too, saw a worthy opponent in the building. She stomped her fuzzy Ugg on the cement and declared, "Why not! There's no way he can *grade* me on this test, right? I'm just gonna do it."

Scottie grinned and handed Amanda the printout, pointing to the office number.

"It's 254," she said. "So, it's on the second floor."

"I think I can manage it, Miss Mom," Amanda said.

"Sorry!" Scottie cried.

"'S 'nothing," Amanda said, giving Scottie a quick hug. "So, what're you gonna do while I get my head shrunk?"

Scottie unzipped her backpack and pulled out a wad of squash-colored yarn. "What else?" She giggled, then pointed behind her. "I think the commons has tables and coffee and stuff. I'll just camp out there and work on my sweater back, and you can come meet me when you're done."

"Cool," Amanda said, her voice wobbling a bit.

"You'll be fine," Scottie assured her.

Amanda stopped rubbing her arms, threw her shoulders back, and pasted on her party face.

"I know it," she said sassily. She spun on her heel and did her Paris Hilton sashay up to the door, to the sound track of Scottie laughing.

Forty-five minutes later, Scottie was no longer laughing. Her sweater back was killing her!

She took a loud slurp of her latte and shifted in her straight-backed wooden chair. It was one of many straight-backed wooden chairs scattered around the student commons' vaulted atrium, along with some big, heavy rectangular tables. Scottie had tried several of the chairs, and each was identically uncomfortable.

Or maybe it was just her knitting that was making her uncomfortable. She peered at her pattern again.

"Okay, I've bound off my six stitches," she muttered. "Now how do I get from there to decreasing two stitches every second row five times?"

Scottie read the line a few more times before she huffed in frustration. She wished Alice was there!

Dropping her needles, Scottie began to burrow through her backpack.

"I may not have Alice," she muttered, "but I *do* have EZ."

Scottie pulled out *Knitting Without Tears* by Elizabeth Zimmermann. Alice had told her about it during a lazy afternoon at the shop.

"The late, great EZ was amazing," Alice had said. "Like Martha Stewart, except completely opposite."

"Okay, you lost me there," Scottie had said, laughing as she looped her way through a string of purls.

"Elizabeth Zimmermann was the one who brought knitting back," Alice said. "She took the dowdy out of it, and some of the labor, too. She's the one who simplified and deseamed sweaters and championed the circular needle and pure wool. And she had such charisma! EZ had quite a cult following."

"Like Jim Jones without the Kool-Aid," Scottie joked.

Alice smirked.

"Just you wait," she'd said. "Once you make your first EZ sweater, you'll know what I'm talking about."

So, Scottie had bought Zimmermann's book—and shoved it to the bottom of her backpack. She'd been too busy working on her non-EZ, totally seamy sweater to read it, and eventually, she'd forgotten all about it.

Now, as she started to read, it took her about thirty seconds to get completely sucked in.

Soft wool, she read, *from the simple silly sheep can be as fine as a cobweb, tough and strong as string, or light and soft as down.*

Scottie read on, flipping page after page until she was hopelessly zoned. The next time she looked up, another forty-five minutes had gone by. She'd been sitting there for an hour and a half, and Amanda's appointment was only supposed to take an hour.

"Where is she?" Scottie whispered to herself, looking up for the first time and scanning the big atrium. Almost immediately, she spotted Amanda.

The weird thing was, Amanda wasn't looking for her. And further-more, she wasn't looking traumatized or excited or thoughtful. She wasn't curled up on a bench beneath one of the soaring windows, and she didn't look pensive or weepy. *None* of the scenarios Scottie had envisioned while she'd waited and knitted was coming true.

Instead, Amanda was standing at a table across the commons, her curvy hips cocked, laughing, flirting, and chatting! With a boy? No! With two girls. Two . . . knitters!

Scottie jumped to her feet and squinted to get a better view of the scene.

The two girls were clearly college students. Their backpacks were bulging with books. They also had quite the edge about them.

One of them, a wiry, sprightly-looking Asian girl, had a tendrilly haircut with cherry-red highlights. Her jeans were covered with strate-gic rips and embroidered patches. Slung around her neck was a coil of fluffy, hot-pink yarn.

The other girl, who had curly red hair, had a scruffy, schoolboy thing going on. She wore a floppy cap, a white, droopy men's shirt, and the coolest sweater vest Scottie had ever seen. Its V neck was at a side-ways angle that almost reached the girl's armpit. This asymmetrical slash was echoed by a slanty cutout in the sweater's abdomen. The arm-holes were edged with jaggedy scallops. And the whole thing was made of tweedy, lime-green yarn.

From the wild looks of the yarn on the girls' needles now, they were hatching even cooler projects than the ones they were wearing.

As Scottie gathered her knitting gear and stuffed it into her back-pack, she kept one eye on Amanda and her new friends.

Is she ever gonna look in my direction? Scottie thought. *I've only been waiting for her for ninety minutes now.*

Scottie began walking huffily across the atrium. But the closer she got to the trio, the cooler Amanda's new friends looked. This pretty much took all the huff out of her. By the time she reached their table, Scottie was squirming with shyness.

"Uh, hi, Amanda," she squeaked. The Asian girl had been showing Amanda a particular twist in her WIP, which Scottie had guessed was a shawl until she saw a couple of sleeves snaking out of it. The redheaded girl turned and gave Scottie a lazy, appraising look while Amanda jumped.

"Scottie!" she said, trotting around the table to give Scottie a dis-tracted hug. "I was just gonna come over and get you. Meet Polly . . ."

Amanda gestured to the Asian girl, who waved one of her frosty metal knitting needles at Scottie and smiled brightly.

". . . and Regan," Amanda finished, putting a hand on the redhead's shoulders. "They're free-formers."

For all of Amanda's awe, you'd think she was saying, "They're rock stars!"

"Oh, cool," Scottie said, nodding vigorously. "So, um, what does that mean exactly?"

"No patterns!" Amanda said, clapping her hands together and bouncing on the balls of her feet. "They just envision and knit."

"Really?" Scottie said to the girls. "But how do you get the shape right? How do you get it to fit?"

"Trial and error." Polly shrugged.

"Let's just say, we're very good friends with the frog," Regan said in a surfer-girl drawl.

"Or sometimes we just wear our mistakes and call it punk," Polly admitted with a laugh.

(It's a purl thing)

"Wow," Scottie said. She tried to imagine herself wearing Regan's badass sweater vest to school. The image was definitely hazy.

"I told Polly and Regan I was surprised to find any knitters here," Amanda burbled, "'cuz I figured everyone would be too busy studying to knit. But guess what? There's like this whole underground yarn movement at U of C!"

"Oh yeah," Polly said. "I mean, it's totally kosher to knit through lectures. Half the people in my Language and Globalization class do it. Guys, too!"

"Guys, too!" Amanda echoed.

"Yeah, and in our dorm, we have knitting/study sessions like, almost every night," Regan said with Polly nodding along. "We always start out drilling one another for our classes, but it usually doesn't take us long to lapse into string theory."

"Get it?" Amanda cried. "String theory!"

"Heh, heh," Scottie said weakly.

"You should come sometime, Amanda," Polly said, cocking her head and sending a cascade of cherry strands into her eyes. "There's no rule that you have to be a student here to knit with us."

"You did tell them you're in high school, didn't you?" Scottie muttered to Amanda. Although, apparently not quietly enough.

"Sure she did," Regan said. "No shame in that. A year ago, I was in high school myself. Thank *God* those days are over."

Oh thanks, Scottie thought. *That makes me feel just great.*

"Regan!" Polly said, giving her friend a little swat. Then she turned to Scottie and Amanda. "All she means is, there's definitely more freedom when you get to college. Hence the free-forming, I guess!"

Polly held up her strange, sleevy-shawly thing.

"I mean," she piped, "can you picture wearing my shlug—which is a shawl-meets-shrug, of course—to high school?"

"No," Scottie admitted, just as Amanda cried, "Yeah!"

"See, that's why you should come knit with us," Regan said. To Amanda only, Scottie noted with a sting.

"Well, I totally can because I'm gonna be coming down here once a week for the next month," Amanda said, shooting Scottie a loaded glance.

I guess Amanda's gonna keep working with the professor! Scottie thought. She couldn't wait to hear more.

"Um, Amanda, shouldn't we get going?" she said. "We've gotta catch the train."

"What?" Amanda said. She'd gone back to admiring Polly's shlug. She glanced back at Scottie absently. "Oh, you're ready to go? Okay, sure."

Amanda dragged herself away from the shlug, and her new buds, with obvious disappointment.

Regan grabbed a notebook from her backpack and tore out a page.

"Here's my e-mail," she said, scribbling on the paper in green ink.

"Can you put your phone number on there, too?" Amanda asked, trying to sound casual.

"Sure," Regan said, scribbling a bit more. "So, call me next time you come down to our fair campus, and I'll tell you how to find our dorm."

"I can tell you're gonna be a fabulous free-former, Amanda," Polly said sweetly.

"You think so?" Amanda said. She was back to being excited and bouncy. "Polly, you don't even *know* how much that means to me!"

As she and Scottie headed out of the student center, Amanda yelled over her shoulder, "Okay, I'll call you soon."

"Bring some cool yarn," Regan called back.

"And fat needles," Polly yelled. "Really fat!"

"Which reminds me," Regan added with a laugh, "baked goods are a customary contribution to our stitch-'n-bitches, Amanda. We like *anything* with chocolate."

Amanda bounced and burbled the whole way back to the Metra stop. She was so excited, she could barely stop talking. She told Scottie how nice Professor Anderson had been, and how he wanted to talk to her more about her reading freak-outs. Then she went on and on about Polly and Regan. *How* cool were they? How sophisticated. How creative! They even dyed their own yarn. With Kool-Aid!

"Yeah, they're amazing," Scottie agreed flatly.

She was happy for Amanda. She really was. Polly and Regan were totally nice, and Amanda *was* made for free-forming.

This is nothing but good, she told herself.

Then why was Scottie feeling so lost?

16 ✴ (Drop Next Stitch)

It was Sunday, and Scottie was packing up her knitting bag when her cell rang. She glanced at the caller ID as she flipped it open.

"Tay!" she said, nudging her backpack aside so she could flop onto her bed. "If you're calling to gloat because your Ollie Cat is *so* much further along than my Squash Blossom, well, you can just *stop* gloating. Because I have *finished* the back from hell! I'm onto the sleeves, bay-bee!"

"Your *second* sleeve?" Tay said. "Because I'm on *my* second sleeve."

"Man, you really must be in love with that guy," Scottie said.

"Watch it," Tay said. "Anyway, that's the thing. I'm on my second sleeve. The end is in sight, and . . ."

". . . and you don't want to go tonight," Scottie finished for her.

"Um, yeah, that's about the size of it," Tay replied. "I want to see if I can finish this sweater tonight."

"Tay, I *need* you at this party!" Scottie wailed.

"What?" Tay said. "Why?"

"Because it's a *baby shower*—"

"I know! *Ugh*," Tay said. "Ever since Jane showed me her stretch marks after class a few weeks ago, my enthusiasm for baby showers has really waned. I *used* to be really into 'em, of course. I mean, isn't everybody?"

Through her laughter, Scottie said, "My point is, Patricia and Alice are throwing the shower."

"Yeah?"

"So, it's bound to be, well . . ."

Scottie glanced at her open bedroom door to make sure neither of her forty-something parents were lurking about before she whispered, ". . . kind of an elderly scene. Not to mention super-girlie."

"Um, Scottie," Tay said, "you know you're only reinforcing my desire to *not* go to this party, don't you?"

"No!" Scottie cried. "See, that's why I need you! Without you whispering snarky things in my ear, it'll be unbearable!"

"So why don't you skip it with me," Tay said. "You can come over here. I'm at my dad's place tonight, which means we've got TiVo and HDTV. We can get some pizza and have a sleeve race."

"I can't skip it," Scottie said. "I want to be there for Jane. Not to mention Amanda. She hasn't been at KnitWit since her little meltdown, you know. She needs the Chicks with Sticks by her side when she reenters the atmosphere."

Scottie neglected to mention the *other* reason she was desperate to go to the shower. She wanted to see Alice. Ever since the night the kittens had been born, Alice had been distracted and just a little . . . off. She'd even canceled their next knitting class.

"I'm closing the shop for three days to get a grasp on my inventory," she'd told their group the previous Tuesday. "If I don't do some serious organizing around here, I'll go crazy."

Which wasn't exactly reassuring.

But maybe this party will get her back on track, Scottie told herself as Tay stalled on the other end of the line. *Come on, a knitting store full of friends? And cake? Maybe this will remind Alice that KnitWit is her family. That we need it. That we need her.*

Tay cut into Scottie's angsty silence with a long-suffering and noncommittal sigh.

"Oh, please, Tay," Scottie wheedled. "I bet *Bella's* not bailing."

"Don't be so sure," Tay said. "That girl is ob-*sessed*. I tried to talk to

•• Chicks with Sticks

her at school on Friday, and she was so zoned on yarn, she barely spoke to me."

Scottie bit her lip. Bella had gotten quieter and quieter at lunch lately, too. She didn't seem to want to break her knitting stride to talk, much less eat. She compensated by nibbling groat muffins and dried fruit between classes.

"The girl's EDing on us," Tay continued.

"What does that mean?"

"Eating disorder?" Tay said. "Duh, it's the scourge of the freshman class."

"Bella's not anorexic," Scottie sputtered. "Have you *tried* one of those groat muffins? They're like lead weights. Each one's gotta have about five hundred calories."

"She doesn't have to be starving herself to be exhibiting ED behavior," Tay recited. "You can diet, or you can do other things obsessively. Shop, exercise, knit . . ."

"Really?" Scottie said.

"It's all about control," Tay said. "At least, according to the shrink they brought in to talk to us in Health class. I think it was really effective. Now all the anorexics who don't want to seem like control freaks have switched over to bingeing and purging."

"See, that's what I'm talking about," Scottie said. "Nobody can make sick jokes like you can."

"Who said I was joking?" Tay said.

"*Really?* Oh my Go—"

That's when Tay started laughing.

"Har, har," Scottie said. "Just for that, I'm three-waying Bella. *She'll* talk you into going."

Scottie clicked over, dialed Bella's cell, and clicked back. Tay was still chuckling when Bella answered on the sixth ring. She sounded bleary and far away.

"Ciao, Bella," Scottie said.

(It's a purl thing)

"Hey, B," Tay chimed in. "It's Tay and Scottie."

"Oh, hi," Bella said. Scottie could hear rapid-fire *click-swishes* in the background.

"So, are you going to Jane's baby shower later?" Scottie said gently.

"What? Oh, was that today? I forgot," Bella said. "I don't know if I can make it. I'm really zoning on this afghan."

"You're on an *afghan* now?" Scottie cried.

"ED," Tay whispered.

"What?" Bella said.

"Nothing," Scottie said quickly. "Listen, Bella, it's been like *days* since the Chicks have gotten together. Can't you break away, for just a bit? There *will* be knitting there."

"Well," Bella said reluctantly, "where is it again? 'Cuz I'm at KnitWit in my favorite beanbag chair, and it's so cozy here, and I've got a kitten in my lap and—"

"Uh, B?" Tay said with a sigh. "The party's at KnitWit. In about a half hour."

"Oh," Bella said. "Well, I guess I can come then. I mean, since I'm already there. Here, I mean. Ow, kitty! Those little claws are sharp—"

Suddenly Bella's connection died.

"Guess she accidentally hit the off button," Tay said. "What with the kitten mauling and all."

"And I guess *I'll* see you at KnitWit?" Scottie said.

"Yeah, yeah," Tay said. "But no gloating! And no booties! I will *not* knit booties. I'm bringing the Ollie Cat."

"Bye, Tay," Scottie said with a laugh before clicking off. She hoped Tay couldn't hear the nervous bobble in her laugh. And she wished she wasn't feeling so shaky as she tucked her sleeve in progress back into her pack.

For a long time, Scottie had yearned for change in her life. *If only, if only, if only.* The words used to cycle through her mind like a mantra. *If only things could be different.*

Now, as she turned off the light and left for KnitWit, she found herself thinking, *If only, if only, if only. If only things could stay the same.*

"Okay, people," Patricia called out. She was standing in the doorway of the KnitWit classroom addressing about a dozen people who were pawing through yarn, sorting out needles, and munching cookies. "Thank you for coming to Jane's baby shower!"

En masse the group whooped softly and clapped (or clicked together their knitting needles).

"In the interest of efficiency," Patricia said, "and *yes,* Jane, because I'm a bossy, type A type—"

"Just look at her latest sweater if you want proof," Jane piped up from her usual chair in the knitting circle. Her belly, Scottie observed, was getting huge, but she seemed much more cheerful about it than Monkey had been.

"Patricia's addicted to size three needles!" Jane continued. "Intarsia all over the place! She frogs daily! It must be perrrr-fect!"

While the rest of the group laughed uproariously, Patricia mock-scowled at Jane and pressed on.

"As I was saying," she continued, "I'm going to assign everybody a project for the evening. We'll work in groups. Alice and Elliott, since you're our fastest knitters, why don't you work on a receiving blanket."

Alice elbowed her husband and said, "Something useful! Elliott will *love* that." Elliott—who looked *just* the way Scottie had imagined him, graying ponytail, barrel chest and all—rolled his eyes and laughed.

"Jane, Michael, and I," Patricia continued, "will collaborate on a onesie and hat."

Patricia pointed at Becca and a few other regulars and assigned them a sleep sack.

Whatever that *is,* Scottie thought. Her hunch about this soiree had been right. As much as she loved being at KnitWit, she felt about as out of place at this party as a baby at a bar.

(It's a purl thing)

Especially when Patricia turned to Scottie, Amanda, Bella, and Tay, who were in their usual spot at the peach love seat. Bella was still working on her filmy sage green afghan, trying to cram in every stitch she could before joining the party. Tay was fidgety and impatient. And Amanda was looking supremely unsatisfied.

Scottie knew why. When she'd arrived at KnitWit about fifteen minutes earlier, she'd spotted Amanda and Alice in the kitchen. Alice was tending to Monkey and the kittens while Amanda was doing her best to apologize for her miniskirt tantrum.

"Alice," she'd been saying when Scottie had poked her head into the kitchen, "I want to explain why I totally lost it."

Alice had waved Amanda off as she poured a bit of food into Monkey's bowl and gave each kitten a loving pat. "No need to explain," she said. "Being a beginner knitter is *hard*. I understand that. Believe me, you're not the first person who's had a knit fit in my shop."

"Well, that's part of it," Amanda said. She talked to Alice's back as Alice began bustling around the kitchen, grabbing a box of cookies and a tray from a shelf. "But it's not quite that simple."

"I know it seems that way now, but actually it *is* that simple," Alice said, arranging the cookies on the tray in a pretty arc. "When you have more experience and you're more comfortable following patterns, your true knitting talent is going to shine, Amanda. I promise."

"But," Amanda said, "see there's this other factor with me."

"I know," Alice said, nodding as she pulled a creamer and sugar bowl out of a cabinet. "One failure and you think your knitting days are over. But I promise you, sweetie, your knitting days are definitely not over."

A shy smile crept onto Amanda's face.

"I think you're right," she said. "But maybe not in the way you think. See, I met these girls—"

"Can you grab the half-and-half out of the fridge?" Alice interrupted with a distracted frown. "Thanks. Now where did I put that sugar? I swear, lately, I feel like my brain is fried."

"I know the feeling," Amanda said quietly. She handed Alice the carton of cream and headed for the kitchen door. Scottie met her in the dining room.

"I sort of overheard all that," she said apologetically.

"That's okay," Amanda said. She leaned against the big table and toyed with a skein of ice-blue R2 paper. "You were right. Alice wasn't mad."

"Told ya," Scottie said. But she wasn't exactly feeling triumphant, not when Amanda was so visibly disappointed. Scottie was feeling pretty disappointed herself. Clearly, Alice wasn't bouncing back from her funk the way Scottie had hoped she would.

"You were wrong about her understanding, though," Amanda went on. "You and Alice may be best friends forever or whatever, but me? I just don't think she gets me. She didn't even listen to what I was trying to tell her."

"I know," Scottie said. She felt all twisty and uncomfortable, whispering about Alice when she was in the very next room. "But it wasn't the best timing. She was all distracted with party prep."

"Oh, so it's *my* bad timing that's at fault," Amanda said.

"No!" Scottie protested. "It's nobody's fault. It was just . . . a miscommunication. Maybe you should talk to her again at class on Tuesday."

"Maybe," Amanda had said, tossing the blue yarn back on the table. "Whatever. Let's just get back to the party, huh? Look, there's Tay."

So that's where they were now, a quartet of pure angst, waiting for their assignment.

"And for our youngest knitters," Patricia said, smiling at the girls, "booties!"

Tay turned to Scottie and shot her a hot, squinty glare.

"Each of you can make a pair—two blue, two pink," Patricia went on. "That way, we're prepared for any outcome."

"Or quadruplets!" Michael cried.

"Egads!" Jane cried. "Okay, enough of *that* talk. Alice got us Swedish Bakery cookies, everyone. Eat up and let's get knitting!"

An hour later, all the girls were finishing their first booties. Even Tay, though she'd grumbled about having to do it every five minutes.

"Hey, nobody said you *had* to make the booties," Scottie said after the eighth (or so) complaint. "You brought your Ollie Cat. Just break it out and work on that."

Tay seemed to consider it for a moment, but then she said, "Nah, Jane deserves these booties. She's gonna have those stretch marks for the rest of her life, after all."

"Check it out," Scottie said to Amanda and Bella. "Tay's turned into a big mush pot. I think the Ollie Cat's softened her up."

Scottie knew her jocularity sounded forced, but she couldn't help it. Between Bella's distractedness, Tay's complaints, Amanda's sad eyes, and Alice's distance across the room, the vibe in the bootie corner was seriously bummin'.

Naturally, Scottie's lame joke did *not* go over.

"I don't think Tay's being mushy," Bella said. "She's just being nice."

"Yeah, and at least she's making blue booties," Amanda said. "It's not like she's gone pink, even if she has gone girl."

"Okay, whatever," Scottie said. Then she eyed Amanda's bootie, which was looking a little squinchy as she bound off the tiny toe. "So how's it going? Do you want to work together on the next one? I could read the pattern. . . ."

"No thanks," Amanda said with faux breeziness. "I've been talking to Regan and Polly a lot the past couple days. I think I'm really getting the hang of the free-form thing."

"Cool!" Scottie said. But that sounded forced, too.

Maybe because it was, Scottie admonished herself.

After that, the Chicks pretty much worked in silence. While the other pods of knitters crunched cookies, tossed one another yarn balls, traded needles, and chatted nonstop, Scottie and her friends burrowed into their projects in sullen silence. Scottie was grateful when Patricia stood up, holding a cookie in one hand and a tiny pastel hat in the other.

"Okay, knitters," she cried, a big grin on her face. "I hold in my hands a completed baby hat and the final cookie, which means, our party is about to come to a close. It's time for a little show-and-tell! We can start, well, with my baby hat! Takhi Cotton Classic in an Erika Knight pattern."

"Awwwwwww," the group sighed.

They cooed, too, over Jane and Michael's almost finished mint-green onesie and the beginnings of a star-covered sleep sack, which turned out to be a triangular wool bag with shoulder straps—a sort of wearable sleeping bag. Elliott and Alice's tiny blanket was the most beautiful item of all—even though it was only half-finished. Alice hadn't been kidding when she said her husband had a knack for delicate beauties. The blanket was cream cashmere, edged in graceful loops of pink, blue, yellow, and green Karabella butterfly.

"I cannot let my baby throw up on that," Jane cried, running up to Alice to give her a hug. "It's a work of art!"

"What about the booties?" Michael cried, waving a knitting needle toward the Chicks as if it were a conductor's baton.

Tay glared at Scottie.

"See what you've reduced me to?" she whispered. "I have to show and tell *booties* to a bunch of old people?"

"Well, I didn't know about this part," Scottie said. She couldn't hide the irritation in her voice. The shower was getting more un-fun by the minute!

"Come on, girls, don't be shy!" Patricia said. "Who's first?"

Tay looked at the ceiling and huffed.

"I'll go," she blurted. She stood up and held out two pale blue booties. The toes were blocked off into little squares, and the cuffs were at least four inches long—much longer than the little nubs that topped Scottie's own blue booties.

"I guess," Tay said, glancing at her friends' versions, "they're more boots than booties."

"Very cool!" Jane said. "Thanks, Tay!"

"Uh-huh," Tay said. She sat back in her chair with her usual slouch, but Scottie could see a small smile on her lips. She knew how Tay felt. Knitting something for someone else did give the yarn a new twist.

Especially, apparently, for Bella. As Tay sat, she uncoiled herself from her beanbag chair and said, "At first, I really didn't want to do these booties. I wanted to work on my afghan."

"Tell us how you really feel!" Amanda whispered.

"Well, I am," Bella said, blinking at Amanda in confusion. She turned back to the group. "But then I realized that booties really rock! You can get through one of them in like twenty minutes. In fact, I made three! 'Cuz, you know, babies always kick their booties off. So now, Jane, you have a spare!"

Wearing her old, enormous smile, Bella held up her three perfect pink booties. Then she flopped back into her beanbag and grabbed her circular needle to resume her afghan. Scottie was amazed. Bella could tune in to her knitting and tune out everything else in an instant.

Must come in handy, she thought, *when you want to escape.*

Since *she* couldn't escape, Scottie got to her feet and quickly, shyly showed off her blue booties. She'd been really pleased when she'd finished the second one—it was perfectly sock-shaped, with even stitches and fuzzy, elastic cuffs. It was everything a bootie should be. But when the crowd *awwwwed* over it, Scottie couldn't feel elated.

Maybe she somehow knew what was coming next.

Amanda wobbled a bit as she stood up, and Scottie suspected that her supertall Mary Janes weren't to blame. As she unfolded both fists, Amanda looked so pale her freckles stood out. On one of her palms rested her first pink booty. Something had gone wrong in the cuff. It looked like nothing more than a tight, scrunchy ball.

Amanda must have tried to loosen up for the next bootie, because this one was huge. The cuff was big enough for an adult wrist, and the foot was roomy enough to warm up a potato.

"Well . . ." Amanda said, shifting uncomfortably, "obviously, things didn't go as planned."

Sympathetic laughter rippled through the room.

"I'm a free-former-in-training," Amanda said with her self-deprecating, crooked smile. "Emphasis on the *training*. But, Jane, I promise to frog these and keep trying till I get it right."

Everyone applauded, making Amanda's cheeks go bright pink. A few of the knitters cheered and called, "You go, girl!" But Scottie could tell that Amanda felt awful as she tossed her needles into her bag.

"What did those free-former girls say?" Scottie said, crouching down to get a glimpse of Amanda's face. "They're very familiar with the frog?"

"Yeah, it's no biggie," Amanda said curtly. "I guess knitting is just going to be a bit more work for me than it is for *normal* people. Just like reading and writing. Dr. Anderson told me about that."

"Amanda, you *are* normal," Scottie whispered urgently. "Stop putting yourself down like that."

Suddenly Scottie felt Alice's presence over them.

She'll say something to make it better, Scottie thought hopefully.

Alice had a hug for each girl.

"You did great!" she cried. "You've come so far so quickly, you guys."

"Well, some of us," Amanda muttered, pointing at the booties she'd tossed onto the peach love seat.

"It's the thought that counts, right?" Alice said, picking up the lopsided pink booties and examining them. "Which is why I want to give you a little advice, Amanda. Free-forming is great, but it's best if you learn your way around knitting from patterns before you try it. Unless you know knitting in your bones, it's going to be an exercise in frustration. Like trying to do modern dance without ever having learned ballet, you know? Only the most natural talent is going to be able to do that."

"I thought you said I did have talent," Amanda murmured, breathing in sharply and looking at the rag rug. "Back in the kitchen."

Scottie's stomach flipped, and—from the stricken expression on her face—it looked like Alice was feeling pretty lurchy, too. Putting a palm to her forehead, she said softly, "I'm sorry, Amanda. Of course you have talent. I didn't mean that you didn't. I was just saying—"

"I know what you're saying," Amanda said. She'd gone back to pale now, her poochy lips tightened into an angry line. "You don't need to spell it out for me, Alice. Because . . . well, because I couldn't read it anyway! I guess there's one way to do things here, and if you can't do them that way, you don't fit in. I hear you loud and clear."

"No—" Alice said. "Wait a minute, I'm confused."

"No, that's *my* job," Amanda said, grabbing her bag and coat in one jerky swoop. "Sorry, I've gotta go."

As Amanda flounced out of KnitWit, Jane sidled up behind Alice and slung an arm over her shoulder.

"That's the thing about babies," she said with a mischievous smile. "They all grow up to be teenagers."

"Jane!" Alice said, batting at Jane's hand. "We were all teenagers once."

But beneath Alice's scolding look, Scottie could see shards of a laugh, peeking through.

Scottie gave Tay a look that said, *What the—?*

Tay shrugged and leaned over to whisper in Scottie's ear.

"Eventually," she breathed, "the generation gap always rears its ugly head."

Feeling shaky and confused, Scottie glanced at the door. Amanda was gone. Perhaps she was already in a cab, racing to Hyde Park, where she could rail against knitting's old guard with Polly and Regan.

Meanwhile, Scottie was still at KnitWit.

And she was wondering if it would ever feel the same again.

17 • (Slip Stitch Knitwise)

By the next day, Scottie had developed a crick in her neck and a painful throbbing in her right ear. Did she have some mysterious ailment? A knitter's cramp?

She wished. No, she had simply spent the entire night after Jane's shower with her cell phone clamped between her head and shoulder. She must have called Amanda a dozen times, only to get her voice mail or that annoying recording that said, "I'M sor-REE! THIS line is BUS-y. Please HANG up and try your call a-GAIN."

Okay, the person who does those recordings has got *to ease up on the caffeine,* Scottie had thought in annoyance. But she'd been compelled to comply and *had* tried her call aGAIN. And aGAIN and aGAIN and aGAIN.

She didn't reach Amanda until the next morning, and that was only because she cornered her at their lockers before third period.

"Let's go to Joe after school," Scottie proposed. "We can rework the booties, if you want. Did you know Joe just started serving *white* hot chocolate? I heard it's fabulous."

"White chocolate isn't really chocolate," Amanda retorted as she threw open her locker without twirling her lock. "It's the brown cocoa that makes it chocolate."

"Oh," Scottie said, deflated. "Well, do you want to go somewhere else?"

"Actually," Amanda said, her words tinged with a thin coating of ice, "I'm heading to Hyde Park. I've got a meeting with Dr. Anderson, and then I'm going to Polly and Regan's dorm. I have to admit, after I left the party last night, I kind of lost it. I called Polly and just cried for a long time. She was *so* great."

Scottie felt the jab almost physically. She flattened her hand over her stomach, pressing down on the twinge. *That's* why Amanda's cell had been tied up.

"You could have called me!" Scottie said. It had just popped out—a pathetic little blurt.

"I wanted to call you," Amanda said, turning away from her locker to look at Scottie for the first time. "But you were still there—with Alice."

"I really think if Alice knew everything the rest of us do," Scottie said, "she would have been a little more sensitive."

"Well, she *doesn't* know all that stuff, which is telling, don't ya think?" Amanda turned back to her locker and gave her reflection in the door mirror a halfhearted glance. She'd been wearing her purple-gold skinny scarf almost every day, sometimes as a belt, once as a headband, but usually tossed around her neck with the casual flair of a fashion model. Today, though, she was knit-free.

That's pretty telling, too. The twinge in Scottie's belly got a little sharper.

"Listen, this is not a big deal," Amanda said. "I mean, not *everybody* meshes with *everybody*. You and Tay and Bella are down with the KnitWit way of doing things. Patterns and stuff. You'll graduate from sweaters to afghans to tote bags. You'll do intarsia first, and lace after that, and beading after that. There's an order to things over there."

"Don't make it sound *too* edgy," Scottie said sulkily.

"It is what it is," Amanda said. "But it's not the *only* way. At least, that's what Polly was telling me. Alice might not go for it, but there are more . . . instinctive ways to knit. I owe it to myself to give free-forming a chance."

"Is that a direct quote from Polly," Scottie said, shutting her locker and leaning against it heavily, "or are you paraphrasing?"

"Scottiiiieee," Amanda wheedled, pushing her own locker shut. "We'll still be the Chicks with Sticks, I promise. We'll knit at Joe and Windy's and at my house and your house and at Wrigley Field. Hey, maybe we can lure Bella out with another hot dog."

Just the mention of that crazy afternoon when the Chicks had seemed like four hodgepodged sisters made Scottie smile. It also brought back the nervous pang in her stomach. She had this crazy urge to grab on to Amanda. To drag her back to KnitWit so Amanda and Alice could work things out. To not *let* her go to Hyde Park.

But Scottie knew she had no right to keep Amanda from her new friends, or from free-forming. She might have even asked to go along, except somehow she knew that Amanda wanted this corner of the knitting world to herself. Clearly, Amanda thought free-forming was something—like her LD—that Scottie couldn't completely understand.

It's just as well, Scottie thought. *If I can't even bring myself to wear Aunt Roz's red sweater to school, then knitting some crazy shlug would pretty much be a waste of time.*

As if she'd read Scottie's thoughts, Amanda tossed in one more zinger: "I told Polly."

"Told Polly what?" Scottie said. She and Amanda had started walking down the hallway—both of them had classes in the language hall that period. Scottie's was Spanish; Amanda's, French.

"Told her about my learning issues," Amanda said. She straightened herself up a bit as she said it and didn't even whisper the word, the way she usually did. "She was *really* cool about it. Turns out, she has an uncle and a friend from high school who both have reading problems. She was all, 'What's the big deal? You just read slow, is all.'"

"But"—Scottie felt awkward—"don't you have a worse case than that?"

"Maybe not," Amanda said. "Professor Anderson told me that a lot more of my problems might lie in my fears than in my actual disability."

"Hello!" Scottie screamed. "That's what I've been telling you."

"Yeah," Amanda said. She was looking both sheepish and proud as she came to a halt in front of her French class. "But somehow it sounds more convincing coming from someone with a Ph.D."

"Amanda!" Scottie squealed. She gave Amanda a quick, hard hug, and this time, there was nothing forced about it.

"This gives me some hope that things could be different," Amanda said, smiling at Scottie. "But I'm also starting to realize, even if I get better, I'm never going to be, like, cured. So the answer is to find the places where I fit."

Suddenly Scottie felt a lot less buoyant.

"I thought you *had* found that place," she whispered. "With us."

"I think I have," Amanda said. Then she shrugged. "I mean, yeah, I have, but maybe not completely. Maybe I need more than one knitting circle. But who's to say they can't overlap, right?"

"Right," Scottie said wanly.

"Listen," Amanda said. "Don't worry so much, Scottie. I'm not going anywhere, I'm just . . . I don't know, shifting gears a bit. I'll say this, though, if you want to be worried about someone, it should be Bella. Have you talked to her today?"

"No," Scottie realized. "Have you?"

"Well, I talked *at* her," Amanda said. "She said she might not come knit with us at lunch anymore because she needs a more quiet, meditative spot to work. With no distractions."

"Like her friends," Scottie said.

The pang in her stomach turned into an anxious stab.

"Are you okay?" Amanda said, looking at Scottie's hand on her belly. "Do you have a stomachache?"

"Nah," Scottie said, trying to be blasé. She considered asking

Amanda if she thought Bella could use a little lunchtime intervention, but something stopped her. Maybe it was Amanda's distracted air as she headed into her classroom, or maybe it was the pain in her belly.

Or maybe, she told herself, *all of us just need a little space.*

As she headed down the hall to Spanish, Scottie tried to ignore the voice in the back of her head—that wheedling voice she thought she'd finally exorcised.

But I don't want space, the voice whined. *It's everyone else that does. Do they need space from* me?

It didn't make her happy, but Scottie tried to oblige her friends. After school, she decided to go by herself to Joe and do her homework in one of the deep, dark, cozy booths. Maybe she'd knit a little, too. And then she'd meet her parents for dinner.

They were going out with some clients in Lincoln Park, and that morning her dad had asked her to go with them.

"They mentioned they'd be bringing their daughter, and I think she's about your age," Dad had said as he and Scottie toasted up English muffins together. "Maybe you could come keep her company. You could tell everybody about your fiber art."

Scottie rolled her eyes. Over the past few days, the word *knitting* had not been uttered once in the hallowed air of the Creator's loft. But *fiber art* had been bandied about constantly.

"I bet everyone would be very impressed to hear that your mother's talent has been passed on to the next generation," her father said.

Scottie had stared at the toaster as her dad gushed. She'd thought about telling him what she was *really* thinking: that she was not a fiber artist. That she didn't know *what* she was exactly. That she'd thought she had a new insta-identity as a knitter, a KnitWit regular, and a Chick with Sticks, but that maybe she'd been wrong. Maybe she was back to being nothing but a big question mark.

She'd *thought* about telling her dad all these things, but then the English muffin had popped, and it had been easier—as she'd busied herself with butter and jam—to simply say, "I'll think about dinner, okay? Can I call you after school and let you know?"

"Sure, sweetie," her dad had said, tearing apart his own muffin and dropping it into the toaster. "We'll make the reservation for six of us, just in case. We're meeting at seven forty-five at Ciabatta, okay?"

Now, as Scottie spread her books and yarn and needles out on a slightly sticky table at Joe, she dialed up her dad and told him she'd be there for dinner. Then she placed her cell phone carefully on the corner of the table.

She had to admit it—she'd agreed to the dinner to tempt Murphy's Law. Now that she was busy for the evening, somebody would *have* to call her.

Maybe it would be Tay, wanting her to come over and lend moral support as she blocked the Ollie Cat.

Or Amanda would call, wanting to dish over coffee about the freeformers' get-together.

Or Bella would break her silence and unleash all the chats that had been buried beneath her frantic *click-swishes*.

Scottie no longer had to restrain herself from calling them because one of them would now be calling her.

Too bad I'm busy, Scottie thought a bit defensively as she opened her trig notebook. *I've got a bunch of trig problems to do, two chapters to read for English, and a history paper due next week. They're not the only ones who need space.*

Of course, deep down, Scottie knew that someone who needed space didn't check her cell phone every ten minutes, just to make sure it was set on *ring* and not *vibrate*. Or to make sure the battery was fully juiced and the keyboard unlocked. Or to turn the ring volume up from low to high, just so she would hear it, should anyone happen to call.

The thing was, nobody did. And a half hour into her afternoon at Joe, the silence, which should have been so conducive to doing homework, was filling her head with static.

How did I go, in a few weeks, from being this loner to being totally codependent? She slammed her trig notebook closed and decided to take a yarn break.

She'd do a few *click-swishes* to clear her head, finish her homework, go do her dutiful-daughter thing, and tomorrow, when everyone had had their *space*, maybe things would return to normal.

Scottie grabbed her Squash Blossom sleeve and started to work on the decreasing. It wasn't long before she'd begun to zone, propping her knees against the table and slumping into the booth. She started to enjoy the bustle of Starkers jostling past, of the cappuccino machine's hissing, and of the sound of girls gossiping in the booth behind her.

Almost without realizing she was doing it, Scottie began to eavesdrop on the gossip. The little tidbits drifted into her ears like a fluffy pop song. She heard it and didn't hear it at the same time.

Molly was seen kissing Jared under the bleachers, and things are so *over between her and Todd.*

Oh my God, I totally flunked the geometry quiz, and it was all because Paul was shooting me those smiles again. Like, through the whole quiz!

Did you catch Trina's sweater today? It was so see-through I could see everything!

Hey, did you hear about Amanda and Matt?

What!?

It took a moment for Scottie to grasp what the girl had just said. By the time she shook herself out of her zone so she could really listen, the girl was well into her story.

About Amanda.

And Matt!

Scottie twisted in her seat and cocked her ear upward.

 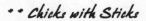

"You'll never believe what she told him," the girl was squealing.

Told him? Scottie thought frantically. *When?*

"In study session," the girl went on, as if she'd heard Scottie's question. "The teacher was out of the room for, like, an eon, so we were all talking. I was sitting next to Matt, who was sitting behind Amanda, so I could hear everything when he asked her out!"

Scottie's mouth dropped open as another girl's voice piped up.

"About time," she said between loud chomps of gum. "Those guys have been flirting shamelessly for weeks."

Scottie realized her needles were absolutely still in her hands. She tossed them onto the table, not caring that a loop had popped off of one of them. She'd fix it later.

"ANYway," the first girl said when she'd recovered, "Matt wanted to go for a walk after school and then go to his favorite place in Chinatown."

"He wanted to take her to his favorite restaurant," the gum-chomper cooed. "That's *so* sweet!"

"I know! But get this! She said no!"

"No!" Gum Chomper cried.

"Yes," her friend said breathlessly. "She told him she was busy."

"With what?" Gum Chomper blurted. "What could possibly be more important than *finally* getting a date with Matt?"

The storyteller paused to take a long slurp of coffee. She was enjoying the drama of her gossip and drawing it out for as long as she could. Scottie almost beat her fists on her legs, she was so impatient. The gum chomper was dying, too.

"Come on!" she cried. "What did Amanda say?"

"She said something about having to meet with, what was it? A free-form knitting group?" the storyteller said. "And going to see some shrink in Hyde Park for her learning disability."

"I didn't know Amanda Scott was LD," her friend replied.

"Me neither." Another slurp of coffee. "I guess she's been hiding it for forever. Maybe she didn't want to tarnish her perfect little image."

(It's a purl thing)

"Of being de facto homecoming queen?" Gum Chomper said. "And the perfect little trust-fundian?"

While Scottie cringed on Amanda's behalf, the storyteller agreed.

"Still, she could have her 'issues' and *still* go out with Matt Altman," Gum Chomper went on. "I wonder why she said no."

"Don't know," the storyteller said. "Amanda's been doing a lot of weird things lately. I mean, have you seen her knitting with *Bella Brearley* in the cafeteria? What's *that* about?"

"That's true," the other girl said. "It's like she doesn't even care what people think of her anymore. She's just given up."

"Ah, sounds nice," the first girl breathed wistfully.

"Really?!"

"No!" the storyteller cried, howling with laughter. "I can't believe you thought I was serious. Hello? I actually *want* to have a life while I'm in high school? Amanda's pretty much consigned herself to dweeb exile now."

But what about Matt? Scottie thought, clenching her teeth.

"But what about Matt?" the gum chomper asked.

Uh, thanks girlfriend, Scottie thought drily.

"Matt?" the storyteller said. "Oh, he took it as a blow-off. You could totally tell. I mean, he tried to brush it off and act as if he'd only wanted to be friends, anyway? But after that, things got really awkward, really quick. Amanda basically killed any potential between them. And don't think she didn't know it. Her hands were shaking. And then she took out these green knitting needles and started working 'em."

"She was knitting in study session? Didn't she get in trouble?"

"Oh, she was reading at the same time," the storyteller said. "Or *pretending* to, I guess. Anyway, she had her book open on her desk, so the teacher didn't give her any trouble. But the *point* is, Amanda and Matt are officially a non-item."

"It's tragic!" The gum chomper sighed.

"Tragic?" the storyteller said. "Are you crazy? Matt Altman is available and crushless! I think it's cause for celebration."

• • Chicks with Sticks

Scottie felt sick as she heard the girls' coffee cups clink.

But she felt even worse as another hour passed and her cell phone never rang.

Okay, so Amanda's gone through this major trauma, she thought, *and she doesn't want to tell me about it. She doesn't have to. She's got Polly and Regan to talk to now.*

After another silent spate had passed—during which Scottie put on mental blinders and yellow-highlighted her way through both her English chapters and a big chunk of history research—she finally packed up her backpack. She felt unspeakably sad as she zipped the bag closed over her needles and yarn and headed for the door to meet her parents.

Amanda was right, she thought. She pushed through the revolving door to the sidewalk, where she was greeted with a blast of cold. *Knitting isn't magic. It's just . . . knitting. That's all.*

Ciabatta was just the kind of place Scottie's mother loved. It was so new, you could still smell fresh paint in the air, yet the reservation list was already jammed.

Two heavy, wine-colored curtains swagged just beyond the front door, which meant you couldn't just *walk* into the restaurant. You had to break through the velvet panels like a diva making her big entrance. Then, to get to your seat, you had to walk down a single aisle banked by two rows of tables.

Or maybe I should call it a runway, Scottie thought as she made her way down the aisle behind her parents. Her mother was positively sashaying through the buzzing crowd. It took five minutes to get to their table because her parents spotted not one, but two people they knew. While her mom and dad schmoozed, Scottie gazed around the restaurant. She saw a sea of black clothing, of jutting collarbones and sharp jawlines, of people who seemed much more interested in eyeing the other diners than in their plates of pasta.

(It's a purl thing)

I wonder why all these people were so hot to come to a restaurant named after a dinner roll, Scottie thought. *They look like they've never enjoyed a carb in their lives.*

The exception was a girl Scottie spotted about halfway down the aisle. Wearing a bright green hoodie over an orange-striped top, she would have stood out even if her hair hadn't been yellow-blond, so bright it competed with the glimmery light fixtures dangling over every table.

Since the girl—sitting with her black-clad parents— seemed to be the only other teenager in the joint, Scottie realized she was probably her dinner mate. Scottie raised her eyebrow. The girl wasn't wearing high-concept eyeglasses. She didn't have a bored air about her. She looked as natural, in fact, as her parents looked artsy-fartsy.

Maybe this night won't be so bad after all.

A moment later, her parents were exchanging air kisses with the girls' parents, Steve and Chloe.

"And you," Scottie's mom gushed to the girl, "must be Isadora!"

"Isa," the girl corrected her as she unfurled herself from her chair. She was tall, broad-shouldered, and had the muscular heft of an athlete.

"Ee-sa," Mom repeated. "Meet Scottie. She's a sophomore at the Stark School."

Isa gave Scottie a wave and a half-grimacing smile. Then she pointed at the seat next to hers. Scottie grinned. If she was reading Isa's signals correctly, the girl was *so* on the same page as her: *Hey, we're prisoners of our parents for the night, but at least we'll probably get the whole bread basket to ourselves.*

As Scottie settled into her sleek chair, Isa leaned over and whispered, "Check it out. There's butter *and* olive oil, and the ciabatta are still warm."

"Sweet," Scottie replied quietly. She smiled as she grabbed a fluffy, hot roll. "Were you at my mom's party this weekend? I didn't see you there."

"Nah, had a game," Isa said, dunking a crust into the dish of green olive oil, which she'd placed directly between them. "Soccer. I'm first string for the JV team at Parker."

"Cool," Scottie whispered. She was impressed. "I'm a knitter."

"Cool," Isa said. She nodded at Scottie's blue-striped scarf, which she'd slung over the back of her chair with her coat. "You make that?"

"Uh-huh," Scottie whispered proudly. "First thing I ever made."

"It's great," Isa said, reaching over to give the merino a quick stroke. "No offense, but I kinda like it more than your mom's paintings. My parents already have two, and between you and me, I don't get 'em."

"No offense taken, believe me." Scottie giggled.

"What are you girls whispering about over there?" Isa's mom asked. She shot the girls a squinty smile through her funky blue glasses.

"Oh, you know, the PSATs," Isa said with a glint in her eye.

"More like the USNT, I'm sure," Isa's mom replied. When Scottie's parents gave her blank looks, she explained, "The U.S. national team is what that means. We've got the next Julie Foudy sitting over there."

As Isa's parents glanced at each other and laughed, Scottie clued her parents in. "Julie Foudy's a famous soccer player."

"Oh!" her dad said, way too brightly.

"Here we are, a couple of wimpy art snobs." Isa's paunchy dad chuckled. "I mean, I'm a twenty-minutes-on-the-StairMaster-and-gimme-a-smoothie kind of guy. And somehow we give birth to this superathlete."

"No!" Scottie's mom cried with a laugh.

"The funniest part is, I've become such a soccer mom," Isa's mom admitted.

"Oh my God, it's true," Isa assured Scottie's mom. "I had to *make* them go to that art opening of yours."

"Yup," Chloe said with a guilty grin. "I *never* thought I could like sports. I mean, we had Isa taking tap lessons when she was a little girl."

"Yeah, but when she refused to do any step except the cancan kick," Steve chimed in, "it was clear where our little girl was meant to be."

"So, what could we do?" Chloe said with a shrug and a wink at her daughter.

"Um, try ballet?" Scottie's mom said.

All four adults burst out laughing. Even Isa chuckled as she took a big bite of bread.

Scottie tried to force a laugh of her own, but it came out as a limp bleat. The truth was, she suddenly felt like crying. Grabbing her knife, she dug a huge dollop of butter out of the dish and began slathering it onto her ciabatta crust. She skimmed the knife back and forth over the stuff until it looked like a layer of oily plaster. She concentrated on nudging the butter toward the edges of the bread, turning it into a perfect ribbon of pollen-colored goop. She had no intention of eating the thing. Her appetite had gone totally dead. But if she kept peering down at her bread plate, she could avoid looking at her parents. She could shut out their chitchat, avoid listening to them gloss the conversation away from errant daughters and back to their favorite subject—the genius of the Creator.

Eventually, though, Scottie had buttered her bread into a pile of mush, and she was forced to lay her knife down.

She longed to grab her knitting needles from her backpack. She *ached* for them. But since Ciabatta wasn't exactly the Stark cafeteria, she kept her pack zipped. She could only sit and seethe as a waiter suddenly arrived with appetizers.

Isa piled her plate with steamed mussels and slices of salami, cheese, and prosciutto from the antipasto platter the parents had ordered. Scottie merely took another roll, which she began to tear into tiny pieces. She made eye contact with no one.

"Scottie," her mother said after a few minutes. "Don't you want any food? The mussels are just succulent and the salami—*mm-mmm!*"

"You know I hate seafood," Scottie blurted. "*And* deli meat."

"Since when do you hate deli meat?" Scottie's dad asked, raising his eyebrows at her before casting a shifty look at Isa's parents.

·· *Chicks with Sticks*

"Since you brought it home from Aunt Roz's funeral!" Scottie said through gritted teeth.

Whoa. Scottie stopped herself from gasping. *Okay, where did that come from? And here's another question:* How *much trouble am I in right now?*

Scottie's mom was staring at her, her jaw clenched. Her dad, meanwhile, was leaping into damage control. After the briefest of pauses, he turned to Steve and Chloe and said, "I don't know where we went wrong. When she was a baby, she loved all the things kids are supposed to hate. Chopped liver, caviar, shrimp, Reuben sandwiches. *Now* she gets picky."

Steve laughed heartily, but Chloe shot Scottie a quick but pointed glance. She looked just like the guidance counselors at Stark—full of concern and sympathy.

Scottie quickly jumped out of her chair.

"'Scuse me," she muttered. "I have to go to the bathroom."

It was a half-truth. She didn't have to go to the bathroom, she just had to *go*. Away. Away from her mom and dad. Away from the feel-good vibes flowing between sporty Isa and her nonsporty parents. Away from Chloe's kindness.

When Scottie slunk back to the table fifteen minutes later, her mother gave her another wide-eyed look.

"I was about to come looking for you," she said, a bit coldly.

"There was a line," Scottie muttered, slinking into her chair.

As the parents resumed their chat, Isa leaned over and whispered, "The waiter took our orders while you were gone. I hope you don't mind, but I ordered you the squash ravioli. And I'm getting this awesome-looking penne with meatballs. If you want, we can split 'em."

Scottie smiled and nodded.

"You should e-mail me your soccer schedule," Scottie said. "Maybe I'll come check out a game sometime."

"Cool," Isa said as she nibbled a bread crust contentedly. "By the

(It's a purl thing) 217

way, when you were in the bathroom, your parents went on and on about your 'fiber art.' I thought you said you were a knitter."

During the drive home, Scottie slumped in the backseat, staring angrily at her parents. While her dad chattered on, wondering which of her mom's latest oeuvre Chloe and Steve would buy, Scottie felt resentment bubble inside her. She knew it wasn't indigestion because she'd barely touched her food.

As her parents laughed over something Chloe had said during the crème brûlée, Scottie now felt words bubbling up. And for the first time ever, she didn't tamp them down. She sat up and broke into her parents' conversation.

"Would you come to my soccer games?" she asked the back of their heads, silhouetted in the headlights of the oncoming cars.

"What?" Mom said absently.

"If I played soccer, like Isa," Scottie blurted. "Would you even come to my games?"

"Scottie," Mom said in exasperation. "You don't play soccer."

"But if I did."

"Of course we'd come to your games," Dad breezed. "We went to all of Jordan's film 'premieres,' didn't we?"

"That's not the same," Scottie protested.

"Scottie!" Mom said, twisting in her seat to glare at her daughter over the top of her yellow hexagon glasses. "What is going on with you tonight? You were so sulky at dinner. Frankly, I was a little embarrassed."

"Oh, I'm *so* sorry," Scottie snarked back. "We all know embarrassing you is the worst thing I could ever do in life."

"What do you mean by that, young lady?" her dad said, sounding a lot less breezy now.

"I mean—" Scottie almost choked on her words. She was trembling, but she made herself press forward. "I mean, I'm not just some extension of you, Mom. And I'm sorry that my being a knitter embarrasses you, but that's who I am. Not a filmmaker, not a *fiber artist,* but a knitter. I know that's a big disappointment to you, but that's the way it is."

"Disappointment . . . ?" Mom sputtered. "Scottie, what are you going on about? I'm thrilled about your artwork."

"It's not artwork," Scottie yelled. She gripped the edge of the car seat tightly. "Or . . . maybe it is. I don't know yet. The point is, *you* don't get to decide what it is. I do. And *when* I do, I think you guys could be a little more supportive. Maybe you could open your eyes to the fact that my knitting is not all about *you.* It's about *me.*"

"Scottie, of course we support you," her dad said. He pulled to a stop at a red light and looked back at her.

"How can you support what you don't even see?" Scottie said. She turned to her mother. "Even when you were painting me, Mom, you never *saw* me."

"Of course she did," Scottie's dad said, shaking his head in bewilderment as he turned back to the road. The light had turned green.

"No, she didn't," Scottie said through a sob. "She looked right through me. She *still* looks right through me."

As Scottie cried, she waited for her mother to protest, to insist that Scottie was wrong.

But she didn't. The rest of the ride home, Scottie's mother stared out the window as if she were in a trance.

Scottie dashed into their building as soon as her dad parked the car. She used her own key to let herself in and stole into her room before her parents had even made it inside. Scottie sighed with relief as she shut her door.

She sat on the edge of her bed, stunned at all the things she'd said. She felt terrified of what was coming next, terrified of hearing her mother's knock on her bedroom door.

On the other hand, she was just as scared that she wouldn't hear it. That her mom would just shake her head and go to bed.

When five minutes had gone by, Scottie slumped off the bed and flipped back her covers. She looked at the clock and groaned. It was 10:40. She'd missed her good-night train. She'd never fall asleep now.

Tap, tap, tap.

Scottie gasped and spun to face the door.

"Scottie?"

Her mother's voice, echoing over the half wall, sounded clogged and teary.

"I just wanted to say I'm sorry," she said to Scottie's still-closed door. "And that you're right. You're *right*. I haven't given you enough credit. The thing is, sweetie, you and I have always been so *different*. I guess when you started knitting . . ."

Scottie raised her eyebrows. Her mother had used the K-word without a bit of hesitation.

". . . I was just excited to have some common ground with you," her mom continued through the door. "But what I really did was take over, the way I always do. You're not me, and your knitting is *your* thing, not mine. I get that now. And I think it's—I think it's really cool."

Scottie didn't realize she'd walked to her bedroom door until she reached it. She opened it up to find her mother, looking puffy-eyed and small, standing in the hallway with her arms crossed over her chest.

"You do?" Scottie squeaked. "Think it's cool?"

"I really do," her mother said, glancing over Scottie's shoulder. Scottie followed her mother's gaze. Her coat was on the floor where she'd thrown it. Snaked on top of it was her blue-striped scarf.

"I've been admiring that scarf of yours for weeks," her mom continued. "It occurs to me now that I might have neglected to mention that to you."

"Yeah, you pretty much did," Scottie said. But her bubbling resentment had disappeared. Scottie didn't know exactly where it had gone.

"I'm sorry," her mother said again. She walked over to Scottie's scarf

• Chicks with Sticks

and scooped it up. She looked at it closely, fingering the stitches, separating them slightly with her fingertips.

Scottie recognized that motion. It was the first thing every knitter did when she picked up a scarf or sweater—in much the way an artist squinted at a painting to decipher the brushstrokes.

"I can make one for you," Scottie blurted. "If you want. It would be better than that scarf. I've had a lot of practice since I made that one."

"I would love that," her mother said. She moved quickly to wrap Scottie in a hug. A nonawkward, pretty wonderful hug. Scottie snuggled into her mother's angular shoulder, enjoying the tang of her hair gel and the faint whiff of ciabatta. "I would *love* a scarf like yours."

"But not this color," Scottie said, pulling away to hold the blue scarf up to her mother's pale, freckly face. She found herself smiling at her mother. No guardrails. No more anger. "My friend Alice has this mustard-colored wool that would be perfect for you."

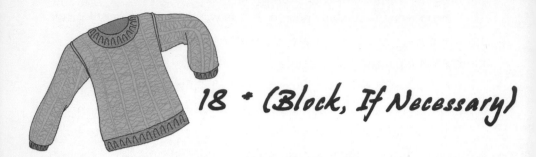

18 * (Block, If Necessary)

All Scottie wanted to do the next day was tell the Chicks with Sticks about the amazing thing that had happened between her and her mother.

Unfortunately, Bella was again a no-show at lunch. And when Amanda arrived at their table, she immediately launched into a breathless monologue of her own. It wasn't the one Scottie had expected, about a certain meltdown with Matt Altman. Instead, Amanda began gushing about all the things she'd learned at Polly and Regan's dorm.

"It was incredible, Scottie," she said. "I mean, I was telling them about my miniskirt disaster, and as we're talking, Regan whips out this circular needle and starts knitting like crazy. And seriously? By the end of the night, she'd made the cutest little miniskirt out of this thready silk ribbon. She'd dropped stitches all over the place, so it looked more like a loose net. Then she put it on over her jeans. It was the coolest look!"

"How'd she do it?" Scottie asked, trying not to feel jealous as she stabbed a ravioli on her lunch tray. Her sweater sleeve was lying in her lap, but somehow she just didn't feel like knitting. Her simple, boat-necked Squash Blossom felt lame compared to Regan's fabulous silk skirt.

"She envisions what she wants as she knits, and slips the thing on about every hour or so, needles and all," Amanda said. "But she said everyone free-forms differently. Some people start with a swatch and build onto that with lots of other swatches. And there are a lot of tricks you can do to add a 3-D effect."

"So, what did you work on?" Scottie said.

"You'll never guess," Amanda said. She reached into her Spade and pulled out a little poof of yarn. It was a loopy flower with orange petals and a lime-green center. It was about the cutest thing Scottie had ever seen.

"I learned to crochet!" Amanda said, pulling a hooked needle out of the bag and waggling it between her fingers. "I think this is really going to open new doors in my knitting."

"That's great!" Scottie said.

But inside she was thinking, *That's great, but, um, don't you have anything else to tell me? About a door being closed, for instance? With Matt?*

"There's something else I've got to tell you," Amanda said. "About a guy."

Scottie almost got teary-eyed, she was so grateful. She held up both hands and said, "Listen, you don't have to go into details if it's too painful."

"Painful!" Amanda said, taking a big bite of a pizza puff. "What do you mean?"

"I mean . . . word has sorta gotten around," Scottie said, grimacing on Amanda's behalf, "and I sorta heard what happened already."

"How could you?" Amanda said, blinking in confusion. "I just met him yesterday."

"Wait. What?" Scottie sputtered.

"I was gonna tell you about Toby, the guy I met at Mandel Hall," Amanda said. "Oh my God, Scottie, he's amazing. He's a poli sci major, but he's *so* not a wonk—he plays guitar in this band, and he writes almost all their songs. And he's totally my type—skinny and pale with dark, kinda messy hair. He could be Paul Rudd's little brother!"

"I thought your type had floppy blond hair and a name that starts with *M*," Scottie blurted.

"Wait, I thought you said you'd heard what happened with Matt yesterday," Amanda said.

Scottie's head was spinning.

"Man," she said, "for someone who can barely read, you have a knack for having, like, three different conversations at once."

The instant she'd uttered it, Scottie slapped her hand over her mouth, while Amanda stared at her in shock.

"Oh my God," Scottie said, her words muffled behind her palm. "I can't believe I just said that. Amanda, I'm so sor—"

"Whaaaaa, haaa, haa," Amanda shrieked. She didn't even start at giggles but proceeded directly to pig snorts. Scottie began to laugh along—if nervously.

"So you're *not* upset about Matt?" she said, shaking her head in disbelief. "I am *so* confused."

"You know what?" Amanda said, wiping the laugh tears out of her eyes and slumping back in her folding chair. "I was confused, too! I left school, and I got on the Metra. Then I got off the Metra and started walking to Professor Anderson's office. And the whole time, I was waiting for the big breakdown. A total tear-and-fear fest because, y'know, the secret was *out*. *And* I'd blown it with Matt. But guess what? The breakdown never came. I actually felt relieved! And the next thing I knew, there was Toby!"

"So you met him in Mandel Hall?" Scottie said, settling into dish mode.

"Not just Mandel Hall," Amanda said, looking sly. "I met him coming out of Professor Anderson's office!"

"Get out!" Scottie yelled. "He's . . ."

"Majorly LD!" Amanda said, bouncing in her seat and laughing loudly. She didn't even seem to notice all the Starkers who suddenly turned in *their* lunchroom chairs to stare at her. "I mean, he's totally in a different category of Professor Anderson's research than I am because *he's* this genius! He figured out all these study techniques of his own when he was a kid. Even though he still has to read slow and hates math almost as much as I do, he does amazingly well in school. He actually skipped a grade in middle school!"

"Wow!" Scottie breathed.

"He waited for me during my appointment, and afterward, we had coffee and talked for *two hours* before I went to meet Polly and Regan," Amanda gushed. "*And* we have a date this weekend!"

"Oh my God!" Scottie cried. "But, Amanda, he's in college! Isn't he old? Are your parents gonna freak?"

"He's just a freshman," Amanda said. "And since he skipped that grade in school, he's only sixteen and a half! Totally age-appropriate."

"Only you could replace Matt Altman," Scottie said, "with a guitar-playing college guy. In the same day!" She grinned and shook her head, trying really hard to hide how wistful she was feeling inside.

Apparently, she did a terrible job at it. With one look at Scottie's face, Amanda was *so* onto her.

"Aren't you happy for me?" she asked.

"I am!" Scottie blurted. "I really am, Amanda. I just . . . I feel left out! I mean, what about the Chicks with Sticks?"

"What about them?" Amanda said. "I mean us."

"Well, I guess that's what I want to know," Scottie said. She knew she sounded sulky and immature, but she couldn't help it. "Are we still an 'us'? Or are you going to be an 'us' with Polly and Regan now? Or with Toby?"

"Scottie!" Amanda said, looking at the ceiling in frustration. "Why can't I be an 'us' with *all* of those people? What do you want, an oath of loyalty?"

"No . . ." Scottie murmured. "Of course not."

Scottie didn't know what she wanted, exactly. She guessed she wanted the Chicks with Sticks to be enough. For all of them.

Not that she was pathetic enough to say that out loud, especially to Amanda, all aglow with free-forming and Toby.

It was much easier to just reach for her sweater sleeve. Scottie grabbed it out of her lap and started knitting and purling intensely. Shrugging, Amanda grabbed her bag, too. She pulled out her crochet hook and a new skein of yarn—some fuzzy lavender-blue eyelash—and began hooking herself another flower.

Scottie wanted to sink into the stitches, to enjoy the yarn vibes traveling between her and Amanda. But she couldn't.

Scottie was sure her angst was evident, but Amanda didn't say anything. She gave Scottie a couple of hard glances as she strung up her funky blossom, but her mouth stayed stubbornly clamped shut.

Only when the bell rang and they were scooping their WIPs into their bags did Amanda say, "You know, Scottie, you could have a little faith in us."

"What do you mean?" Scottie said, a hint of irritation in her voice.

"Just what I said," Amanda said. "I'll see you later, okay?"

"Sure," Scottie said with a shrug.

As she shuffled through her afternoon classes, Scottie kept pondering Amanda's comment. She heard it in the back of her mind all through physics, during her trig teacher's hour-long sine and cosine tear, and as she knitted her way through study session. *Hey, Amanda got away with it yesterday.*

When she saw Amanda at their lockers at the end of school, Scottie finally had something to say.

"Listen," she said as Amanda chunked open her locker door, a dreamy smile (Toby-induced, no doubt) on her face. "You say to have faith in the Chicks with Sticks. But how can I when not one of you wants to get together tonight. *Tuesday* night. Class night!"

"But class is canceled this week," Amanda said, blinking in surprise. "Remember? Alice is doing inventory or something."

"I know, but *we* could still get together," Scottie said. "If Bella hadn't totally checked out and if Tay wasn't obsessing over the Ollie Cat. And what about you? How come you haven't asked me to hang out this afternoon? Do you have a date or something?"

Amanda looked guilty and thrilled at the same time.

"But I thought you guys were going out this weekend!" Scottie wailed.

"We are," Amanda said. She couldn't quash a little smile as she added, "Tonight, we have a phone date."

"See?" Scottie said. She slumped against the locker bank. "Everything's . . . unraveling."

"I'm going to class next week," Amanda protested. "I figure by then, I may actually have some free-forming chops to show Alice. And Tay'll be there, too. She told me in math class. The only reason she hasn't called you about tonight is she has plans with Josh. She's gonna give him the Ollie Cat!"

"Really?!"

Scottie gripped her stomach, instantly nervous on Tay's behalf.

"Exactly," Amanda said, reading Scottie's reaction. "That's why she's been so silent the past few days. She's so nervous, her nails are almost completely bitten off and her hair looks like a scrub brush. I gave her some styling product to use before the big date, and she actually took it!"

"Whoa," Scottie said. "This is serious. What are they doing tonight?"

"Oh, the usual," Amanda said. "The skate park, followed by video games. It's not like *Josh* knows it's a date."

"It's not like *Josh* knows anything," Scottie muttered.

"Well, he's gonna soon," Amanda said. "Tay said she'll give him the Ollie Cat during their walk home."

"Wow," Scottie said. She suddenly felt incredibly tired. "Things are changing so fast. You and Tay are on the verge of having boyfriends, and Bella's checked into a knitting nunnery or something."

"Yeah, things are changing." Amanda sighed impatiently. "Things are *always* changing, Scottie. And plenty of things aren't, too. You'll see next Tuesday, when we're all back in class at KnitWit."

I guess—Scottie sighed as she and Amanda left the school—*I just have to have faith.*

The thing about faith is, it's constantly being tested. Scottie spent the next week enduring trial by voice mail.

When she called Bella's cell Tuesday night, she was immediately transferred to Bella's singsongy greeting, which meant she'd turned her cell totally off!

Okay, I can understand being on a meditative knitting kick, Scottie thought as she slapped her own cell shut, *but to turn your cell off for reasons other than school or a movie?! That's extreme!*

The next morning, when Scottie called Tay to find out how Josh had liked the Ollie Cat, she got voice mail, too.

And when she dialed Amanda for the dish on her phone date? Voice mail.

She couldn't reach *anyone,* in fact, until she saw Amanda at lunch. Her date had been dreamy, she reported with her mysterious new smile. But as for Tay's? Amanda was in voice-mail limbo on that front, too.

"And guess what else?" Amanda said, the Toby smile falling away from her frosty pink lips. "Tay wasn't in math class today. She's out sick."

"Sick?" Scottie said. "Did she seem like she was coming down with something yesterday?"

"Not even," Amanda said, cracking open her Diet Coke. "She had energy to burn. Nervous energy, probably. She even answered two questions in math, and Tay *never* raises her hand in math. It's unheard of."

"Well," Scottie said, biting her lip, "let's just hope she caught a cold hanging out yesterday with Josh."

"Maybe they walked home really slow," Amanda said, "holding hands without their gloves on."

"Maybe they kissed on the sidewalk," Scottie filled in with a giggle. She took her first bite of grilled cheese and opened her knitting bag to pull out her sleeve.

"Maybe they kissed for so long in the cold night air that they *both* got sick," Amanda said hopefully. "Maybe we keep getting Tay's voice mail because *they* keep calling each other, leaving mushy messages between sneezes and nose blows."

"*So* romantic!" Scottie said with a full-out laugh now. "Hey, let's call her over and over until she's *forced* to use the call waiting."

Laughing herself, Amanda grabbed her cell and speed-dialed Tay. After her first bounce to voice mail, she laughed and hit *redial*.

After the second voice mail hit, Scottie decided to try herself.

Voice mail.

And voice mail again.

"Okay . . ." Scottie said when she'd finally given up. "Maybe she's sleeping."

"Don't worry," Amanda said, grabbing her own needles, on which she was knitting a triangle of dusty pink merino to go with her crocheted flowers. "We'll try her after school. She can't hold out forever."

But she *could* hold out for a good long time. Wednesday after school and Wednesday night were all about voice mail, voice mail, and more voice mail. Tay wasn't talking.

When she didn't show up for school again on Thursday, Scottie really started to get worried.

"C'mon," she pleaded into Tay's voice mail at lunchtime. "Just call and let us know you're not dying of pneumonia or something. Please! We miss you. . . ."

But over the course of the afternoon, Scottie's cell stayed silent.

Have faith, have faith, have faith, Amanda said in Scottie's head.

And maybe she was right! After school, just as Scottie was about to stick her "L" card into the turnstile, her cell phone rang. Scottie knew it wasn't Amanda, who'd just headed to tutoring. She actually held her breath as she stepped out of the stream of commuters and flipped open her phone.

"Hello?" she said.

"Scottie."

It was Tay! Her voice was flat, and Scottie could barely hear her over a roaring in the background.

"Tay!" Scottie cried. "Where are you? On the train? I can barely hear you. But who cares! Fill me in! Are you feeling better? I left you like twenty voice mails."

"I know, that's why I'm calling," Tay said. "To tell you to stop, Scottie. Stop calling me! I don't want to talk to you!"

Then she hung up.

Scottie felt like she'd been slapped. Her hands shook as she clicked off her cell. In a daze, she slid the phone into her coat pocket and stumbled back into the short line to get to the turnstile.

But just before Scottie thunked her card into the slot, she stopped. She stood in the crux of the stile, frozen with indecision, until a growly voice behind her belted out, "Make up your mind, girlie! Move it!"

Scottie jumped backward, knocking right into the growling guy. He smelled like sweat and cigarettes and sneered down at her as she stumbled around him.

She *had* made up her mind. Rushing out of the station, Scottie ducked her head against the wind and began stomping down the sidewalk, heading east.

It must have been ten degrees colder at the lakefront. The wind was so whippy Scottie's scarf flapped around her face. The roar of the pea-soup water was almost loud enough to drown out the torrent of traffic on Lake Shore Drive.

Scottie was already shivering, but she forced herself to start tromping across the grass.

Tay wasn't on the train, Scottie told herself. *She was here.*

But as she walked on, spotting nobody but one homeless man and a few wind-addled seagulls, she started to have her doubts.

Well, she thought miserably, *she was here,* or *she was on the Ashland Avenue bus, which is notoriously noisy. Or she was on the observation deck of the Hancock Building, or . . .*

The burst of certainty Scottie had felt in the train station was flickering out on her. The sunless sky was dimming, too. She was *so* ready to turn back and head home. Screw the CTA, she'd take a cab.

"And you know what else?" she yelled into a rush of wind that hit her suddenly with an extra-punishing blow. "Screw faith. I'll knit alone."

Way ahead of her, somebody peeked out from behind a tree. Somebody who'd obviously been startled by Scottie's crazy shriek. Somebody, like Scottie, who'd thought she was all alone here.

Scottie moved closer as the girl jumped out from behind her tree, a tree with a perfect curve for slouching and knitting.

"No way!" Scottie cried. "Tay!"

She trotted up to Tay, grinning a big, fat, incredulous grin.

It's fate! she told herself as she approached her friend.

"What are you doing here?!" Tay yelled.

Or not, Scottie thought, skidding to a halt.

"I had a hunch that you'd be here," Scottie said, almost yelling against the wind and waves. "Why won't you talk to me? Why can't I call you? What happened with Josh, Tay?"

"You want to know that bad?" Tay said. "Okay, I'll show you."

Tay flipped open her messenger bag with a vicious *thwack* and yanked out a forest-green sweater. It was Midnight Pine, to be exact. As

(It's a purl thing)

Tay shook the sweater out, Scottie couldn't help admiring it. Post-blocking, the stitches had sorted themselves into near-perfect rows. The sweater was slightly A-shaped. It was both slouchy and slick, cozy and cool. Tay had done an amazing job on it.

There was just one problem.

"Weren't you supposed to give this to Josh?" Scottie asked.

"I *did* give it to him," Tay said. "On Tuesday night. What an idiot I was."

Tay shook her head and laughed harshly.

"Do you know why I chose Tuesday to give it to him, Scottie?"

"Why?" Scottie squeaked.

"Because I thought the Chicks would sort of . . . be with me," Tay spat. "Because it was class night, I thought my friends would be with me in spirit while I made this incredibly scary and incredibly *stupid* gesture."

"He didn't like it?" Scottie cried. "How could he not like it?"

"Oh, he liked the sweater," Tay said. "He thought it was the coolest thing ever—until he realized that I'd made it for him. Until he figured out *why* I'd made it for him."

"What did he say?" Scottie cried.

"Nothing really," Tay scoffed. "Things just got incredibly awkward. He joked around it, at first. Then he tried to weasel out of our plans to go to the movies this weekend. And finally, 'cuz I dragged it out of him, he told me he had no romantic feelings for me, whatsoever. *Even* if I went girl. To him, I'm always going to be the ugly tomboy he used to guy around with."

"Used to?"

"What, did you think we'd stay friends after that?" Tay yelled, throwing the Ollie Cat on the ground. "Since Tuesday, he's done everything possible to avoid me, including dropping the name of Ashley Torres like six times."

Ashley! Scottie thought in horror. "Who's that?" she quavered.

"Only some ditz who goes to Josh's school," Tay cried. "She's a cheerleader! She has *fake nails*. She's had breasts since the sixth grade."

"Oh my God, Tay," Scottie blurted. "What can you see in a guy who would like someone like that?"

"I see someone who was my best friend," Tay choked out. "And because *you guys* talked me into knitting him a sweater, he is gone, Scottie. Completely gone! Out of my life. Poof!"

"We didn't mean—"

"I was so stupid to listen to you," Tay sputtered. "I was so stupid to think *knitting* was some sort of answer. Knitting is going to make Josh love me? Knitting is going to make the Chicks *best friends forever?* Yeah, right."

"What are you saying?" Scottie said.

"I'm saying, please do what I told you and stop calling me," Tay said. "Stop trying to get me to knit with you. Just . . . stop!"

Scottie was so stunned, she couldn't think of a thing to say. Not that she'd exactly been articulate up to that point. As Scottie stood there, her mouth hanging open, Tay swiped up her sweater and stomped away.

Scottie stumbled in the opposite direction, her vision blurred from the wind and her tears. She vacillated about every ten seconds or so between aching for Tay and feeling bereft for herself.

We're over, Scottie thought as the first sob escaped her windburned lungs. *The Chicks with Sticks are* so *over.*

She had only one thing left now to have faith in.

19 ✴ (Bind Off and Break Yarn)

Scottie stood on the landing outside of KnitWit and tried to breathe. It was so cold outside, even the short walk from the bus stop had knocked all the air out of her.

But Scottie knew the main reason she was breathless was fear. It was Tuesday night at 5:10, and the odds were *very* good that she'd be the only Chick in tonight's class.

Over the past few days, Tay's anger hadn't waned a bit, Bella had continued to ditch lunch in favor of knitting alone, and Amanda's phone dates with Toby had become a nightly ritual.

Sure, she'd told Scottie she'd come to class, but she'd said it several days ago, and she'd been wearing her little Toby smile at the time. Scottie had learned that you couldn't count on Amanda remembering *anything* she said under the influence of the Toby smile.

As she reached for the purple glass doorknob, Scottie's confidence wasn't exactly bolstered by the state of the KnitWit blackboard. In all the erasing and rechalking of messages, half of the bubbly letters in the shop's name had been rubbed out. So had Scottie's little corner of graffiti. THE CHICKS WITH STICKS ROCK had been replaced with, "Be back in five. A."

Really? Scottie's anxious, internal whine was back. She fought it off and plunged through the door. The moment her eyes adjusted to the foyer's pinky gold light, though, she skidded to a confused halt.

Oh my God, she thought. *KnitWit's been robbed!*

She didn't stop to wonder why on earth the burglars might have wanted all the "Lost Kitten" and "Apartment for Rent" flyers from the foyer wall.

And as she stumbled into the dining room—where the bookshelf normally full of vintage craft magazines, pattern printouts, and knitting tomes was empty—she actually wondered why burglars would take care to pack their booty in boxes and stack them neatly along the wall.

It was only after a full minute of staring at the boxes that Scottie realized what was really happening.

Burglars weren't carefully packing up KnitWit. Alice was.

"Hello? Is anybody here?" Scottie yelled in a panic.

At the same time, Alice rushed in from the tiny bedroom, and Elliott appeared in the kitchen door. Both looked exhausted and very surprised to see her.

"W-what's happening?" Scottie asked shrilly. "What are you doing packing? Alice? Weren't we supposed to restart class tonight?"

"Oh, honey," Alice said. "Didn't you get my voice mail? I left one for everybody in the class."

Again with the voice mail, Scottie thought. She was really starting to hate that mode of communication.

"I guess I forgot to turn my cell back on after school," Scottie said. "Alice, what's happening?"

"What's happening is . . . I'm going to do it!" Alice announced. Her voice was a little breathless, but Scottie couldn't tell if it was with excitement or fear.

"Do what?"

"What I've been thinking about more and more," Alice said. "I'm closing KnitWit, Scottie. It's time to move on."

Scottie gasped, feeling tears immediately spring to her eyes.

"Just like that?" she cried.

"No, not just like that," Alice said quietly. Behind her, Scottie heard Elliott slip back into the kitchen. "I think this has been coming for a while. I've loved KnitWit, but I don't think I'm doing the best job anymore."

"That's not true," Scottie protested. "I need you. We all do! You're such an amazing teacher. Not to mention friend."

"Not to everybody," Alice said, slumping onto the arm of the La-Z-Boy. "Scottie, you saw how I hurt Amanda's feelings. She's probably not the first one. And I mean, c'mon. I was looking to *kittens* to rejuvenate me? I think that's a pretty sure sign—I'm burned out. I need to make a fresh start. Maybe find some other way to be people's . . . knit wit. Maybe I'll give that book a shot."

Scottie started crying quietly.

Everything's disintegrating, she thought. *It's like the Chicks are this sweater that's being frogged to death. The question is, what happens when the sweater's all gone? When there's nothing left to unravel?*

She wanted to ask Alice this question, but she knew it would be cruel. Alice had given her so much, and now it was time for Scottie to give back to her, no matter how much it hurt. She stumbled across the room and hugged Alice hard.

"You're at least staying in Chicago, aren't you?" she squeaked.

Alice laughed and got to her feet.

"Of course I am," she said through her own tears. "How could I leave just as winter is coming on in full force?"

She laughed a little and looked around the half-packed shop.

"It's strange how not-strange this feels," she says. "KnitWit has been my life. For years! But now that it's time to leave, it doesn't feel like mine anymore. It's time."

"I wish I felt that way," Scottie said. "I was just getting to know it. And you. And knitting and everything."

"It's just a place, Scottie," Alice said. "The magic's in the people who came here."

Or not, Scottie thought, springing a new font of tears.

"Listen," Alice said, walking into the dining room. "I'm going to have a going-out-of-business sale, where I insist that you come stock up on yarn. And maybe a kitten."

This only made Scottie want to cry harder, but she swallowed her grief back and nodded.

"But I want you to take some yarn with you tonight," Alice said. "Why don't I pick something out for you—something really special."

"O-okay," Scottie said with a shrug.

Alice smiled and began to search, as she always did, through the bowls and boxes and crates scattered around the shop. Scottie leaned against the La-Z-Boy. She couldn't even begin to wonder yet what knitting would be like without KnitWit.

Who's going to find my yarn for me now? asked her old plaintive voice as Scottie sniffled and gazed around the half-empty shop.

At that exact moment, she spotted something.

Three things, actually. A trio of yarn skeins poking out of a laundry tub next to the peach love seat.

Before she knew it, Scottie was kneeling on the floor, holding one of the yarn bundles in her hands.

It was a flossy wool, a chunkier weight than she'd worked with before. Threaded through the yarn was an orange-pink that reminded her of KnitWit's foyer, a stunning streak of lime that made her think of the too-bright grass at Wrigley Field, the indigo of her aunt's eyes, and a shot of yellow that reminded Scottie of nothing in particular; it just made her happy.

In the yarn, Scottie immediately saw mittens that could protect your hands on the darkest winter mornings, a hat with earflaps that dangled pom-poms from two long cords, a scarf wide enough to cover your mouth and nose when walking into the wind. This yarn would keep Scottie warm all winter.

"Alice?" she called over her shoulder as she gathered the skeins into

(It's a purl thing)

her arms. "You don't have to pick anything out for me. I found some yarn on my own. It's perfect! It's *me*."

And that was how Scottie was able to leave KnitWit with a smile on her face, even though it was for the last time.

She even realized, as she clomped down the stairs, that she just might survive without the Chicks with Sticks.

If she had to.

But if she had to, she needed to say good-bye first.

On the sidewalk, Scottie lifted her bare hand, already envisioning the fabulous chunky mitten she was going to knit with her new yarn, and called out, "Taxi!"

A few minutes later, she arrived at Joe. She pushed through the throng of Starkers milling around with mugs of mocha and shots of espresso. She didn't stop for coffee or a chat with anybody from school. She headed straight toward the back.

She needed to see the initials she and her friends had carved into Joe's fireside coffee table—so she'd know it had all really happened. She wondered if the C W/ S would still be there. Or if, like everything else, the scratchings had disappeared by now, covered over with other people's statements.

After pushing past what seemed like dozens of kids blocking her path, Scottie finally made it to the coffee table. What she saw there made her burst into tears.

Amanda, Bella, and Tay were *all* sitting around the table, their feet propped on the scarred wood, their hands *click-swishing* away. Well, except for Amanda's. She was hanging up her cell phone and looking crestfallen—until she glanced up and saw Scottie.

"No way!" she shouted. She jumped out of her chair and threw her arms around Scottie. "I was just calling you. Why haven't you been answering?"

·· *Chicks with Sticks*

"Yeah," Tay said, standing up with her own sheepish smile. "You know, it's really uncool to make your friends leave you a million voice mails."

"What?" Scottie choked through her tears. "How? What's going on?"

Bella popped out of her chair. Scottie noticed that she was wearing the skinny jeans she'd gotten at Trixie's Attic along with the pearly brown sweater she'd been working on the day she'd bought them.

"Fate!" Bella cried, dropping her current WIP to clap her hands together. "That's what's going on, Scottie."

Scottie hiccuped and dried her eyes on the napkin Tay had handed her. She flopped onto the threadbare sofa where Tay had been sitting. She looked at her friends as they settled back into their seats and grinned through her hiccups.

"I thought this would never happen again," Scottie said, her voice still choked. "*How* did this happen again?"

"I'm not sure if I can explain any better than Bella has," Amanda said, her eyes wide and gleeful.

Scottie twisted in her seat and stared at Tay.

"All those things you said at the lake," she said. "I thought . . ."

"I thought I meant them, too," Tay said. "I was hurting so bad, and I guess I pretty much blamed you guys for that. But here's the thing. As the week went on, my fingers were, like, *itching*. I had to get my hands on some wool!"

"What did you do," Scottie said, "with KnitWit closed and all?"

Tay grinned and held up her needles. They held a neat little square of Midnight Pine yarn.

"I did some frogging," she said.

Scottie threw back her head and howled.

"That stupid sweater deserved it," she said.

"Anyway, as I was tearing out all those stitches," Tay went on, "I remembered that mitten that we frogged at Wrigley Field. And I realized—this whole mess wasn't your fault. Josh was *never* gonna love me.

On one level, it still hurts really bad, and on another, you know what? I'm glad I get to spend next spring at Wrigley Field instead of Comiskey. I get to play *Doom* whenever I want now. And I can knit in public without worrying about *him* thinking that I've gone girl. Not that I have or anything!"

"Well, thank God for that," Scottie said with a teary grin. "I'm glad you're back!"

Scottie looked across the circle.

"You, too, B," she said to Bella. "You look . . . different."

"As in, not freakishly obsessed?" Bella blurted.

Scottie glanced at Amanda and Tay before shrugging and saying, "Well, yeah!" Bella lotused her legs—with some effort in her tight jeans—and cocked her dreadlocky head.

"I guess I was looking for something, you know?" she explained. "Like . . . an *identity*."

Scottie and Amanda exchanged another glance before Scottie said, "Yeah, I know."

"I guess I went a little overboard," Bella said. "Like the time I went to that Transcendental Meditation workshop with my parents and didn't speak for an entire week. 'Cuz I was looking for transcendence, you know?"

"Okay, not really this time, but go on," Scottie said with a giggle.

"Yeah, what snapped you out of it?" Amanda said.

"My mom and dad!" Bella said. "They sat me down and said, 'You've individuated enough, young lady. Now if you don't get some balance in your life, we're taking those sticks away.'"

"You're kidding!" Amanda shrieked before dissolving into laughter.

"What happened to their whole 'Free to Be You and Me' thing?" Scottie squeaked through her own laughs.

"Eventually, the generation gap always rears its ugly head," Bella said with a sage nod. "But of course they were right! I mean, I *missed* you guys. I even missed yoga. And I definitely missed knitting over lunch. That whole meditative knitting thing was kind of unfun! Plus, I was always hungry!"

"You know what *is* totally fun?" Amanda said. "Free-forming. I want to teach you guys how to do it. I mean, if you think you might be into it."

"Hello?" Scottie cried. "I've only been waiting for you to ask me all week!"

"Cool!" Amanda said, bouncing in her chair.

"Hey, first things first," Tay said. "We've gotta finish."

"Finish what?" Scottie said, blinking at her friends.

"You forgot?" Bella cried. "Scottie, you of all people?"

"Forgot what?!" Scottie shrieked. "What are you talking about?"

"The progressive blanket!" Amanda said. "Tonight was our night to stitch our squares together and send it on to the next knitter."

She held up her own square, a funky assemblage of crocheted flowers.

"I *totally* forgot," Scottie cried.

"I did, too, actually," Amanda said. "And then I got Alice's message. When that annoying little voice-mail voice said, 'November FIF-teen,' I remembered. I don't know what made me come here. I guess I just hoped, since we couldn't go to KnitWit, that you guys might show up here."

"That's just what I was thinking," Bella said, fingering her own lacy square of peach silk. "I'm telling you guys, it was fate!"

"B, I gotta agree with you this time," Tay said, shaking her head in wonder. She gave Scottie a shy smile and pointed at the bit of coffee table where the girls had carved their initials. "I had a hunch."

Scottie smiled at her friends and took a peek at the table.

Their initials *were* almost gone, fading beneath a sea of other scribbles.

Scottie didn't care. She slumped happily into her seat and pulled out her beautiful new wool. She'd use it to knit her square for the progressive blanket. There'd be plenty left over for her mittens, hat, and scarf.

See that's the thing with yarn, she thought as she took out a couple number 12s and began to cast on. *It's pretty forgiving. Whether your sweater's unraveled or you've ripped it out in a fit of frogging—when it's all over, the yarn stays with you. It might be a bit worn and squiggly. It might seem like a completely different yarn afterward. But it's no less strong. You can steam it out, reroll it, and knit it up into something new.*

Epilogue
✳ (End with Right Side Facing)

As Scottie walked into Joe, she loosened her pink-lime-indigo-yellow scarf and slipped off her chunky, pom-pommed hat. The first whiff of spring was in the air, and it was getting too warm for her favorite hat-scarf-mitten ensemble.

Not that you'd know it in here, Scottie thought, looking around the coffeehouse as her eyes adjusted to the dim light. It being Tuesday, the place was swimming in wool. And chenille and linen and R2 paper and Debbie Bliss baby cashmerino.

"Hey, Scottie!" a voice called as she shrugged off her jacket. It was Maryn. She was just heading to the fireplace, carrying a frappé in one hand, a couple of hot-pink needles in the other.

Smiling, Scottie fell into step beside her.

"Thank God you're here," Maryn burbled. "Amanda keeps trying to push her free-forming thing on me, and I just can't do it. I need patterns in my life! I just do! In fact, I was wondering if I could get the pattern to your Squash Blossom."

"Totally," Scottie said. "I've made some changes in it so it looks even more petally. It's got scallops on the bottom!"

"Love that!" Maryn cried. She headed over to her usual spot at the corner of the fireplace, a few feet away from Amanda, Polly, and Regan.

Polly was immersed in her latest experiment—the shlugger, a combination of a shrug, a shawl, and a baseball jersey.

"It has the potential to be *very* punk." Polly giggled to Scottie when she peeked in on the action.

Amanda waved at her. She was talking on her cell, wearing her Toby smile *and* a blossomy miniskirt of her own invention. Scottie pointed at the skirt and did a little dance of approval.

"Watch out," piped a voice behind her. "Scottie's doing her happy dance."

Scottie turned to smirk at Tay, who was cuddled into the couch with John. In John's enormous hands was a ball of blackberry-colored yarn—or half a ball anyway. He was in the process of converting a skein of sport-weight wool into a ball. At the same time, he was cajoling Tay.

"So is *this* going to be the sweater you knit for me?" he begged. "I mean, I never thought of purple as my color, but, hey, I'll take it."

"No way," Tay insisted with a playful smile. "I told you about the curse of the love sweater. I will be knitting you nothing. Nada! Not while you're my boyfriend."

"So, I have to break up with you to get a sweater out of you?" John said.

"That's about the size of it," Tay said, giving her stabby *click-swishes* an extra bit of sashay.

"Guess I'll buy myself a purple sweater, then," John grumbled. "Maybe after practice . . ."

He unfurled his extremely tall, basketball-player self from the couch and kissed the spiky top of Tay's head. While a wash of pink flooded Tay's cheeks, John looked beseechingly at Scottie.

"Will you *please* try to convince her to knit me something," he said. "Anything. A pair of socks. A *single* sock!"

"Sorry, dude," Scottie said, waving good-bye. "Nobody tells Tay what to do."

"Got that right," John said, giving Tay's shoulder a sweet squeeze. "See ya, Tay-Tay."

"Bye," Tay whispered, going even pinker.

As soon as John had left Joe, everyone screamed, "Tay-Tay?"

"Watch it!" Tay glowered. "Especially you, Scottie. Don't make me bring up your little secret."

"No!" Scottie shrieked.

"What?!" Amanda cried. She'd just finished her conversation with Toby and was perched on the edge of her chair.

"Let's just say someone graduated from 32AA to 32A recently," Tay said. "And that someone is *very* happy about the development."

"Shut up!" Scottie squeaked, covering her face with her hands.

"In fact," Tay said, "I walked into the Stark girls' room the other day and found Scottie there, so enraptured by her curvy profile in the mirror, she didn't even hear me come in!"

"Good thing you weren't Tim Caldwell," Amanda squealed to Tay.

"Oh my God," Scottie said, going red at the mention of her crush. "If you know what's good for you, you will both stop right there. Because you *know* how much dirt I've got on you guys."

She couldn't keep the laugh out of her threat, though. She didn't have time to follow through, either. Bella had just burst into Joe, along with a few other regulars at the Chicks' Tuesday S&B. Bella was walking alongside Tiff, and behind them sashayed Angie, Rose, and T'angela, who'd all gotten hooked on knitting after getting cut from *American Idol*.

Bella oozed flower-girl chic in her bell-bottomed brown cords, ice-blue poncho, and the bloom-bedecked head kerchief Amanda had knitted her. Her lanky lope was even bouncier than usual. After dispensing hugs all around and flopping into her beanbag chair with her latest frothy afghan, she cried, "So guess who e-mailed me today?"

"Alice?!" Scottie cried.

"Alice!" Bella confirmed. "And guess what else? She got it!"

"She got the book deal!" Amanda cried. "You're kidding!"

"The editor made an offer this morning," Bella squealed. "She said she'd seen a ton of knitting memoirs and a ton of knitting pattern books, but she'd never seen a knitting memoir that was *also* full of patterns. They're drawing up the contract now!"

"Oh, wow," Scottie cried. She was so happy for Alice, she had to restrain herself from hopping up and doing another dance.

Instead, she pulled out her needles and started *click-swishing* along with her friends. She eyed their bucket of flyers on the coffee table. The purple pamphlets were running low. Scottie grabbed one to take to the copy shop. She'd run off another stack of them and replenish the bucket the next day.

As she settled into the scented eye pillow she was knitting for her mom's birthday, Scottie glanced at the flyer in her lap:

Never mind the frogs, come stitch with
the Chicks with Sticks
All knitters welcome, from beginning to advanced.
(Even boys.)
BYOY, but needles are available for borrowing.
Baked goods welcome!
(Chocolate only.)
We meet every Tuesday afternoon at Joe.

Scottie smiled at the goofy drawings the Chicks had made in the borders of the flyer. Tay had cartooned a smiling frog with webby feet. Amanda had doodled flowers in every corner of the sheet, and Bella had drawn a plate of baked goods featuring brownies, groat muffins, and, lurking in the stack, a Chicago hot dog.

Scottie's contribution? At the top of the flyer, she'd scrawled a saying that had been repeated often during the Chicks' long winter of knitting together. By now, nobody could even remember who'd coined the phrase.

They just knew it was true:

Even a Work in Progress can keep you warm.

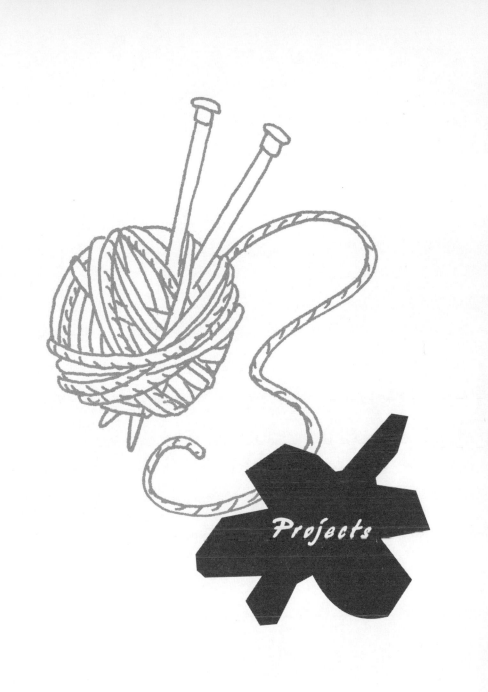

Projects

The Knit-On (and on and on) Friendship Scarf

Want to lasso your own knitting buds into a progressive project like the Chicks' patchwork blanket? The Knit-On Friendship scarf is an even cozier collaboration. Instead of sewing together a collection of squares, each knitter will simply knit onto the scarf's topmost section. It's an instant gratification thing. Your scarf grows before your very eyes, and you don't have to do any sewing.

1. Make a few preliminary decisions with the friends in your knitting circle. Everyone should knit with the same yarn weight and the same needle size, or use whatever needle size will get them closest to the main gauge. It will probably add to the scarf's consistency if you also use the same material, be it wool, cotton, or silk. But that part's up to you. You should also decide together how wide a scarf you want, and the first knitter should cast on the appropriate number of stitches. Finally, you can decide how many rows each knitter should work so that each section is the same length. This isn't a requirement—again, it's up to you.

2. Knitter #1: Get your knit on. Work in any color(s) and pattern you please. Just stick to the preordained number of stitches and rows.

3. When you're finished, cut off your yarn, leaving enough length to work the tail back in at the end of the project.

4. Thread a blunt-edged yarn needle with a piece of yarn that's more than twice the width of the scarf. Carefully run the threaded needle through each stitch on the knitting needle. Then gently pull the knitting needle out of the stitches. The scrap yarn is now holding all the stitches instead of the needle. Bring the end of this "holding yarn" around and tie it so it forms a loop. This way, the yarn won't fall out in transit.

5. Pass it on. The next knitter can now cut that holding-yarn loop, replace it with her own needle, add on her own yarn, and knit as you did—in any color(s) and pattern she likes.

Aromatic Eye Pillow

For many of us, the very act of knitting is soothing. But sometimes you need more than needles to de-stress. On those trying days, sling this nicely weighty, flower-scented pillow over your eyes and check out for a few minutes.

In keeping with the whole relaxation theme, this pattern is easy and breezy. It's basically two rectangles sewn together, with a slight curve built in to fit your face. If you're feeling less confident with the sticks, just leave out the shaping and make a squarer pillow. Ahhhhhh!

SKILL LEVEL: Beginner

MATERIALS AND TOOLS:
- 50 yards (approx 1 skein) of smooth, soft sport-weight yarn (like Lion Brand Microspun)
- U.S. size 6 needles (or whatever needles needed to get gauge)
- tapestry needle
- an old pair of tights or knee-highs
- 2 cups of uncooked rice
- dried lavender (optional)
- sewing needle
- thread

GAUGE:

24 stitches and 32 rows = 4 inches over stockinette

FRONT:

Cast on 20 stitches.

Row 1: Knit.

Row 2: Purl.

Continue working in stockinette, knit one row, purl one row, until work measures 3 inches, approximately 22 rows. End on a purl row.

Begin shaping with decreases:

Row 1: K1, k2tog, k across.

Row 2: Purl across.

Repeat these two rows four times more for a total of 5 decreases. 15 stitches will be on the needles. Work even for two rows.

Begin shaping with increases:

Row 1 (RS): K1, m1, k across.

Row 2 (WS): P across.

Repeat these two rows four times more for a total of 5 increases. 20 stitches will be on the needles. Work even for approximately 22 more rows, or until work measures 7½ inches from the beginning. Bind off.

BACK:

Cast on 20 stitches. Work in stockinette as for the front, until work measures 3 inches, approximately 22 rows. End on a purl row.

Begin shaping with decreases:

Row 1 (RS): K12, k2tog, k1.

Row 2 (WS): Purl across.

Row 3: K11, k2tog, k1.

Row 4: Purl.

Row 5: K10, k2tog, k1.

Row 6: Purl.

Row 7: K9, k2tog, k1.

Row 8: Purl.

Row 9: K8, k2tog, k1.

Row 10: Purl.

You have made a total of 5 decreases and 15 stitches will be on the needles. Work even for two rows.

Begin shaping with increases:

Row 1 (RS): K10, m1, k across.

Row 2 (WS): P across.

Row 3: K11, m1, k across.

Row 4: P across.

Row 5: K12, m1, k across.

Row 6: P across.

Row 7: K13, m1, k across.

Row 8: P across.

Row 9: K14, m1, k across.

Row 10: P across.

You have made a total of 5 increases and 20 stitches will be on the needles. Work even for approximately 22 more rows, or until work measures 7½ inches from the beginning. Bind off.

FINISHING:

Weave in ends. Spritz pieces with water, pat into shape, and lay flat to dry.

Using the tapestry needle and yarn, sew the front and back

pieces together, leaving one of the small sides open to stuff the pillow. Make sure you have the right sides facing out.

Cut off the foot of the tights or knee-highs. Pour the rice and lavender into the foot. If you want a drapy pillow, don't stuff the foot full; for a firmer pillow, pack in the rice and herbs. Sew across the cut edge of the foot with the sewing needle and thread. Make sure that no rice can escape!

Place the rice-stuffed foot into the eye pillow, and using the tapestry needle and yarn, sew the open end of the pillow shut using mattress stitch.

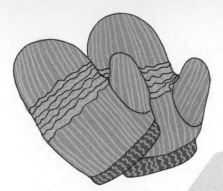

Midwestern Mittens, Extra-Chunky

Nothing's cozier than mittens, especially these woolly wonders. This cinchy pattern is a great way to break into double-pointed needles for the first time.

A few pointers: Dividing the stitches unevenly after casting on will make for easier ribbing. Note that whenever you're told to cast on or work a number of stitches, the first number is for smaller/girly hands and the number in parentheses is for larger/guyey hands. (But not your boyfriend's hands. Knit for your sweetie at your own risk.)

SKILL LEVEL: Intermediate

MATERIALS AND TOOLS:
- 100 yards of moderately chunky yarn. Try Lion Brand Landscapes (50% Wool, 50% Acrylic, 50 gms, 55 yards)
- 1 set of U.S. size 10.5 double-pointed needles, or size needed to obtain gauge
- 1 stitch marker
- stitch holder or scrap yarn
- yarn needle

SIZES: small/medium (medium/large)

GAUGE:

12 stitches = 4 inches stockinette in the round

MITTENS (make two):

Cast on 20 (22) stitches

SM/MED divide as follows: 6 st on first DPN, 4 on second, 6 on third, 4 on fourth.

MED/LG divide as follows: 6 st on first, 6 on second, 6 on third, 4 on fourth.

Work 6 rounds in K1, P1 ribbing. Work additional rounds, as desired, for a longer cuff.

Round 7: Increase round. Switch to stockinette (knit every stitch). Work first needle even. Second needle, M1 stitch, work even. Third needle work even. Fourth needle M1 (M2), work even. 22 (24) stitches total.

THUMB INCREASES:

Rnd 8: Begin increasing for thumb gusset. In first needle knit the front and back of the first stitch, place marker, knit into the front and back of second stitch. K around. Knit two rounds even.

Rnd 11: Increase round. Knit into the front and back of first stitch, k1, slip marker, k1, knit into the front and back of next stitch. K around. Knit two rounds even.

Rnd 14: Increase round. Knit into the front and back of the first stitch, k2, slip marker, k2, knit into the front and back of next stitch. K around. Knit two rounds even.

Slip the first eight stitches on needle 1 onto a stitch holder or piece of scrap yarn. These will become the thumb later on!

HAND:

CO 2 onto the empty needle. Begin knitting with the 4 stitches on needle 1. K even until the stockinette portion of the mitten measures approximately 5 inches (measure from the end of the cuff). Put the mitten on to check the sizing, especially if your hand is very small or very big. You are ready to begin the decreases when the mitten is at the tips of your ring and first fingers.

DECREASE:

Rnd 1: Needle 1: K2tog, k4; Needle 2: K5 (k2tog, k4); Needle 3: K2tog, k4; Needle 4: K5 (k2tog, k4)

Rnd 2: K even.

Rnd 3: *K2tog, k3*, repeat ** around.

Rnd 4: K even.

Rnd 5: *K2tog, k2*, repeat ** around.

Rnd 6: K2tog, 2, repeat around.

Rnd 7: K2tog, k1, repeat around.

Rnd 8: K2tog around.

Break yarn and thread through loops, pulling tight on the inside, and weave ends in.

THUMB:

Put the thumb stitches on the needles as follows: 3 st on needle 1, 3 st on needle 2, 2 st on needle 3. Using needle 3, pick up 2 st from the cast-on stitches from the thumb.10 stitches total.

TIP: To avoid holes, twist the stitches before and after the cast-on stitches in the first round by knitting into the back of the stitch.

Knit 6–7 rounds even.

Begin decreases:

Rnd 1: Needle 1: K2tog, k1; needle 2: K2tog, k1; needle 3: K2tog, k2tog.

Rnd 2: K2tog around.

Break yarn, thread through stitches, pulling tight.

Weave in all ends.

Charming Stitch Markers

When knitting in the round, you're going to see your stitch marker at the end of every row. So, it might as well be pretty, right? Personalized? Even better. Make your mark on your marker with a funky charm. You'll find plenty of options at your local craft store, from beads to pom-poms to feathers. You can even fashion your own charm out of polymer clay.

MATERIALS AND TOOLS:

- 1 package of ring-size memory wire
- eye pins or head pins
- beads
- needle-nose pliers with wire cutters

Dangles:

Thread some beads onto the eye pins (or head pins). Using the needle-nose pliers, bend the free end of the pin into a loop and trim the end with the wire cutters.

Using the wire cutters, cut a round and a half off the memory wire. Using the pliers, bend one end into a small tight loop. Thread a beaded eye pin onto the memory wire. Bend the free end of the memory wire into a small tight loop.

Use 'em and share 'em!